HUNTERS IN
THE STREAM

HUNTERS IN THE STREAM

A Riley Fitzhugh Novel

TERRY MORT

McBooks Press

Guilford, Connecticut

McBooks
Press

An imprint of The Rowman & Littlefield Publishing Group, Inc.
4501 Forbes Blvd., Ste. 200
Lanham, MD 20706
www.rowman.com

Distributed by NATIONAL BOOK NETWORK

British Library Cataloguing in Publication Information available

Library of Congress Cataloging-in-Publication Data available

Names: Mort, T. A. (Terry A.), author.
Title: Hunters in the stream / Terry Mort.
Description: Guilford, Connecticut : McBooks Press, [2021] | Series: A
  Riley Fitzhugh novel | Summary: "Riley Fitzhugh goes through officer
  training and is assigned to PC 475, nicknamed Nameless by her crew.
  Along the way Fitzhugh meets Ernest Hemingway and, toward the end, tells
  him about the Nameless's adventures. Hemingway thinks about adapting the
  story for his own"— Provided by publisher.
Identifiers: LCCN 2020048898 (print) | LCCN 2020048899 (ebook) | ISBN
  9781493058365 (hardcover : alk. paper) | ISBN 9781493058372 (electronic)
Classification: LCC PS3613.O7786 H86 2021 (print) | LCC PS3613.O7786
  (ebook) | DDC 813/.6—dc23
LC record available at https://lccn.loc.gov/2020048898
LC ebook record available at https://lccn.loc.gov/2020048899

∞™ The paper used in this publication meets the minimum requirements of
American National Standard for Information Sciences—Permanence of Paper
for Printed Library Materials, ANSI/NISO Z39.48-1992.

Chapter One

"But what about me?"

I didn't have an answer for her. Frankly, I hadn't really thought that much about it. So she kind of surprised me. I had a flashback of that scene early in *A Farewell to Arms* when Catherine says something like *"Oh darling, be good to me,"* and Frederick thinks *"Huh? What the hell?"*

She had come to L.A. to get discovered for the movies, but she probably realized by now that she'd have just as good a chance back home in Milwaukee, so she was thinking about Plan B. I liked her well enough, but not enough to think in terms of next week, let alone the "Future" with a capital F. I had waited until I got my orders before I said anything to her, or anyone else. But when the word came for me to report for officer training in New York, it was time to say goodbye to L.A., and this was part of it. I had volunteered for the Navy. I wanted to do it. But when those orders finally arrived, I wondered whether this was really such a good idea. Call it volunteer's remorse. I consoled myself with the thought that anyone would have felt the same way. That wasn't much consolation, but it would have to do. There was no backing out now.

"I don't think you'd like the Navy," I said to her, finally. It was lame, but she was standing there glaring at me, waiting for me to come up with something, and this was all I had at the moment. I smiled, too, but it was unconvincing, or insincere, take your pick. Anyway, it didn't work.

"That's not what I meant," she said. "And you know it. You're a real bastard, you know it? A real bastard!"

"But . . ."

"Go to hell!" she said.

She turned around and left, and that was that. As final scenes go, it was thankfully short. It could have been a lot worse. On the other hand, it wasn't the way the movies play the scene of the young hero going off to war. You know, there's a close-up of the girl, all dewy eyed, and she says, "Oh darling, take care of yourself and come back to me, safe and sound." Then the guy says, "Sure I will," which is an easy promise to make. What else is he going to say? But it didn't play that way this time. Does it ever? Maybe just in the movies, which is why they call Hollywood "The Dream Factory." The Reality Factory is down the road in Oxnard. And most everywhere else.

I wasn't really going off to war, not officially, because the war hadn't started yet. Not for us, anyway, although they were already killing each other pretty freely in Europe. We'd be in it soon, though. No doubt about that. I figured I was just getting ahead of the game and might have deserved a little credit for that. But she didn't see it that way. She thought something meaningful might be going on between us. It goes to show you how perspectives can differ. Well, as Hemingway's hero said, what the hell.

The Navy idea came to me even before I met her. A few weeks before, I was having a drink with my buddy in the FBI, Bill Patterson. He was all excited because he was getting transferred out of L.A. to a job as a field agent. Now he'd have a reason to carry his pistol, loaded. He was supposed to carry it all the time, but he never felt the need. Before this he had been an analyst in the Los Angeles office, which meant paperwork and research and not much else. But he was diligent, and his good work on potential fifth column risks at home had won him a promotion. He'd had some good ideas about counterintelligence, and the Bureau was happy to reward talent.

"Where are they sending you?" I said.

"Cuba. Havana. Palm trees, rum, and beaches. Same as here. But quite a few more bad guys to keep an eye on."

"Like?"

"Like those guys who support Franco and think Adolf's a swell guy. They call themselves the Falange. Same Fascist Party as in Spain. Some of the same people, in fact. Lots of cloak-and-dagger potential. Then there's the other guys. The Spanish Reds."

"Commies?"

"Yep. A lot of them came to Cuba to escape Franco's firing squads. We don't think much of them, either. Those two will be at each other's throats, for sure. We don't care about that, of course. They're welcome to kill each other as long as it doesn't affect our interests. In fact, the more of that, the better. But that sort of thing always seems to spill over onto our plates."

"Out of curiosity, when did we annex Cuba?"

"Oh, they're still technically a foreign country. But we have an embassy there, and I'll be attached to that. In the spy business, they call this arrangement a 'fig leaf.' Between us girls, Mr. Hoover wants to expand our intelligence business and doesn't want the Army and Navy boys to steal a march on us."

"What are the bad guys all up to?"

"It's not entirely clear. That's why the Bureau's sending me. And a few others. To find out. But think of the possibilities, once we get into the war. All those friends of Adolf, just ninety miles from Florida? U-boats and hidden fuel dumps? Sabotage? Spying on shipping? Running spies and saboteurs up to the Gulf Coast? Plenty of opportunities for mayhem. Interesting stuff for me, after sitting at a desk all this time. Want to come along? Maybe I could get you hired as a civilian assistant or something. Seriously. Your experience as a debonair L.A. sleuth could be useful."

"No thanks. I think I've had enough of sleuthing for the time being. But you could help me out with something, if you wouldn't mind."

"If I can. What's on your mind?"

"I was reading about the Navy's V7 program for training officers. I was thinking of joining up."

"Really?"

"Dumb idea?"

"No. We're all going to be in this war sooner rather than later. Just don't tell John Q. Public quite yet. FDR wants to keep it as a surprise. And the Navy's as good a place to be as any. Better really. As long as you're an officer."

Bill knew about that. He was an Annapolis grad and had come to the FBI after doing four or five years of active duty. He looked like a harmless professor, but he wasn't.

"If I could have foreseen all this stuff, I would have stayed in," he said. "At the time it seemed like peacetime Navy promotions would be too slow. The Bureau seemed a better bet. Who knew? But the Bureau's going to be plenty active, too, so I don't mind." He studied me for a moment. "How old are you?"

"Birth certificate says almost thirty."

"I'm pretty sure the V7 program cutoff is twenty-seven."

"Details."

"And you're supposed to be a college graduate."

"Or have 'equivalent professional experience.'"

"You think being a private eye, chasing art thieves, and associating with mobsters qualifies?"

"Yes. Besides, I associate with you, too. And the cops."

"True. And I do think the work experience would qualify, as long as you emphasize the law enforcement angle and downplay the skirt-chasing private shamus thing. But how are you going to get around the age limit?"

"Blinky Malone."

He thought about it.

"That could work."

Blinky Malone was L.A.'s finest forger. He'd done passports and visas for me, and a few other things. True, his work couldn't pass really professional scrutiny, but who in the Navy Department is going to look all that carefully at a birth certificate? Blinky could also whip up some transcripts and letters of recommendation, if the equivalent work experience didn't measure up. Give Blinky a day and he could have me graduating from UCLA, magna cum laude, at the age of fourteen. Bill knew Blinky and the quality of his work, because Blinky was also an FBI informer.

"There's also an FBI background check, you know," said Bill.

"That's why I'm buying you a drink."

"You want me to do some creative writing?"

"I don't think you'll have to. You know the old expression, my life is an open book."

He didn't say, "Which book?" Bill had an educated man's contempt for saying the obvious.

"I suppose that here and there you might have to overlook this and that," I said. "But there's nothing that should keep me out. Nothing that's likely to *come out*, anyway. And the word is they're looking for people. I figure the longer I wait and the closer we are to getting into the war, the harder it'll be to get accepted. Too many candidates. So now's the best time."

"You're right about that. So how old are you going to be?"

"I can pass for twenty-five, easy. I don't smoke."

"I tell you what. I'll look into what's required for the FBI check and see what I can do. It only figures that they'd ask the local office to do the background check, so my getting involved will seem normal enough. And at this stage of the game, you won't be the only one using your contacts to get a place. A few letters of recommendation wouldn't hurt. Blinky could draw some up. And I'll be happy to write something swearing you're a combination of Eagle Scout and Wyatt Earp."

"I'm going to ask Ed Kowalski, too." Ed was a respected L.A. homicide lieutenant. He was also a friend. Well, sort of.

"That'll help. He enjoys a good lie. Between all of us we can probably get you in."

"Thanks, Bill."

"Save it. Some lonely night when you're standing the midnight watch in the middle of the ocean, you'll think back on this moment and wish you'd never opened your yap. You know what Dr. Johnson said about the Navy?"

"No. But I bet you do."

"He said, 'No man will be a sailor who has contrivance enough to get himself into a jail; for being in a ship is being in a jail, with the chance of being drowned, and a man in a jail has more room, better food, and commonly better company.'"

"Is that the exact quote?"

"Pretty much. We all learned it at the Academy. And here's another line you'll need to know." He rattled his ice cubes at the bartender. "I'll have another."

"I already know that one," I said.

It helps to have friends who can get things done. With Bill's help and Blinky's artistry and a few other maneuvers here and there, it all worked out. In just under a month, I was sworn in and ready to leave for the Navy's officer training program in New York. As for that girl who wondered about our future together, I saw her a few days later riding down the coast highway in an Oldsmobile convertible with the top down. She was laughing and had her hand resting behind the driver's head. I recognized the guy she was with. I'd seen him in a recent Western movie. He didn't have a big part, but I guess the paycheck was big enough to cover an Oldsmobile.

Chapter Two

The first month of training was like a regular boot camp in which we all learned the difference between port and starboard and how to march in formation—something that sailors almost never do but for some reason need to know about. We learned how to polish our shoes and belt buckles, and we learned the difference between an officer and a chief petty officer, and the difference between the wretched moles who worked in the engine rooms and the simian deck hands who toiled with ropes and paint chippers. In short, we learned that if you were in the service, it was better to be an officer.

And during the time that we were learning to march and learning the difference between port and starboard, the Japanese bombed Pearl Harbor, and suddenly things got much more serious, and we started our three months of officer training.

We learned about navigation and how to find our position on the planet by measuring the angles of the stars, and we got so that we could get as close as one hundred miles to the school solution. Sometimes even closer. We practiced taking sightings from shore points and then working out a series of plots and maneuvers on paper, trying to move a theoretical ship from point A to point B and all the while keeping it in the water and off the West Side Highway. We went cruising in New York Harbor, tooling around in Yard Patrol craft (YPs) and learning the basics of ship handling and signaling and formation sailing. That part was enjoyable. We studied gunnery and small arms, something I knew a little about, since as an L.A. private dick I was licensed to carry a .38 police special. I didn't carry one very often, because those things are bulky and heavy when they're loaded and spoiled the cut of my suit coat. But still, I knew which end of a gun was dangerous, and I'd seen more than a few dead people with bullet holes in them, so I was a step ahead of most of my classmates.

Then there were classes in leadership, and the best instructors boiled the subject down to a few principles—let your men do their jobs, because they know more about their specialties than you ever will, expect them to do those jobs correctly and let them know you expect it, look after their welfare, treat them fairly, try not to let them con you, and don't be an asshole. "Admirals and captains can be assholes, but not ensigns. You have to earn that right." Those seemed fairly easy and sensible, but they were hard for some guys to understand and accept. Those were the guys who were impressed with the authority of their position, or, more accurately, thought their position actually carried some authority. I saw that kind of thing more than a few times later. We learned that the chief petty officers and first class petty officers believed they ran the Navy—and that they did run some of it and were to be treated with respect—but that even as junior officers, our jobs were equally important, and we should treat our men as men and as specialists who worked for us. Nothing more, nothing less. We worked for the officers who were senior to us and ultimately for the skipper who was the closest thing to God on earth, even though he might be a complete dick. The skipper, I mean. This last bit was not part of the curriculum but was passed along from the instructors, sub rosa. Finally, our gold braid meant that we could give an order, but nothing guaranteed that the order made sense or was worth following. It was up to us to make sure it did.

We also learned the rules and regulations. This became important once we started active duty, because we would ultimately be responsible for enforcing those same rules. There were some in our class who came to believe that the Navy "book" was sacred. There were others of us, like myself, who already knew that any and all rules were the work of Man and could therefore never be infallible and should be administered accordingly. This was only good sense, and the best officer instructors more or less said so. There were a few instructors who were true believers, though, and we all wondered how they got their jobs and worried about where they'd get sent next. Not many of us wanted to run into them again.

After one month of boot camp and then three months of officer training, we received our commissions as ensigns. Then we got our orders to report to our next assignments.

I don't know how I felt when I read my orders. I was assigned to the PC 475. It was a ship without a name, a patrol boat and sub chaser homeported in Key West. None of the vessels in that class had names—just numbers. I had hoped for something a little more glamorous—a battleship or a cruiser or a destroyer. I guess I felt a little let down, because I thought I had done well in training. Most of the other officer candidates were guys just out of college, and as far as I could see, they were still a little wet behind the ears when it came to the ways of the world. Ask them directions to the "Tables Down at Mory's," and they could tell you. Ask them how you got the clap, and they'd need a moment to remember what they'd read. That's how they seemed, anyway. Of course, they'd learn soon enough, but they did seem a little callow, even after making it through the course. We all did make it through, however, and the Navy Bureau of Personnel scattered us throughout the Atlantic and Pacific fleets. When I made a mild complaint about my orders to one of the instructors I'd gotten friendly with, he told me a small ship could actually be a lot better. You had more responsibility, much less "military" bullshit and spit and polish, and as long as you got a good skipper, life could be satisfying and even enjoyable.

"Of course, if you get a jerk for a captain, it's another story. No place to hide in those little buckets."

"I suppose you know what Dr. Johnson said about sailors," I said.

"Ha! Of course. We all memorized it at the Academy. Truer words were never spoken, if you get Captain Bligh's younger brother. Or some crusty old mustang with a perpetual hangover."

"Mustang?"

"Old enlisted men who've been given a commission, mostly because they were good at their specialties and the Navy needed officers for some specific kind of job—usually deck or engineering. They can't go any higher than lieutenant, except very rarely. They're ex-chief petty officers and so on. Most of them were in the Navy for twenty years and more before getting their commissions. Real salty. Some of them have a hard on for college boys coming in as shiny new ensigns. Even us graduates from boat school." By which he meant the Academy.

"I know an ex-bosun's mate out in L.A.," I said.

"Well then, you know what I'm talking about. Besides, you're no college boy. You know the difference between real blonds and the other kind, so you shouldn't have any trouble if you do get one for a skipper. They sometimes get command of these specialty vessels. Tugboats and patrol craft. I wouldn't be surprised if your PC has one for a skipper. They're not all assholes. And they usually know their business."

"Maybe I'll get lucky."

"Words to live by. Speaking of that, I've been meaning to ask you—are those actresses out in Hollywood really as good-looking as they seem, or is it all a trick of photography and makeup?"

"They're actually better looking in person."

"I was afraid of that. Man, is your life going to change."

"It already has."

Chapter Three

Southern California is a desert with ocean frontage. South Florida is a swamp with even more ocean around it. I prefer the desert. The air is dry and the sea breezes are cool. Florida air is damp, and in the summertime breathing it is just one step above drowning. But in early spring there wasn't much to complain about. That would change, but for now it seemed like the living conditions would be OK. The nearest mountains were a thousand miles away, so that was a little disorienting. But at least there were palm trees and beaches. Lots of beaches.

I checked in at the Key West commanding officer's headquarters, and the Navy yeoman in the front office looked at my orders and gave me directions to my ship. It was tied up along one of the new piers that had just been built by civilian workers who were overrunning the place. Most of the civilians on the islands were happy about the coming hostilities because it meant work for them, building the base back up. It had been left to languish pretty much since the end of the last war. That's how we seemed to treat every war—we figure it's the last one in history, so why bother worrying about the next one, since it was never coming.

I walked through the busy work parties and the noise of construction all the way to the end of the island, where there were two rather elderly looking destroyers tied up and a few more yard patrol craft out on moorings. A PBY flying boat was moored out there, too. It wasn't much of a fleet, but then Key West wasn't much of a naval base. Not yet. And in an obscure corner of the dockyard, I found her—the PC 475.

I felt a little funny looking at the ship. My ship. She was new and shiny and seemed almost elegant, but there was something else about her that seemed to say, "You're mine, poor fool, and it's too late to back out now." It was a feeling in my stomach like loneliness and indigestion, both at the same time. But I was also excited. Our destinies were entwined, mine and that ship's. And I actually said it that way to myself. There are moments when you can forgive yourself for a touch of melodrama or sentiment, as long as you keep it to yourself. Seeing your first ship for the first time qualifies as one of them, as far as I'm concerned. Whether our destinies would be dramatic or humdrum remained to be seen. But my first impressions of the 475 were positive, on balance. I did wish she had a name, though—something elegant or beautiful or nautical or brave, something that would underscore and enhance her handsomeness. But she didn't. She was just the 475.

She was just over 170 feet long, painted haze gray, of course. There was a three-inch fifty gun on the bow. It was standing in the open—not in a turret—and would be operated manually by sailors cranking gears to swing it side to side and elevate it. The gun would be useful to take on an enemy sub on the surface and maybe to blast away at a small target on the shore. But that was about the extent of it. It wouldn't trouble anything in the air. You couldn't crank it fast enough to follow the flight of an attacker, unless it was a blimp. The superstructure in the middle of the ship was topped by an enclosed bridge, the place where I expected to be spending many hours standing watch, conning the ship. There were round windows (or ports). Just above was a flying bridge where the signalmen were stationed. From there a mast rose straight up to the masthead lookout station—a one-man bucket. The after portion of the main deck had twin forty-millimeter guns and a pair of twenty-millimeters as well as two depth charge launchers on each side and two racks of depth charges. In action against the U-boats, the crew would roll those deadly drums off the stern. This vessel was designed mostly to hunt submarines.

The number 475 was painted on the hull all the way forward. It was gleaming white and outlined in black and looked damned fine against the gray of the hull.

There was a gunner's mate second class standing watch on the quarterdeck. That seemed strange. Usually that was an officer's job, even in port. He looked spruce enough in his dress whites.

I walked up the short gangway, saluted the flag on the stern, and saluted the quarterdeck.

"Request permission to come aboard . . . sir." I added this even though the gunner's mate wasn't an officer, because it was standard phraseology. He returned the salute. "Permission granted, sir." And I stepped on board.

"Ensign Fitzhugh, reporting for duty."

"Yes, sir. Welcome aboard, sir. We were told to expect you." He smiled, and his friendliness seemed genuine. "The messenger will show you to the captain."

A scrawny seaman saluted and asked me to follow him, and we stepped through an open watertight door and walked a few steps down a narrow passageway. And I noticed that peculiar smell that all Navy ships seemed to have—some combination of paint and fuel oil and something I never could identify but that smelled somehow electrical. It was not an unpleasant smell, just distinctive. And I got so I liked it. Maybe in future years it would bring back the memories of my Navy days the way Proust's taste of a madeleine brought memories back to him. And if you're wondering how I know about Proust, I have to admit that somebody told me. Though I read a lot, I hadn't gotten to Proust yet, and frankly I didn't expect to anytime soon. Somehow a Navy ship didn't seem the right context for reading a Parisian aesthete whose life-changing event was eating a cookie.

The seaman knocked on a door, a voice said, "Come in," and I took off my hat and stepped into the captain's cabin.

"Ah! Doctor Livingston, I presume," he said. He was an average-sized man dressed in work khakis with lieutenant's bars on his collar. The commanding officer of any vessel is called "Captain," regardless of his actual rank. I'd guess he was in his early forties, but he also seemed to have maybe a little extra mileage on him. He had thinning gray hair, a bushy white mustache, and no extra flesh on his bones. His face was tanned and weather-beaten, and his blue eyes were just a little bloodshot, more from eyestrain and sun glare than hangover, I hoped. But in spite of the appearance of moderate wear and tear, there was something friendly and humorous and ironic in his expression, something that said he'd been to the ballpark and back more than a few times and had had his share of laughs. It was as though he constantly expected something ridiculous to happen, and he was looking forward to it. Something also said that if there was any bullshitting to be done, he'd be the one to do it. He was twenty years too old to be a regular Navy lieutenant. And I thought—"Mustang."

"Ensign Fitzhugh reporting for duty, sir."

He stood up and smiled and shook my hand.

"Good. Welcome aboard. Your first name's Riley, I believe."

"Yes, sir."

"Glad to know you. My name's Ford. Ted Ford. The crew calls me Model T, but I don't recommend you try it. At least not in my hearing. Humorous contempt is for the enlisted men. It's their constitutional right, you might say. I was one for eighteen years, so I know how the men talk and what they talk about and where they try to hide the booze and just about everything else that goes on belowdecks. All that stuff you don't know anything about, yet."

"No, sir."

"Good. Well, I expect you'll learn. Who said the beginning of wisdom is knowing you can't find your ass with both hands?"

"Socrates, sir?" I figured that was as good a guess as any.

"Maybe so. People say he was a smart fella. Probably sounds better in the original. Greek, wasn't he?"

"Yes, sir."

"Have a seat."

There was one other metal chair in the tiny stateroom.

"I'm glad you're here," he said. "There's a lot of work to do. I've seen a copy of your file. You did well in training."

"Thank you, sir."

"That's why they sent you to this vessel. They send the dumb ones to the battleships, where they can't get into too much trouble. This is a handy little ship. The men call her the *Nameless*. Scratch a sailor and you find a comedian. Lord Nelson said that, unless I'm mistaken."

I nodded and smiled. This seemed to be a good beginning.

"She's brand new," said the captain, "but she's like a debutante with bad breath and a wooden leg."

"Sir?"

"Ignored. Neglected."

"Sir?"

"Ignored and neglected by the boys in the Navy Department. We're short of most things. Mostly men. Fact is, so far you're the only other commissioned officer, aside from me. Which means, for the time being at least, you're the exec. Congratulations."

"Sir?"

"No need to thank me. You were the best candidate for the job."

This was a bit of a shock. I was fairly sure even a small ship like the 475 rated some officers that were not lowly new ensigns. Certainly someone with some experience should be ordered here as executive officer, a ship's second in command.

"Will there be anyone else joining, sir? Any other officers?"

"Supposed to be," said the captain. "But you know what they say about supposed to be. There's supposed to be a heaven, but I'll believe it when I see it. And I'm not all that anxious to get there. Right now I prefer the kind of angels that smell good and sit on barstools."

"Sounds like a country song, captain."

"Yes, it does. Probably is. Anyway, the sad story is we're shorthanded and might just stay that way, so we'll have to make do. No choice in the matter."

"Yes, sir." If I had learned anything in officer training, it was that "yes, sir" was an all-purpose response to just about anything, unless the skipper says something like "Do you think I'm some sort of jackass?"

"Normally, only officers stand the deck watch when we're underway. And there's only the two of us, so far. But the captain doesn't stand watch, you know. I could, but I don't want to. I'll be in the bridge enough as it is. Which leaves just you. And I suppose you're the kind who likes to sleep now and then."

"Only when necessary, sir."

"Well, relax. The good news is we've got a senior warrant officer who can fill in till we get another couple of officers. And we have a quartermaster chief who can as well. They both know more about ship handling than you do and almost as much as me. That gives us three for underway deck watch. Four hours on, eight off, so you'll have time to work on your suntan and memoirs. How's your navigation?"

"Fair, sir."

"That's honest, anyway. The chief quartermaster is a fair hand at it too. You'd expect that from a quartermaster, since that's their specialty. And I know which end of a sextant to look through and where the sun and stars are, generally. So between you, me, and the chief, we should manage to find our way around without having to stop and ask directions. What did you do in civilian life?"

"I was a private detective in Los Angeles."

"Like in the movies? Did you wear a hat and trench coat?"

"Only in the rain, sir. And it doesn't rain much in L.A."

"Well, well. I'm guessing you don't shock easy."

"I don't think so, sir."

"That's good. Why in hell'd you leave that to join this outfit? Kill somebody important? Run off with the mayor's girlfriend?"

"I figured there was a war coming, sir."

"You figured right, seems like. Well, if you were a private dick, you've been around and probably know the difference between duck feathers and pussy hair."

"I think so, sir."

"I'd be surprised if you didn't," said the captain. "'Course, it ain't that hard to tell if you look at 'em side by side. But real-life experience is good. Maybe the men won't be able to fool you more than half the time. That'd be better than most new ensigns."

He took a cigar from his pocket.

"Care for one of these?" he said.

"No, thanks, Captain. I don't smoke."

He nodded and lit his cigar with a Zippo.

"A fine thing, a Zippo. Just about perfect in conception and design. When I joined the Navy, I promised my Aunt Lucy I wouldn't smoke cigarettes. She didn't say anything about cigars. She was a nice old lady, but she didn't understand the first rule about giving orders—be precise. You said your first name is Riley. Is that the name you go by?"

"Yes, sir."

He nodded.

"I like to know what a man likes to be called. I once went hunting with a fella. He was a southerner, kind of a redneck like me, and he had a damned good bird dog. That dog could smell a quail in a garlic patch, and when I asked that ole boy what the dog's name was, he said, 'Well, his name is Henry, but he don't like it, so he *goes by* Monroe.'"

I had to laugh. Captain Ford paused and studied me for a moment.

"Now, I'm glad to see you smile at that," he said, "because there are two kinds of people in the world—those that think that's funny and those that don't get it. I prefer the company of the first. A fella with no sense of the ridiculous is depressing to be around. A Navy ship is a small community. I don't say it's a family, because a good crew gets along better than most families. And a good crew has no room for long faces."

"Yes, sir."

"Luckily, there ain't anyone on God's green earth that's as irreverent as a sailor. Makes him mighty fine company. The best. The trick is not to spoil it."

"Yes, sir."

"Generally speaking, it's only the officers that can screw the pooch and make life miserable on board a ship. Usually they learn better over time. The good ones, anyway. The ones straight from boat school take the longest, because they think they actually learned something at the Academy. But even they catch on eventually, most of them. Since you come right from civilian life and an actual job, maybe you'll catch on quicker."

"I'll do my best, sir."

"Your file says you're twenty-five. You look a tad older."

"That could be a mistake in the file, sir."

"The Navy doesn't make mistakes, which means you're younger than you think. Be sure and write and tell your mother. I expect she'll be surprised to hear it. Is she still alive?"

"No, sir."

"Oh. Sorry about that. Well, that sort of thing happens. You married?"

"No, sir."

"That's good. Married men sometimes get distracted by goings-on at home. They start thinking about what the missus is up to and gradually lose interest in scraping paint."

"Hard to believe, sir."

"I know. But it's true. On my last ship we had a gunner's mate whose wife ran off with a carnival barker. The fella was a weight guesser, and when he guessed she was fifty pounds lighter than she was, she fell in love right there. Came as a shock to that gunner's mate. Had to give him compassionate leave to go home and straighten things out. He came back, but he was never the same. He had suffered a disappointment."

He looked at me with a sly expression. I knew an opening for a straight line when I heard it.

"What was it?" I said.

"The disappointment? He didn't say."

"Maybe it was that she came back."

"No. That wasn't it. She stayed gone. The last he saw of her, she was running the kettle corn stand. That was the wrong job for a fat woman. Or the right one. Depends how you look at it. 'Course, most things do. But it was a sad story. Wouldn't you say?"

"If you say so, sir. But it's a little hard to believe."

He nodded in approval.

"I thought so, too, at the time. Could be that gunner's mate was pulling a fast one and just wanted some time off. Now and then, a sailor will get inventive. They don't always tell the honest truth, or any other kind for that matter."

"I'll remember that, sir."

"You'd be wise to. Well, the good news about us being shorthanded is that you'll have a room to yourself. Just across the passageway there. The bad news is you're going to work your ass off getting this bucket ready for sea. But God help the Germans once we do. I pity the poor bastards. You know they scuttled the *Graf Spee* down in Montevideo. That was in '39. Must have heard about plans for the *Nameless*. Get your gear squared away, and then we'll have a tour around."

"Aye, aye, Captain."

"I have to admit I like hearing that, Riley. Nothing like being the skipper. Nothing in the world. I'd rather be captain of a Navy ship than king of Ruritania, wherever that is. Never thought I'd get here, but I have, and I aim to do a good job at it. You do the same, and we'll get along just fine."

"I'll do my best, sir."

"Well, let's hope that's good enough."

I left him and breathed a sigh of relief. I figured I'd been tested and passed, because I knew when to smile, which meant I wasn't visibly nervous and could spot a dab of intentional bullshit. Captain Ford was a mustang, but all indications were that he was OK. He had a sense of humor. Aside from fairness and knowing what he was doing, that was about all you could ask from a skipper. No other pedigrees required.

And the more I thought about our conversation, the more I realized that Captain Ford had also given me some practical lessons in how to be an officer.

Chapter Four

A Navy ship of any almost any size—any size bigger than a PT boat, say—is organized pretty much the same way. The executive officer—the exec—is second in command to the captain. Then the men are organized in departments, like engineering, deck, communications, navigation, supply. Those are the basics. Bigger ships may have more departments. The department head is usually a fairly experienced officer, and the bigger the ship, the more senior he is. In his department there are divisions, and each division is in charge of junior officers. The deck department, for example, might have a gunnery division and two other divisions dividing up the work of keeping the ship in good repair. On a bigger ship like a cruiser or a battleship, gunnery is naturally a department on its own. The engineering division is responsible for keeping the ship's power plant working; the communications department operates the various signals, both visual and radio, sending and receiving messages, coding and decoding, and so on. Each department is manned by sailors who are specialists in that discipline, as well as neophyte seamen who have not yet qualified and therefore do the bulk of the routine work. Meanwhile, when the ship is underway, some of these same officers take turns standing watch on the bridge, which is the control center of the ship. This Officer of the Deck, or OOD, is responsible for handling the ship, giving orders to the helmsman, and making sure the ship is following the course and speed the captain has dictated—and making sure the ship doesn't run into any trouble of any kind, such as collisions with other vessels, reefs, and storms, and, in fact, any and all things that could endanger the ship. The captain can't be on the bridge at all times, nor does he want to be, and the OOD is therefore in charge. Only the captain and the exec can tell the OOD what to do. Even officers who may outrank the OOD cannot give him orders or countermand anything he does.

Ship handling is an acquired skill, and probably the most satisfying thing a young officer does. It takes a little work and experience to get qualified. An officer who does not qualify is considered something of a failure, regardless of his other virtues. Ship handling is, after all, the essence of the service. But because we had only one commissioned officer to stand watch—me—we needed one of the chief petty officers to fill in. A chief petty officer was the Navy's top enlisted man, the equivalent of an army sergeant. The other watch stander was a senior warrant officer. A warrant officer was a specialist who ranked below the lowest commissioned officer—an ensign—but above all enlisted men, including chiefs. He had wardroom privileges. The wardroom was the officers' lounge and dining room.

Because the 475 was undermanned and because, aside from the captain, I was the only commissioned officer, we did away with divisions and just kept a departmental organization. Most departments were run by senior petty officers who were specialists in that particular discipline. The deck department was run by Chief Warrant Officer Tom Wheatley, communications by a senior signalman, and so on. We would stay that way until the Navy Department sent us some more officers. Then the new boys would slide into appointed slots and the enlisted men would continue in their departments but report to their appointed officer, who would report to the exec. As it turned out, for the next year we never did get any new officers. There was a good reason for that. There weren't enough to go around. Like the 475, the Navy was shorthanded.

We were supposed to have a crew of seventy, but we were twenty short of that. The men didn't seem to mind too much. The ship was new, so maintenance was not difficult, and there was more room in the crew's quarters. Being undermanned wouldn't really become a problem until we were deployed and operating at sea for weeks at a time. Then the crew might start to get rundown from extra work and lack of sleep, but until then, no one would complain.

All the department heads reported to me, the exec. It seemed ludicrous that I was second in command of a Navy ship. After all, I was only a couple of weeks from training school. But there was no choice, and it didn't take too long to get into the swing of things. That meant paperwork and administration and a lot of dull bureaucracy. It also meant arguing with the base supply officers, trying to get the things we needed. Before I arrived, the captain had organized the various departments and put together the watch assignments, so that part of the job was already done, thankfully.

In my first week aboard ship we got underway in order to start the process of shaking down all our systems and organization and making sure the 475, aka *Nameless*, could do the things she would be required to do. For me, that primarily meant learning to stand OOD watch and learning how the ship handled. Fortunately, we never had to operate with anyone else, never had to travel in formation and keep station, never had to go alongside a supply ship for underway replenishment or do any of the more complicated maneuvers. And it didn't take too many trips out into the Gulf before I had a decent idea of the basics. I had learned the theory in training. Now it was a matter of practice and experience. The captain was helpful, and so were CWO Tom Wheatley and Quartermaster Chief Russo, the two other OODs. It was in everybody's best interest to get me up to speed as soon as possible. So it was a busy week.

I also got to know the men. When I first reported, the captain called the men together, and they fell in according to their departments. The captain then introduced me to them all and invited me to say something to them. I told them I was just out of officer training, and that they all probably knew what that amounted to and what it didn't amount to. That brought some smiles. I told them I had a lot to learn but that I was a pretty fast learner, and I'd work hard at it. I said the captain had praised them as a good and professional and dependable crew, and I looked forward to working with them. And I finished by saying I'd do my best by them and for them, and I expected they'd do the same for me and the ship. And that was it.

"Good speech," said the captain, afterward. "The men liked it. And I passed the word through the usual gossip channels that you used to be a private eye in L.A. and that you'd lost count of the starlets you'd serviced. So the men are predisposed to respect you."

"Starlets? What about the fully fledged stars, Captain?"

"I didn't want to go too far. Bullshit doesn't stretch like saltwater taffy. But if you want to drop a few hints about Betty Grable, it's all right with me. I doubt she'll complain."

"Well, sir, she hasn't so far." That was the truth, so far as it went. I'd met her once at a cocktail party.

The captain did a mild double take and then nodded.

"Good to know," he said. He paused for a moment. "Well, we got our work cut out for us. You know, I figured we'd get into it with the Krauts, but I'm sort of surprised it happened the way it did. Hitler must be a dumb son of a bitch to jump on us just because the Nips did. But now we got a two-ocean war on our hands."

"I suppose the Germans had a treaty with the Japanese."

"Treaties never bothered Adolf before. Well, it's a mistake, and he'll regret it."

"What's it mean for us?"

·"Hard to say. But if I had to guess, the *Nameless* will spend the rest of the war looking for U-boats. Whether along the Atlantic coast or maybe in convoy duty or maybe right here in the Gulf."

"You think the Krauts would send U-boats here?"

"Those bastards will go anywhere they can sink a ship, and just think of the easy pickings here. All those tankers moving oil from Galveston and New Orleans, not to mention the ones coming up from Venezuela. Plus there's all sorts of normal merchant ships carrying bananas and toilet seats and what all from one place to another."

"Lots of targets."

"Like a kid under the bleachers with a brand-new slingshot. You know those Venezuela tankers travel all alone. Most merchantmen do, I should say. Aside from a jackass or a mule, there ain't a more independent critter than a merchant captain. Hates the sight of another ship and wouldn't listen to his own mother. Those tankers'll pass by here on their way up the coast to New York and from there over to jolly old England, some of 'em, anyway. Man, if I was a U-boat commander, I'd be itching to get right here in our backyard. Because you know the only thing that's in their way right now?"

"Us?"

"And a few others like us. But not many. Not many. Well, we'll know what the Navy wants us to do about it all. I figure the base commander will tell us pretty shortly."

He did.

Captain Ford came back from a meeting of ship commanders and the naval base commander. He called me and the department heads together. We met in the 475's wardroom. The wardroom was usually reserved for officers as their lounge and dining room, but under the circumstances it was the only place big enough and private enough to have a meeting. Plus, the *Nameless* was already operating in unconventional ways. One more break from convention wouldn't matter much, if at all.

"Gents, I figure we got only a couple of months before the shit hits the piano player, and we'll need all of that time to make sure we're ready to take on the U-boats, because the word is they'll be coming here as sure as Adolf is a dick-less vegetarian. That's what our intelligence boys think, and you know as well as I do that they're never wrong. Seems that the Krauts have been planning for this for quite a while. They've got spies scattered around the

Gulf who tell them that there's nothing to stop them but a few patrol ships like the lucky *Nameless* and a few ancient destroyers. Plus there's a couple of PBYs and a blimp to help out, but that's about it. Over time there'll be more ships and more planes, but for the foreseeable future, we'll be going it pretty much alone.

"Now I'm sure you're all familiar with that best-selling novel *The Bobbsey Twins Sink a U-Boat*, and I feel confident that if we ever do see one, we'll be able to do just as good a job. But the problem is—finding the bastards. I'm told that there're some tricky new electronic weapons that we'll eventually get, like radar and some other gizmos. But for now all we've got is our eyes. Once we spot one, we've got sonar, of course, but that ain't worth a damn for searches over big stretches of sea. We have to see 'em before we can attack 'em. That means constant patrolling with the few ships we have. We've got PBYs, like I said, and they can cover a lot of territory, but we don't have enough of them either. We've got some dive bombers, but they have a tendency to run out of gas quickly, so they'll be kept on the beach. Their job will be to respond, if and when somebody spots a U-boat and calls for help. We've got some civilians who're volunteering to cruise around the Gulf in their fishing boats and yachts, and if they see something suspicious they'll radio Key West and have them send a plane. Or us. In short, we're as thin as Popeye's girlfriend, and we're limited by how far the human eye can see. And we just plain don't have enough eyes. Not nearly enough. What's more, the bastards can see us too, and if they want to fight, they can either hit us with a four-inch-caliber deck gun—which as you damn well know is bigger and can shoot farther than our three-inch fifty—or they can sink us with a torpedo, if they feel like wasting one on a patrol ship with no name. But if they want to run away, all they have to do is pull the plug and submerge. At which point we're left with our thumb up our ass, like the fat boy whose date ran off with the quarterback. So in words of one syllable, we are in deep shit for the foreseeable future. At least six months. Probably more like a year. And so is every other ship that floats on water. Any questions so far?"

"Any good news, Skipper?"

"I'm glad you asked that. Yes, there is. The Andrews Sisters have a new hit record, and Mae West does not wear falsies. That was a rumor spread by subversives. They've been rounded up and shot for spreading gloom and despondency. What's more, Sloppy Joe's Bar has definitely not run out of beer. So there's plenty to feel good about."

"What's next, Captain?"

"Well, like I said, we're gonna be busier than a two-peckered stud horse. Just nowhere near as happy. The Krauts will be coming our way, sure as

Himmler's a fairy. So this base is on lockdown, which means there's no extended leave for anyone. Every day we're in port—and there won't be many of those—there'll be liberty for one section. They can go into town, but that's it. Another section can have the run of the base, so the non-com's club will be available. The duty section will stay aboard, of course, and stay alert. The one good thing about being on this sandy pancake is it's small enough so that if we have any kind of emergency, the whole crew can get back here fast. We will continue our underway training during the day, which is another way of saying we'll be on patrol for real. The CO figures the Huns will take awhile to get organized, so we'll have some time before they show up, maybe. But we can't take any chances. You can bet they've already got plans for this sector in their file cabinets. So I figure it won't be long before we start smelling knockwurst and sauerkraut. Any other questions?"

"What's the name of the Andrews Sisters' new hit?"

"I don't remember exactly. Something that rhymes with Nantucket. Now get the hell out of here and tell the men the score. And don't just tell 'em what's happening. Tell 'em why. They ain't going home for a while, and they got a right to know the reasons. One more thing—all the mail has to go through the exec. He'll be the censor. We don't want the men accidentally giving out any classified information. Censorship is Navy-wide, so don't let the boys think they're special. Most of 'em don't write the truth to their wives anyway, but they might make up something that's useful to the enemy."

"Who's gonna check the exec when he writes to all his Hollywood sweeties?"

This brought a good-natured laugh.

"I asked him about that," said the captain, with a sardonic smile, "and he said he'd only write to the ones he knows will be faithful. So he won't need a censor. That's all, men."

Chapter Five

I have a friend who was a professor of art at UCLA. He's an Englishman, and he just recently returned to England to work for the British Secret Service. He once gave me a book called *The Wind in the Willows*.

"Many people think it's a children's book," he said. "It isn't."

So I read it and understood what he meant. And early on there's a passage that I see quoted every once in a while: "Believe me, my young friend, there is *nothing*—absolutely nothing—half so much worth doing as simply messing about in boats. Simply messing."

And I remembered a line from Huck Finn—"It's lovely to live on a raft." Those were the same kinds of feelings you got at sea, even—or maybe especially—on a Navy vessel. The first time I stood OOD watch, I understood. I stood on the bridge, in the pilot house, overlooking the bow of the ship as she cut through the blue waters of the Gulf, and on that day at least the water was as smooth as a lake, so that the bow wave was creamy and symmetrical. Dolphins were riding in that wave, doing their version of Hawaiian body surfing, and jumping and diving and looking for all the world like their only object was to enjoy themselves. The Greeks believed that dolphins would rescue sailors and carry them to shore and that they were the special pets of Poseidon. On that perfect day, standing watch on the bridge of the *Nameless*, you could almost believe it, if you wanted to.

The captain was in his chair on the side of the pilot house. He was as relaxed as a curled-up cat. I knew he was there to keep an eye on me and to coach me in the ways of ship handling in general and in the moods of the *Nameless* in particular. And I was glad of it. But he didn't seem all that concerned. Well, we were in the middle of the Gulf and there was no one else around. Behind me was the helmsman standing at the ship's wheel. He would do exactly what I said, when I said it, and only that, unless the captain countermanded my orders. But the thought that a mere word from me would alter the motion of this vessel and the lives of the fifty or so men in it was melodramatic, pleasant, and more than a little inflating all at once. That being said, I was also a little nervous. Next to the helmsman was the engine order telegraph, which we used to send orders to the engine room—all ahead full, all ahead standard, all back one-third, and that sort of thing, just the way you see it done in the movies. The quartermaster of the watch was a second class petty officer. He was standing by the chart table. There was a gyro compass in front of me indicating our course. We were steering 180 degrees—not "one hundred and eighty," but "one eight zero." But the captain was having me run through some course changes just to give me a better and better feel of how the ship handled.

"I imagine they explained all this in training," he said, "but it never hurts to repeat the important stuff, like telling your girl you love her. Or in your case, 'them.' A ship doesn't turn in a line, even though it seems to. She kind of slides through the water when she turns. The stern slides out from under you one way and the bow out the other, while you stand sort of in the middle. The screws work like hell to push her straight forward, but she won't do it in a turn and insists on sliding a little to the side. Kind of like skidding. When you're turning right, she's sliding left and vice versa, of course."

"Is that why ships are called females, Captain?"

"Nope. They're called females because every damned one of 'em is beautiful, even the old and ugly ones."

We were in our assigned cruising area between Key West and Havana. We would patrol around in prescribed patterns until the evening, when we would put into Havana on some official business having to do with the Cuban navy. Ninety miles of open sea—it didn't sound like much, until you were in it. Then the idea of seeing the squatty conning tower of a U-boat, much less its periscope, seemed like something else again. A landsman never thinks much about the curvature of the earth, but you very quickly understand it at sea. A small thing like a periscope becomes invisible only a few miles away, and giant ships can disappear below the horizon. That's one reason some lookouts are perched on the highest points of the ship. The higher they are, the farther the horizon, and the farther they can see. That doesn't change the fact that a U-boat periscope is mighty small and difficult to see at almost any distance, and a U-boat conning tower, which is low in the water, can become invisible after only a half dozen miles, even when the sub is completely surfaced. And since your ship sits higher in the water and has a higher superstructure, he can see your masts when you can't see him. It may be lovely on a raft, as Huck said, and it's also lovely on a ship, but when you're at sea in wartime, things become a little more complicated.

On this day, though, it was hard to think anything could go amiss. It was early in the war and there had been no reports of U-boats in the Gulf. Not yet, anyway. The Atlantic coast was another story.

"Those merchant skippers are so used to cruising just offshore and thinking they're safer than a nun in a convent," said the captain. "Well, they're getting some surprises, just like those old-time nuns, when the Vikings came calling. U-boats are torpedoing 'em so close to land that the crew can just about step over the side and walk to shore, if they ain't burned to cinders or blown to pieces. People on the East Coast ain't got it through their heads yet that we're in a war with the Germans, so the cities are all lit up like New Year's Eve, and that makes a fine backdrop for a U-boat, when he's lining up a shot on a tanker. Perfect silhouette. By God, it makes me almost wish my old pappy had never left the old country."

"Which old country was that, Skipper?" By now I was used to feeding the captain straight lines. I knew when he wanted a cue.

"Kentucky," he said. "If he'd of stayed there, I wouldn't be sitting here on this floating target. I'd be making bourbon whiskey. Only I wouldn't be making it like he did. I'd be making it legal."

"Is that why he left Kentucky?"

"Could be. I never believed that story about him and the sheriff just having a friendly race. Who knows where I'd be today if that sheriff hadn't blown a tire."

"I can't believe you really regret winding up in the Navy, Captain."

"No, you're right. I don't. Best thing that ever happened to me. But that don't stop a fella from wondering about might-have-beens. I once knew a girl called Elaine . . ."

The lookout called down from the mast.

"Contact off the port bow, sir. Looks like a fishing boat."

The captain and I both looked through binoculars.

"Yes, sir. I see him," I said. "Looks like a single man in a skiff. He's a long way from home." At the time we were twenty miles off Havana.

"Yep. They'll do that, these Cuban fishermen. Sometimes on purpose."

We studied the man for a few moments. We slowed to take a better look and to make sure our wake didn't swamp him. He waved as we got closer.

"He's OK. Just being friendly," said the captain. "He doesn't need anything."

We waved back and kept on our way, increasing speed to all ahead standard, which gave us a good fifteen knots.

"That fella in the boat reminds me of the time I was in Havana in a snug little sailor's bar, right down on the waterfront," said the captain. "That was before I knew better than to go into such places. I got to talking to some of the local guys—fishermen—and they told me about an old boy who went out to sea in a little skiff just like that fella we passed. Well, that ain't very remarkable. They all do it, like I said. Anyway, they watched this guy hook into the biggest marlin any of 'em had ever seen. They were right there near him when it happened, and they saw that fish jump. Looked like a U-boat, only prettier. And that old boy had him hooked really good. He hung on like that fish owed him money. Which he did, if the old boy could land him. But that fish wasn't having any of it and towed that skiff straight out to sea, just like what happened to them old whalers when they harpooned a big one. It's called a Nantucket sleigh ride, which was mentioned in that song by the Andrews Sisters, I believe."

"What happened to them?"

"The Andrews Sisters? Nothing that I know of."

"No, I meant to the fisherman and the fish."

"Hard to say. They disappeared over the horizon, and that was the last anyone ever saw of that fish or the old boy who hooked into him. The story's a legend around here. Kind of like 'The Flying Dutchman.'"

"Sort of a sad story."

"Yes, it is. The old boy had a wife and nine children, some of them his. 'Course they were all grown by then and didn't suffer any, because the boys had a good business running rum up to Florida, and the girls all worked nights in the bars of the city. Mama stayed home and bulked up on fried plantains, black beans, and rice. That's a Cuban specialty you should try, by the way. So, she stood her bereavement without any strain. She and the old boy didn't get along, anyway. Well, that was understandable, since they'd been more or less married for forty years, and there weren't any exciting discoveries coming their way."

"I wonder why that fisherman kept at it. Fishing I mean. Seems as though his family was in pretty good shape."

"Hard to say. Just liked doing it, I guess. 'Course, for all anyone knows, that fish towed him clear to Tampa. Could be there right now, rolling cigars. That's a big business in Tampa, and Cuban cigar rollers are always in demand. They get top dollar. Local rollers ain't a patch on your average Cuban."

With sunset approaching we were just outside the harbor entrance to Havana. I was hoping the captain would take over, because I wasn't looking forward to conning the ship through the opening of the harbor. From my perspective it looked narrower than it really was, and my first flush of OOD pride was draining away. Even worse, I wasn't at all confident about my ability to get her into whatever berth the Cubans had assigned. And of course the captain understood.

"I'll take it from here, Riley," he said.

"The captain has the conn," I announced.

"Ain't necessary, Riley," he said. "Anyone else takes over or whenever you relieve the watch, then yes, you tell the world. The captain always takes it just by giving an order."

"Sorry, sir."

"No worries. Just another item for your book of memories."

We went gliding through the harbor entrance as smoothly as you please. On the left was the stone lighthouse and the massive masonry fort called the Morro.

"It wouldn't take much to blast a ship out of the water from there," I said.

"Nope." He smiled his ironic smile at me. "I figure that's why they put it there."

Beyond, after the long, narrow entrance channel, lay the city, old and dignified and a little shabby. Mostly faded white.

"The place always reminds me of Miss Havisham," said the captain. "I figure you know that story."

"Yes, sir, I do."

"She's all dressed up, but her dress ain't as fresh as it once was. Still, there are worse places for a sailor. And I've been in most of 'em. Pass the word—set the sea and anchor detail."

The quartermaster announced this over the 1MC, which was the ship's intercom and loudspeaker, and the men from the deck department ran to get the mooring lines ready to pass to the Cuban line handlers on the dock.

We headed for the first set of docks on the right side of the harbor. The captain ordered all stop as we glided toward them, and then all back full for a few seconds to take off the remaining forward motion.

"I expect they taught you this in training, too" he said, "but it doesn't hurt to repeat something. When you're coming into a slip or a dock like this, the best way is to pull up opposite and stop. 'Course, she won't stop on a dime, so you have to anticipate, maybe even back the engines to slow her down. Then when you're stopped where you want to be, you put the rudder over, reverse one engine and go forward with the other, and the old gal—or the new gal in our case—will just pivot around smooth as you'd want, so that when the bow comes almost around to where you want it, you put your rudder amidships, stop all engines, let her swing come to a stop, and then go ahead slow and slide into the berth like you know what you're doing."

Which we did. The deck gang had lowered the fenders and thrown the mooring lines, and the men on the docks pulled them in and looped them over the bollards, and we were there. Our men ran the gangway ladder onto the dock.

"Pass the word, secure the sea and anchor detail. Sections one and two will have liberty commencing at 1800 hours. Section three will have the duty." The captain turned to me. "I'll be staying aboard tonight, Riley. There's a conference with the Cuban navy in the morning that you'll want to attend, 0900 in the wardroom. But there's nothing going on tonight, so if you want to see the sights, go ahead."

"I'd like that, sir. I haven't been here before. Any recommendations, Captain?"

"Well, you might try the Floridita Bar. If I remember correctly, you take a right along the waterfront here until you come to O'Reilly Street. Ain't far at all. Turn left on O'Reilly and follow it till the end, turn left again and look for a sign. Their specialty is daiquiris, but I'd stay away from those if I was you. Rum drinks can cause problems next morning, if you have more than a half dozen. But I expect you know that. I have to keep reminding myself, you ain't some wet-nosed fraternity boy fresh off a panty raid."

"O'Reilly Street? Funny name in Cuba."

"Yep. Named after an Irishman who worked for the Spanish king back in the days when people took religion seriously and fought about it. Decent soldier, he was, apparently. I may be wrong, but I think he had something to do with building the fort at the harbor entrance. Must've been a modest fella. Didn't name it after himself, like some would have. The full name is Castello de los Tres Reyes del Magos de Morro. The Spanish like long names. The Magos are the three Magi, which is curious. I'm almost positive those old boys never visited Cuba, though they did get around some. Navigated by the stars, same as sailors."

Chapter Six

When the ship was secure and the liberty sections had left on the eternal twin missions of the sailor in port, I changed into civilian clothes and left for the Floridita. O'Reilly Street seemed to represent all that a very old colonial city was—buildings that were once elegant but now needed some paint or a good power wash, people who were a mixed bag of Spanish and Indian and black, some of the women pretty and everyone either indifferent or friendly. No one overtly hostile. They were used to Americans, knew we had money to spend and were not hard to satisfy. The prostitutes were especially glad to see an American Navy ship come into port. They and sailors are ancient allies, of course. There weren't many beggars, and the ones who were there were satisfied with a nickel. Someone told me you could get a good bowl of soup for a nickel. A shot of rum was probably even cheaper. No one seemed to care much about the litter or the newspaper pages blowing here and there. The streets hadn't been swept for a while, but were not too bad. There wasn't much car traffic, and the buses were very old and smelled like it.

I found the Floridita where the captain said it would be. It was small and dark with a long bar along one wall and the standard large mirror on the wall behind. There were a few tables scattered around the rest of the room. But it was clean and not crowded. There were no angels on the barstools, but it was early yet. There were a couple of prostitutes at the other end. They smiled at me, but that meant nothing. They have a well-developed sense of who's in the market and who's not interested. There was a guy in the middle of the bar eating a club sandwich. There was no one else. I sat down at the end of the bar and leaned my back against the side wall.

The barman came over, smiling.

"Senor?" he said.

"I hear daiquiris are a specialty of the house."

"You have heard correctly, senor."

"Maybe I should try one. What's in them?"

"White rum and grapefruit juice and a few other little touches for color and a little flavor. Sugar if you want it, but that is optional. If you would permit me, I would recommend a double."

"OK. But no sugar, please." I figured if I didn't have more than a couple, the next morning wouldn't be a problem.

He made one and presented it with a flourish. It was a frozen concoction in a tall glass. It tasted good, and I could see that after the first one you might think having three or four more would be a good idea. It wasn't too sweet. I suppose the grapefruit juice balanced out the rum.

"You like, senor?"

"Yes. Very good."

The barman smiled and then looked toward the door, and his smile broad-ened. It was a smile of recognition. A tall blond woman in a clingy black dress was standing in the doorway. She had stopped and was looking around, as if checking to see if someone was there, someone she was not expecting exactly, but someone who might have come without letting her know. She looked specifically in my direction.

For a moment I thought she might be that mainstay of the Hollywood detective picture—the femme fatale. She had the look. And she knew how to enter a scene. But that idea faded quickly, and I was soon thinking that there may be something different about her. A femme fatale is usually pretty one dimensional. This woman seemed to offer something more than that. Not a femme fatale. A *femme interessante*. Or whatever the term would have been in Spanish.

She was the kind of woman people describe as beautiful, even though she wasn't, particularly. It was more her manner than her looks that created the impression. She was assured. And it was not an act; it was genuine and there-fore appealing. She knew she'd be the center of attention in any room, and because she was accustomed to it, she gave it no importance. She was what the French call *soigne*, a word that is hard to translate but more or less means well-groomed and not overdone—"clean," in the way the lines of a sailing yacht are clean. Her blond hair was shoulder length and probably her best feature. Her face was tanned, and yet she was nothing like the blond women and girls of California whose tans suggested health and outdoor sports. She looked as if she would be as comfortable in a smoky bar as on a beach, and that was a rare combination in my experience. Most of the women I knew were either one thing or the other. Or neither. She had a slightly long face and nose. Her features were nothing out of the ordinary, nothing to suggest the perfection of a UCLA cheerleader, for example. In short, she wasn't even pretty. But then some beautiful women are not what you'd call pretty. Not at all. Would you say that Garbo was pretty? Dietrich? Sometimes a young girl's prettiness matures into beauty, but it doesn't happen the other way around. A beautiful woman doesn't become pretty with age; she just stays beautiful in her own way, right up to the end. This woman's eyes were large and brown and luminous, and there was an expression in them that was sly and mischievous and a little hard. I'd seen that look plenty of times but not with this level of complexity. Most of the Hollywood tough girls had only one level of gum-chewing hardness. This one was nuanced and multifaceted, humorous and skeptical. She looked like she'd be a handful, as the expression goes. She was sexy as hell.

Of course, I didn't know all this right away, that first night. I learned most of it later. But the elements were all there that evening when she walked into the Floridita. She was a package of signals that you saw but couldn't unravel and decode until later, after she let you know her, after the two of you had talked well into the night, after she'd let you take her to bed. Or maybe it was after she took you. Is that the only way you ever really get to know a woman? I don't know, but I do know it's one very good way to do it.

She surprised me by coming up and sitting on the stool next to me, although there were plenty of open places along the bar.

"You're sitting in a famous seat," she said with a smile. Was I about to make a friend? It seemed like it.

"Really? No one told me. What's it famous for?"

"That's all right. He's not around."

"Who?"

"The famous man who usually sits there." She took out a Chesterfield and lit it with a gold Ronson. Then she signaled to the barman. "I'll have one of those, Constante," she said, indicating my daiquiri.

"Si, Marty," said Constante.

"Do you like that drink?" she said to me.

"It's pretty good. Tastes a little like those slushy things you get at the county fair."

"You're right, although it's been awhile since I've been to a county fair. Do they still sell those funnel cakes?"

"They do in Ohio."

The bar man delivered her drink and she took a good-sized swallow. I noticed she had long, slender fingers. She wasn't wearing any rings.

"They give you plenty of rum," she said. "But it doesn't overpower you with the taste. So beware. What are you doing in Havana? You don't look like a tourist. Are you a gangster?"

"I'm an officer in the Navy. We're here for some sort of meeting."

"What kind of meeting?"

I smiled at her and said nothing.

"I see," she said. "Good. It's wise of you to be discreet in this town. It's filled with all sorts of riffraff and the wrong sorts of people. Politically, I mean."

"Spies?"

"Lots of them. Amateur and professional."

"I've heard that. Do you live here?"

"Yes. For my sins. Are you career Navy?"

"No. I'm a new boy. Just along for the war. My name's Riley Fitzhugh. I heard Constante call you Marty."

"Short for Martha."

"Which do you prefer?"

"Doesn't matter. Either one. What did you do before the Navy?"

"Promise not to laugh?"

"No, not if it's funny. What were you? Some sort of defrocked priest? Like something out of Graham Greene?" She paused for a moment, as though conscious of having said something wrong. "I'm sorry. Have I made some sort of snotty literary reference? I didn't mean to, if I did. It just popped out."

"Don't worry about it. As a matter of fact, I know who he is. I don't much care for him, though. Kind of gloomy."

"He's better when he doesn't try so hard. So what *did* you do before the Navy?"

"I was a private detective in L.A.," I said.

"I thought you said you were from Ohio."

"Hollywood by way of Youngstown."

"Ah! Really? Hollywood, huh? And not an actor? That's surprising. I'd have guessed you were. But I don't think being a PI is funny," she said. "It's kind of interesting. Like something out of the movies or that magazine, *The Black Mask*. Do you read that?"

"Now and then."

"Have you ever shot anyone?"

"No. Someone else usually takes care of that. I arrive on the scene after the body has been discovered."

"That's smart. But I'll bet you carried a gun. I'll bet it was a snub-nosed police special. A thirty-eight."

"No, I didn't carry one. But I had one around."

"Did it spoil the cut of your clothes? Is that why you didn't carry it?"

"That's exactly why." And I wasn't being a smart-ass. That was actually the reason. "They're heavy, especially when they're loaded. And uncomfortable. The cops have to carry one, but I don't. Or didn't."

"I know," she said. "Women are lucky, because we can carry ours in a purse."

"Do you have one?"

"You bet. So don't get fresh, see?" She was playful, in a friendly way. There was no undercurrent of anything. "Did you lurk around in the shadows taking pictures of lovers doing naughty things? You don't seem that type."

"Thank you, I think. There are guys who do that, of course, but oddly enough my most recent cases had to do with art theft and forgeries."

"You were a high-class type." This wasn't a question, nor was it a mockery. It sounded as if she was being sincere. Of course, at that moment I wanted to think that.

"Missing persons also came up now and then," I added. This was true, but I also figured it would make a better impression than mentioning insurance fraud.

She thought about that for a moment.

"How can a missing person come up, I wonder? Isn't that a contradiction? A missing person who comes up is no longer missing. Isn't that right?"

"Yes, now that you mention it. I should have said missing person *cases*."

"Yes, that's better."

"You remind me of my captain. His old auntie disapproves of tobacco and made him promise he would never smoke cigarettes. So he smokes cigars. He told me that as a lesson in giving proper orders. Be precise."

"Yes. I understand. I think I would like your captain."

"You probably would. I like him. He looks like Mark Twain with a Navy haircut."

"How perfect. What other things did you investigate? Routine infidelities?"

"They were sometimes part of the mix. Not always. They usually went along with something else."

"I'll bet. I wonder, is 'routine infidelity' one of those tautologies? You know, like 'honest truth?' Oh, wait . . . I ran across a word just the other day—*pleonastic*. Do you know what it means?"

"Never heard it before."

"I hadn't either, but I looked it up. It means a phrase with unnecessary words, like 'widow woman.' I don't know how that differs from a tautology, but it must somehow, otherwise there wouldn't be two different words. 'Routine infidelities.' 'Routine' is unnecessary because infidelities are nothing unusual. They are by definition routine. An L.A. private dick must agree with that."

"I do. Although I never thought about it."

"That's because they're so routine. You see? Your lack of interest in the subject proves the point."

I had to smile. This was more conversation than I usually got from strange women in a bar. And different. In Hollywood they generally just want to know if you're in the business and if you knew anyone who could help them get a screen test. And depending on whether you were interested or not, you would tell them yes or no, sometimes skirting the truth. Even the "honest truth." What you told them had a lot to do with how they looked. Which meant you said yes more often than not, because let's face it, aspiring starlets rarely look like Margaret Dumont or Ma Joad. The thought made me smile.

"What's funny?" she said.

"I was just wondering whether 'honest truth' was pleonastic."

"Yes. I'd say so, definitely."

"I suppose you're a scholar of some sort," I said. "Probably teach logic at the university."

She laughed at that. She had a pleasant laugh.

"Teach logic? Hell, no. I don't even practice it. Far from it. I'm a reporter. But we call ourselves journalists. It's fancier."

"A journalist? That explains your questioning technique."

"I suppose it does. Is it too aggressive? I'm sorry. It can be rude, even when it's only meant to show interest."

Hmm. Interest is good, I thought.

"I don't mind," I said. "Do you work for a Cuban paper?"

"No. I don't work for anyone right now. The fact is, I've been writing a novel. Just finished the wretched thing. Ugh. I sent it off the other day. Good riddance."

"Really? I impressed."

"Are you?"

"Sure. Working around the movie business, I got to know a lot of writers. I like them as a group and individually. I admire what they do, although they're always grousing about the business. I've thought that maybe when the war's over I'll go back and give it a shot."

She made a face, a grimace.

"It's a dog's life, Riley. Believe me. You'd be better off going back to chasing art thieves."

"What's your book about? Or is that too boring a question to ask a writer?"

"No. Not at all. Any genuine interest is always welcome. God knows there won't be much interest in it once it's published. So—what's it about? About a hundred pages too long. About three months overdue. About this far away from being dreadful. About an unhappily married woman who has an affair with some guy. The usual stuff. I doubt it would interest you."

"Frankly, the way you describe it, I doubt it, too. It doesn't sound like it even interests you."

"It doesn't. Too close to home, maybe."

"Where's that?"

"Home? Just down the road, out in the country. Not far from here. We're the local gentry." She paused and thought of something. "Are you going to be in Havana long? Or can't you say?"

"I can't say because I don't really know. Not too long, probably."

"Based in Key West?"

"Are you a spy?"

"No. I volunteered to be one, but they rejected me."

"Hard to believe."

"Sez you." She smiled at me to mock the tough girl language.

"I guess it's no secret that we have a base in Key West," I said. "But I have a feeling we'll be calling in Havana regularly. I hope so. It seems like an interesting place. Certainly beats Key West."

"Yes. It certainly beats Key West. Most things do." She apparently had something against Key West; it wasn't that bad, after all. "In fact, Cuba is a sunny little tropical paradise," she said, "except for the natives who have to live in shacks and shipping containers. And it's so pleasant most of the time that I feel like a heel sitting here writing trash, while there's a war on. People are getting killed while I'm getting bored. It's frustrating and does absolutely nothing for my self-respect."

"That sort of why I'm here, too. That feeling."

"Really? Is that why you signed up?"

"Basically. I don't mean to sound like Jack Armstrong, the All-American Boy."

"Sponsored by Wheaties?"

"Yes. Breakfast of Champions. But that is why I joined, more or less. Chasing art thieves in Hollywood didn't seem worth doing anymore. Not when this whole thing was going on."

I was a little embarrassed by that. I figured she'd just think it was a line. But she didn't. She reached over and touched my arm, just for a second.

"I like Wheaties," she said. "And I like all-American boys—as long as they voted for Roosevelt. Did you?"

"Sure." I didn't, but this was no time to get into politics.

"For a while I worked for the New Deal," she said, lighting another Chesterfield. "It was worth doing, I thought, but in fact it didn't matter at all. Led to nothing. Not what I did, anyway. I wrote long articles about how miserable life was for southern factory workers, but no one ever read them. They didn't make a penny's worth of difference. What we needed to get out of the Depression was a good war. Well, we got one. And here I sit in sunny Cuba."

"Well, if it's any consolation to you, I think there might be some action in the Gulf sooner rather than later."

"So I've been told. I'd still rather be in Europe. Oh, well. I'll give you my address and phone number," she said. "You must come out and visit. We usually have some people around. It's part of my penance for living here. You might enjoy meeting them. Now and then a writer or artist turns up."

"Thanks. I'd like that."

"We must do our bit for the boys."

"We?"

"Me and my old man. Do you play tennis?"

"Pretty well."

"Good. How about shooting things? Like pigeons."

"Clay or feathered?"

"Oh, feathered."

"Never done it."

"You'll get your chance, I'll bet." I wasn't sure what she was talking about, but it didn't seem to matter.

She wrote down her address and phone number on a bar napkin, finished off her drink, stubbed out her Chesterfield, and then stood up to leave.

"One's usually enough for me. So long, Riley. Please call me. I'm serious. I wouldn't say it if I didn't mean it." She waved at Constante and said, "If His Nibs comes in, tell him I was here earlier, flirting with a good-looking sailor."

And she left.

"Who was that?" I asked Constante.

"Marty? Martha Gellhorn is her name. She is the wife of the famous writer Ernesto Hemingway."

"I see. And this would be his famous barstool."

"Yes. But I knew he was not coming in today. He is out on his boat."

"Apparently he didn't tell her his plans."

"Are you married, senor?"

"No."

"Then perhaps you do not know that husbands do not always tell their wives everything."

"Really? Hard to believe."

"Yes. But true. I am married, so I know these things."

"Well then, you probably know whether it works the other way around, too."

"Who can say, senor? I think that would depend on the wife. This Marty, though . . . she is very beautiful, I think."

By the time she walked out, I had come to think so too. It hadn't taken very long.

Chapter Seven

The next morning at 0900, two officers of the Cuban navy came aboard the 475, or as we had all come to think of her, the *"Nameless."* One was a captain, the other a full commander, so we had side boys at the quarterdeck to render the appropriate honors. A first class bosun's mate piped his whistle as they came up the gangway, saluted the flag and the quarterdeck, and requested permission to come on board. Captain Ford and I were there to greet them and, after introductions, we went to the wardroom.

"Your ship is very fine, Capitan," said the Cuban captain. He was a stout man in a full-dress uniform with the ribbons of many medals. You couldn't help wondering what he had got them for, but there were certainly plenty of them. The commander was similarly bedecked, though he didn't have as many ribbons. He was slim and silent. Both were handsome examples of pure Spanish blood, dark from the sun, not from any heredity.

"Thank you, sir," said Captain Ford. "She is new and we are still in the process of getting acquainted, but I think she'll do nicely."

We sat around the wardroom table. It was covered in the usual green baize. Blake, our one and only steward, served coffee. The Cubans and Captain Ford all lit up cigars, and the small room soon filled with thick blue smoke, the kind that men who like cigars consider something like the air of heaven. It gave me a headache, but I was only an ensign and was expected to take it, which I did.

Cuba had declared war on Germany only a few days after we did, so they were our staunch ally, except for the Falangists, who were German sympathizers. The Cuban navy, though, was shorthanded and ill equipped. They were better supplied with senior officers than with men or ships. In fact, their fleet mostly consisted of motor torpedo and gunboats. They had plans to buy more vessels from us on credit and maybe even to build some. But that was in the future. Mañana.

Although their navy was small, the Cubans had a sizable army. You had the feeling that these troops were designed more to keep the natives in line than to repel invaders. Revolutions were always in season somewhere on the island, especially in the wild and mountainous east. Besides, the place was run by a dictator, and uneasy lies the crown on the head of a guy who knows most people hate him.

The Cuban officers had two items on their agenda. The first was to tell us that they were our firm friends and that they would do everything in their power to help defeat the coming scourge of the U-boats. The United States had shared our intelligence with the Cuban government, and so everyone knew the U-boats were on their way. As part of this presentation, the captain and the commander were saddened to tell us that their resources were limited and that the few vessels they had were not able to do much more than some coastal patrolling. That meant we would bear the brunt of the offshore patrols. Well, we were not surprised by that. Frankly, we and the Navy preferred it that way. This was not meant to be an insult to our allies, but simply to say that problems of language and different signal codes made it difficult to work together closely. There would have to be coordination of efforts managed through the staff on shore, which meant in our case the Office of Naval Intelligence in Havana. The less of that we had to worry about, the happier we would be.

The other item was unexpected.

"We have had word, Capitan Ford," said the more senior Cuban, "that the local fascists are planning to build and man some fueling stations on the far eastern end of the island. There are places that are desolate and mostly uninhabited. A few Indian fishermen and charcoal burners live out there, but no one else. And their villages, such as they are, are not permanent. The area is ideal for a clandestine fuel dump. Is this the correct word? Clandestine?"

"It's a five dollar word for secret, so, yes."

"Good. And I hardly need to tell you that such facilities will be very welcome to the U-boats that have just made an Atlantic crossing and are running low on diesel fuel and fresh food."

"For sure. You say these are being planned? I assume that means they're not in place yet."

"So far as we know. But we cannot be certain of that."

"I don't suppose these dumps will be visible from the sea, maybe disguised as a fishing village," said Captain Ford. "That would be too easy."

"No, Capitan. They will be hidden from sight. All along the north shore there are dozens, even hundreds of tiny islands and inlets, all covered in palms and jungle. You have your Keys, we have ours. Yours are gentlemen and show themselves in a long line that is beautiful to look at from the sea. Ours crouch along the shore and hide themselves behind thick mangroves. You could steam by a few hundred yards out to sea and not see any sign of people, if there were no men working or no U-boats moored and refueling."

"How about from the air."

"The same is true. The jungle will cover them. The men building these places know what they are doing. At least we must assume they do. But even an amateur would realize there are only two ways to spot the dumps—from the sea or from the air. They will protect against both. How many fifty-gallon drums of fuel could you stack under a camouflaged tarpaulin? Or bury in a covered trench? Plenty. There are no roads or villages nearby. The few people who live there travel by boat when they need supplies."

"How did you come by this information, then?"

"We have persuaded one of the fascists to cooperate. Unfortunately, he was killed while trying to escape, so that we only know the broad outlines of the plans. The exact locations and scope of the operations are still a mystery. All we know is that they will be on the north coast tucked away in the mangrove keys and swamps."

"What about the army?"

"As I said, there are no roads and the jungle is thick. Even if we knew where the dumps are, there would be no way to get there except by sea. The army has no amphibious capability, and as I have said, our navy is not designed or equipped for that kind of action either."

"I suppose these stations will get their fuel from supply ships."

"That is the only reasonable conclusion, Capitan. They could not be supplied locally for many reasons. There are no roads, and any major purchase of diesel fuel would be noticed. The only practical possibility is that a German merchant ship will anchor just offshore at night and ferry drums of fuel and supplies to the camp. Then in the morning, if necessary, the merchant can sail over the horizon and wait out the day, as though on its way south or to some port in the Bahamas. Then it could return at night, if it has not finished unloading. They can do this indefinitely. A darkened ship unloading to a darkened camp in an area no one goes to—that is how I would do it, Capitan."

"Me too."

"Naturally they would maintain radio silence and communicate by signal light. Our only possible advantage is that many of these keys are surrounded by shallow flats or reefs. So, either the cargo ship will have to send boats in from fairly far offshore, or the German agents will have to find a key that is not only remote but with deep water close by."

"By the hundred fathom curve, maybe," said Captain Ford.

"Yes. Perhaps. Although there are other keys that have deep enough water close to shore. And no reef to worry about."

"And of course the U-boats could also come at night and the supplies would be ferried out to them. In the daylight they could submerge and wait for night to finish loading, if they need to."

"Exactly, Capitan."

"I see. So we'll be steaming around in the dark looking for shadows along a coastline that's a hundred miles if it's an inch. Life would be simpler if we had radar. But we don't. Not yet. But we have taken a number."

"Capitan?"

"I mean we are in line to get radar, but it's a long line and we're toward the back."

"I understand."

"And since you don't have the tools to deal with this problem, not yet, at least, I guess it's up to us."

"I am afraid so, Capitan. It seems clear that finding and destroying these dumps will be an important part of the campaign against the U-boats. If they are starved of fuel, they will not be able to stay here long. That will cause Admiral Donitz a headache because he will have to rotate his boats. Some will be coming, some going home, some on station here. But if they have a fuel dump that is regularly supplied, one or two boats could stay here almost indefinitely."

"The merchant ships supplying the fuel would also supply torpedoes, food, and ammunition. For the subs and for the base."

"Of course. And can be easily relieved by another ship carrying new food and fuel. Tramp freighters with neutral registration and neutral flags offer a good disguise. And besides, as you will know, the Gulf and the Caribbean are alive with shipping. No one will pay attention to one more tramp steamer."

"I see the problem. Well, Captain, this appears to be our baby, at least for the time being. Have you or your people spoken to our diplomatic people here?"

"Your consideration does you credit, Capitan. And your embassy and naval intelligence people here have been advised of this situation and have communicated it to your commander in Key West. This has all happened in the last few days, you see. I thought it best to tell you personally, but if you have any concerns, please feel free to discuss it with your ambassador and the naval attaché here."

"I assume that there will be no diplomatic problems, if we should find such a place or places, and if we make a landing to take it out or even bombard it from the sea. It would be best if we didn't have to send a signal asking for permission before we could hit it."

"Feel free to do what you think best to destroy the enemy, Capitan. A fuel dump will make a very fine explosion and fire. As I said, it will be in a remote area, so there is no danger to our civilians except perhaps for a few Indian fishermen. And they know how to run away when the shooting starts. They have had many years of practice."

"I'll bet. And there's no chance that we'll run across any friendly little bases out there."

"No. If you see a fuel dump, it will be the enemy. We have no need of such facilities. And if you do find the supply ship in our territorial waters, please feel free to board her, burn her, or sink her, with our compliments. As for the U-boats, well, that goes without saying."

That ended the conference, and the two Cubans left the ship with all appropriate honors on the quarterdeck.

"What do you think, Captain?" I said, when they had gone.

"They sure have fancy uniforms for patrol boat skippers. Probably have lieutenants and ensigns scrubbing decks."

"That commander didn't say much. I wonder what he was doing here."

"I suppose for the same reason you were here. As a witness. Makes good sense. Down here, every senior officer is a potential politician. Which means they never really know when, or if, they're gonna have to explain something to someone. Helps to have someone who can vouch for you. Same with us, for different reasons. But, they're our allies, and the idea of a Nazi fuel dump out in the boondocks of Cuba is enough to worry the Good Humor Man. That Cuban captain is right—with the right kind of supply base, one or two U-boats could stay here till Adolf goes bald."

"I heard our propaganda boys have put out the word that he wears a rug."

"Yeah, and they also say he dresses up at night in one of those fancy fräulein outfits."

"A dirndl?"

"That's the varmint. Can you imagine that picture? It'd make one hell of a pinup. Well, it seems like we've got something to think about. I'm gonna spend the rest of the afternoon looking over charts of this northern coastline. But . . . I want to be sure we have our diplomatic ducks in a row. A Cuban navy captain telling me it's OK to bombard a piece of his country is one thing. The politicians might look at it differently. Cuba may not be much of an ally, but there's no sense in causing more trouble than we need to. Hustle on over to the embassy and double-check. Our naval attaché is a good fella. Make sure this is kosher."

"Aye, aye, sir. I also think there might be a friend of mine stationed there. An FBI agent."

"Really? Well, he might know something worth knowing. Look him up. We're in no hurry to leave. The men will appreciate another night in Havana, especially after being locked down in Key West. Tomorrow will be early enough to get underway again. By the way, did you find the Floridita last night?"

"Yes, sir."

"Anything interesting?"

"Yes, sir."

"Blond or brunette?"

"Blond. But married."

He nodded.

"That's often the way."

Chapter Eight

I walked over to the American Embassy. My friend Bill Patterson had his office there. He had some nebulous diplomatic title, but he was an FBI agent and a spook. He had sent me a postcard a few months back saying that he'd arrived in Havana and that I should call him, if and when I was in the neighborhood.

The Marines at the embassy gate saluted smartly, and I stepped into the impressive old colonial structure. The man at the reception desk told me that Bill was in his office. He called him and in a matter of moments Bill came bounding down the massive staircase.

"Look what the cat's dragged in," he said. "The Navy's pride and joy!"

He was dressed in a white linen suit, white shirt, and black tie. All he needed was a Panama hat to look the role of a successful sugarcane or to-bacco planter. He still had his FBI haircut, though, and a milk and cookies manner that gave him away. He was permanently disqualified for undercover work, unless it was to infiltrate the Boy Scouts. But looks were deceiving. He looked boyish but was in his early forties. An Annapolis grad, he left the Navy for the FBI because he was afraid there weren't going to be any foreign wars and knew there'd always be crime to fight.

"You're just in time to take me to lunch," he said.

"Somewhere cheap, then. I'm just a lowly ensign."

"Fair enough. Then I'll take you. But it's all cheap here, pardner. Every-thing. It's great to see you!"

We went to a place around the corner. It was small with only a few tables, but the smell was rich and complicated and delicious. The tables were covered with shiny white paper, the kind butchers use to wrap meat. And the flatware was some kind of very old metal with a patina of ancient scratches. The chairs were a mixed bag collected individually over the years. We were the first ones there at lunch hour.

"Quaint," I said.

"This place is famous for *boliche*," said Bill. "It's a kind of pot roast with a spicy sausage stuck right through the middle of the beef. Great stuff. Potatoes and carrots and all the fixings. OK?"

"Sounds good."

"Good is not the word." We sat down and ordered beers. "Are you stationed on board ship?"

"Yep. The PC 475, also known as the *Nameless*, not officially, but by her crew. We'll be protecting you from U-boats, primarily."

"Yes! I saw her come in yesterday. Trim little craft."

"I think so. But we don't think of her as a trim little craft, Bill. We think of her as a squared-away fighting ship and a credit to the Navy."

"My sincere apologies."

"Accepted. The captain is a good guy, but we're shorthanded. I'm the exec, if you can believe it."

"Why not? Well, word is you'll be having something to do pretty soon."

"So I hear. What have you heard?"

Bill looked around to see if anyone was listening, but we were alone, for the time being at least. Still, he lowered his voice.

"That's not my area, you understand, but the embassy is small and everyone knows everyone else, so naturally the word gets around. And what I hear is that our people are worried sick about the merchant shipping in both the Caribbean and the Gulf. They figure it's going to be easy pickings for the U-boats, and there's not much we can do about it for the time being. You guys and a few others like you are our only assets. I'm not telling you anything you don't know."

"No. We had a meeting this morning with the Cuban navy."

"All of it?"

"Just two senior guys. They had some interesting intelligence for us about possible Nazi sympathizers establishing supply dumps in the boonies east of here. I was wondering if you guys know anything about it."

"Yeah, we do. Something's definitely in the works. We don't know where or how soon or how many there'll be. But it's happening. This island has got more spies and agents running around than you can shake a dick at. There's all sorts of rumors about plots and sabotage here and on the mainland. A lot of it is just bullshit, but this supply dump stuff is real. It only makes good sense, if you're the Krauts. Dozens of remote locations on a big island loaded with sympathizers and agents. And if one place gets discovered and blown up, it's easy enough to build another."

"Who are they?"

"The sympathizers and agents? It's a mixed bag. You got the Falangists who supported Franco's gang and who think Adolf's a swell guy." He stopped and looked thoughtful for a moment. "You know, I studied history at the Academy, and I remember that it was Ferdinand and Izabella who kicked the Moors out of Spain."

"Columbus's Izabella?"

"The very same. She didn't care for them, since they weren't Catholics. She also kicked the Jews out, but that's another story. Anyway, don't you think it's ironic that this guy Franco brought an army of Moors from Africa to overthrow the government? And he's doing it with the backing of the Church. Funny, huh?"

"Hysterical."

"Anyway. The fascists are just one gang of troublemakers here. And they're probably the biggest group of potential problems. We estimate that there are a couple hundred thousand who lean that way. Then there's the commies. They hate the Falangists but don't like the Yanquis one little bit and will sign up with anyone who'll help them in the short term."

"The enemy of my enemy is my friend."

"For the time being. But they're keeping a list of names for the firing squads, after the revolution. Then you've got people who don't like Batista and know he's robbing the country blind and think they'd do a better job of it. They're not commies and they're not fascists. They're just your garden-variety oligarchs and kleptocrats. And finally there're the real German agents who know what they're doing and pretty much stay out of sight. They're good. The fact that we don't know who they are or how many there are proves it. We hear reports, but that's all we hear. But they're here. That's for sure. And the worry is they're building a fifth column to take over the government. All told, it's quite a crew."

"No Italians or Japanese?"

"Not that I know of. They don't like the food. But rest assured, if a Nip in a kimono ever walks into a Havana bodega and orders raw fish and sake, why, our highly trained agents will spot him in no time."

"But the Germans are the brains behind these dumps?"

"Sure. What could be more logical? You know, when the Germans knocked France out of the war, they were able to build sub bases on the French coast. That really cuts down on the travel time to the Atlantic shipping lanes. I'm sure they told you in boat school that they're tearing up the Atlantic convoys."

"Yes. It was mentioned."

"Well, the Gulf of Mexico is a damned sight farther away, but it's plenty rich in targets and well worth the trip. Plus these merchant captains don't travel in convoys. They have no escorts. They're like coeds at a convention of rapists. And there's no one here to stop the U-boats, except a few hardy sailors like yourselves and the boys down in Gitmo. The Krauts'll have a field day, if they can get their fueling and supply situation worked out. Hence the dumps. Just think, if the U-boats could refuel from the eastern tip of Cuba, they could go into the South Atlantic, the Caribbean, come up here to the Gulf, or even head to the US coastline. What's their cruising range?"

"Eight thousand miles."

"Right. So if you reduce the number of trips one U-boat has to make to and from their French bases, think of the time saved and the extra territory they could cover."

"They'd have to go back for repairs and maintenance some time."

"Of course. But not as often. It'll be a sweet setup for them, if they can pull it off."

"What are the odds of finding out where these places are going to be?"

"So far, not so good. But we're on the case. So are the Cubans, and they know a little bit more than we do about the local agents. They nabbed one and he talked some, but their methods were a little rough, and he didn't survive."

"Yeah, the Cuban officers said he was shot trying to escape."

"Sure he was. Anyway, they'll be rounding up a few more, but I have a feeling the ones they nab will be small fish. The Krauts wouldn't trust this kind of mission to local lowlife. They'll have some of their own people doing the real work. Maybe even drop some regular supply troops off to manage the operation. It wouldn't be hard to do."

"The Cuban officers this morning said we'd have carte blanche to take out these dumps when we find them, but my skipper wants to make sure this won't cause a diplomatic fuss if we do."

"You have orders, certainly."

"Yes, I'm sure the captain has them in his safe. But I don't know that they cover this sort of thing. I kind of doubt it. We just found out about it. This is a potential diplomatic problem, and the skipper knows how that sort of thing can get out of hand. He's been in the Navy twenty years and knows what CMA stands for. He wants me to check it with the politicos. Who knows? We could run across one of these places tomorrow on a routine patrol. We want to be sure of our position, before we get underway and start looking. And we sure as hell don't want to have to call up Key West, so that they can call Havana and ask permission, before we do anything."

"I get it. Well, the best thing to do is go back to the embassy and talk to the powers that be and get some sort of OK, in writing. A memorandum of understanding to go with your CO's orders. Your commanding officer's in Key West, right?"

"Yes. We report to the Gulf Sea Frontier."

"That's good. Our boys are tight with them. We have a good understanding, if nothing else. Let's eat, and then I'll see to it you get to the right folks."

The food was heavy and delicious. You could cut the beef with a fork and the sausage was plenty spicy. On the side there were carrots and potatoes and onions all steeped in the gravy. We washed it down with icy bottles of Hatuey beer.

"This is great," I said. "What kind of sausage is this?"

"Chorizo."

"It's good."

"You know what Bismarck said about making sausage. Well, with chorizo you not only don't want to see it getting made, you really don't want to know what it's made *of*."

"'What the eyes do not see, the heart does not feel.'"

"Words to live by. Enough chili will mask just about anything. How many parrots and stray cats did you see coming over here?"

"I don't remember seeing any."

"I rest my case."

When we were finished we had some strong black coffee, and Bill lighted a good-sized cigar and puffed away contentedly.

"You take up smoking these things yet?" he said.

"No. They give me a headache."

"Too bad. You're missing one of the great pleasures of Cuba."

"Speaking of that, I went to the Floridita last night."

"Ah! *Bueno*. How many frozen daiquiris did you have. The record is sixteen doubles, I've heard."

"Impressive. I had three or four. That was enough."

"Yes. You're not in shape yet to go after the record."

"I met an interesting woman there. Martha Gellhorn."

"I'm not surprised. You don't waste any time as a rule. Seems I've heard the name. A Yanqui, correct? Lives here?"

"Yes. She's married to Ernest Hemingway, the writer."

"That's right. That's where I heard the name. Hemingway, eh. Well, he's an interesting cat. Our boys don't much care for him. But he's well connected. Very friendly with the ambassador and with the ONI head—a Marine colonel."

"Your boys, meaning the FBI? Why the difference of opinion?"

"Well—and this is confidential—we keep a dossier on him."

"Why? What's the point of that?"

"Mr. Hoover doesn't care for any Yanks who went over to Spain in '36 and were sympathetic to the commies. Hemingway was one of them—one of many. Most of them were writers and such. Political naïfs and tools, most of them. And mostly harmless. But Mr. Hoover isn't as broad-minded as I am. There's a dossier somewhere on each one of them, but since this Hemingway lives here in Cuba, he's part of our portfolio. I'd be surprised if his file has anything in it you couldn't show to your maiden aunt. Routine stuff. But he doesn't like us much, either. Calls us draft dodgers, which I really don't care for, one little bit. And he once referred to some of the senior boys as the Gestapo. That ruffled more than a few feathers."

"How many of you guys are down here?"

"Enough. Anyway, this guy fancies himself some sort of secret agent. He's made a deal with the ambassador to bankroll a kind of half-assed spy ring—a bunch of local characters who go around collecting bits of gossip and rumors. He gathers up all this trash and gives it to the ambassador, who gives it to us to check out. It's all worthless and a waste of our time. 'Pedro So and So is banging Maria Whatshername.' Hemingway seems to think he's a real hard-ass operator, but all he's doing is making busy work for us."

"Maybe he'll turn up something about these German supply dumps."

"Not much chance. His only contacts are pimps and cockfighters and the occasional whore. They know where you can buy dope or the best place to catch the clap, but they don't know much else. Not only that, he's getting into your business too."

"What do you mean?"

"He talked the ambassador and the local Navy boys into letting him take his fishing boat out on the Gulf to look for U-boats. The Navy gave him a radio and something called 'huff duff'—I suppose you know what that is. It's new since I was in the service."

"Yes. It stands for 'high frequency direction finder.' We've got it too. It's a way of pinpointing a radio signal. It gives you a compass bearing to where the signal originated. If a U-boat sends a radio message, we'll know where he is at that moment. It's one way we can get a fix on them, but once they stop transmitting and change locations, they're gone. And, of course, a U-boat's not going to stay in one spot for long. And huff duff only has a range of about thirty miles. It's better than nothing, but only just barely."

"Well, anyway, this guy's got his boat's rigged out with that gear and—get this—his plan is to attack a U-boat by going alongside and throwing grenades into the conning tower. Does that make any sense to you, admiral?"

"Nope. You know as well as I do that no skipper in his right mind would let a strange vessel get within pistol shot, let alone grenade range. What kind of boat does he have?"

"A thirty-eight-foot wooden fishing boat."

I had to smile at that.

"A few bursts from a fifty-caliber machine gun would turn it into kindling. The Krauts wouldn't even waste a shell on it, let alone a torpedo."

"Well, that's Martha's husband for you. Have you read his books?"

"One or two. Now that I think of it, I think he dedicated his last book to her. The one about Spain."

"Any good?"

"Yes. Very."

"Well then, maybe you have a clue about what he's like. The word around the shop is he seems to believe his own press clippings."

"What's he use for a crew?"

"A couple of Cuban fishermen and two or three drinking buddies."

"Christ. Amateurs on parade. But I guess he can't do any harm. A few more eyes on the water can't hurt. As I said, we're shorthanded. And if he sees a U-boat, maybe he'll radio the position before committing suicide."

"There's that, I suppose. Still, he makes us professionals a little testy. There are those who think he's just a blowhard."

"Say it isn't so."

"Ah. That's a good song. Who wrote it?"

"Irving Berlin, I think. Either him or Cole Porter. Ozzie Nelson recorded it. He's got a decent band."

"Ozzie Nelson. His girl singer's a dish. Married her, I think. Do you miss Hollywood?"

"Not yet. There are nights when I miss some of the people."

"Blonds?"

"Most of them. But not all."

"I can believe it. I'm happy to be doing fieldwork, but I have to admit I look back on the days in L.A. with some nostalgia."

"It wasn't all that long ago."

"Maybe you'll meet someone who'll make you forget all those California friends."

"That'll be the day."

"Maybe you have already. Met someone, I mean."

"No sense getting ahead of ourselves, Bill, although she did give me her number and asked me to call."

"I would call that an expression of interest."

"Probably. And . . . if the famous author is out looking for U-boats, I suppose that means he'll be away for long stretches."

"A formula for loneliness at home."

"She doesn't seem like the type who gets lonely. Bored, maybe. That's more likely."

Bill looked at me and grinned.

"So . . . what's she look like?"

"Nice."

"Of course. Well, from what I hear, the husband has a temper, and if I remember correctly, you don't have any next of kin. So you can leave me instructions about what to do with the body. I'll have it taken care of."

"Good to know. Well, that was some lunch. The cat and parrot sausage was something to remember."

"You won't have to. It will remember you."

"It's no wonder these people like a siesta. But I'm glad to know about this place. Next time I'll bring a date."

"It's not exactly the Polo Lounge, but it has its own charm. Let's go. I can smoke the rest of this cigar on the way back to the embassy. We'll get you squared away with the powers that be, so you can tell your skipper it's OK to fire any time he sees a Kraut in the mangroves."

"Sounds good. What do I owe you?"

"Nothing. It's on the embassy tab. Speaking of Krauts, have you heard that Hitler likes to wear a dirndl at night and dance the polka with Goebbels?"

"Yes. And I heard he's a very good dancer."

"I wonder who leads."

"And I wonder whose music they dance to."

"Wagner?"

"Ozzie Nelson?"

"Say it isn't so."

Chapter Nine

The next day I had the eight to noon watch, and we were ready to get underway.

"Want to take her out, Riley?" said the captain.

"Yes, sir," I said.

"All right."

I ordered the mooring lines singled up and then ordered "take in the stern line," followed by "take in the bow line" and "all back slow." After blowing three blasts on the ship's whistle, we edged away from the pier into the main channel. When the bow was well clear of the end of the dock, I ordered "all stop." When we had lost most of the way, I ordered "right full rudder, left ahead slow, right back slow," and the *Nameless* swung ninety degrees to the right as sweetly as you could want, and then it was all ahead slow as we headed for the mouth of the harbor.

"Nicely done, Riley. She pivots like Ginger Rogers. We'll head north for a spell."

"Come to course zero zero zero," I said to the helmsman as soon as we were clear of the harbor. And soon we were in the deep blue water of the Gulf Stream.

The meeting the day before with the ambassador and the ONI went well enough, and they gave us a memorandum that said we had the permission of the Cuban government to undertake combat actions against any known or suspected enemy installations on Cuban soil, while being careful to avoid hazarding Cuban property and innocent citizens.

"I wonder what 'being careful' is supposed to mean, exactly," I said.

"Politician talk. Reminds me of a story I read awhile back. Guy named Nash Buckingham wrote it. Ever hear of him?"

"No, sir."

"Well, he's an old-time duck hunter and writer. Southern fella. Anyway, this story is about some guy who goes duck hunting with an old Black guide, and they go out into this marsh, and there are ducks flying around everywhere. So this ole hunter blasts away and blasts away and can't hit a thing. The ducks are flying over his head, grinning. After a while the hunter decides to take a break. He's used up more powder than an old maid getting ready for a date. He and the guide're hiding in this duck blind thinking over their sins, and the hunter is feeling discouraged. Just then a flock of ducks lands in the middle of the pond, not twenty yards away. Well, real sportsmen wouldn't shoot sitting ducks, would they? No sirree. So this hunter asks the guide, 'What'll I do,' and the guide says, 'Jes' shoo 'em up, so's they'll fly.' So the man says, 'OK.' He stands up real slow and then all of a sudden shouts, 'SHOO!' And the ducks turn around to see who's making all the noise, and then they figure it's time to leave. So, *technically* the hunter gave those ducks a fair chance, but as the old guide put it, 'There wasn't no time at all between de "shoo" and de "shoot."'"

"Meaning, the Cubans want us to be technically correct when we open up. Maybe give the locals a chance to get out of the way?"

"More or less. But the only technicalities they're *really* worried over are their own. I doubt the boys in Havana give a used cigar about some raggedy fishermen. What they really want is to be on record that they told us to be careful, and they want to be able to prove it to anyone who raises a fuss afterwards. Like the old Roman philosopher said, 'Follow the letter of the law and let the spirit take care of itself.'"

"Who was that, sir?"

"Fella named Fordicus Maximus. Ever hear of him?"

"No, sir."

"Not surprised. But just between you and me, I think the locals will clear out long before we show up. Soon as the Krauts land and start setting up shop, those fishermen and charcoal burners will decide somewhere else is a lot healthier. The only property we'll damage will be palm trees and mangroves, and that stuff grows back. So I figure that memo is big enough to cover the asses that need covering, including ours. I'll put it in my safe along with my orders." He gave me the combination to the safe in his stateroom— "In case I am incapacitated, as the saying goes. We'll send a copy to Key West by message and give them a paper copy when we're back in port. All neat and proper, until someone changes his mind about things."

"Yes, sir."

"And now that we're squared away with the political boys, we need to think about how we'll handle things if we find one of these supply dumps. Or one of the steamers supplying them."

"Yes, sir."

"Ever want to be a pirate, Riley?"

"No, sir."

"That's a shame, because you're going to have an opportunity that any ten-year-old boy would give up kissing girls for." He turned to the messenger. "Pass the word for Gunner's Mate Williams."

The messenger on watch used the ship's intercom, the 1MC, and issued the order. A minute or two later, a solid-looking veteran named Williams appeared in the pilot house and saluted the captain. He was a first class petty officer and the most senior gunner's mate on board. He was a stocky man, heavily tattooed on his forearms. He was slow moving and apparently slow thinking, but he knew his job and, as I was to learn, was utterly dependable.

"Have a good time in Havana, Williams?" said the captain.

"Pretty good, sir. Won a few bucks at a cockfight."

"Run into Honest Lil?"

"I happened to see her at the Rug Room."

"How'd she look?"

"She's got some miles on her, Captain."

"I expect she does. Kinda sad, when I think of it. There was a time when she wasn't old and ugly. Back then, she was just young and ugly. But on her better days she could pass for Chiquita Banana, if you didn't look too close. Remember those days, Williams?"

"Yes, sir. She always smelled good, too."

"That's a fact. How's she smell now?"

"Not as good, Captain."

"That's a shame. Well, I've got a job for you. It looks like we might have some shore party action in our future, and I'm not talking about the kind Honest Lil sells. And we're so damned shorthanded, we're going to have to scramble a little."

"Yes, sir."

"When I did my inventory of small arms, there were eight M1 rifles, three Thompson submachine guns, and twelve forty-five pistols, plus plenty of thirty-caliber and forty-five-caliber ammo. Plus there were a couple of twelve-gauge scatter guns. And a box of twenty fragmentary grenades and a couple of white phosphorous. That correct?"

"That's correct, sir."

"OK. I want you to select six volunteers—five seamen and one petty officer—for a small arms team—sort of a combination landing party and boarding party. The petty officer will be second in command under Mr. Fitzhugh, so pick someone with a head on his shoulders. You'll be responsible for small arms training, but if and when we go into action, I'll need you to stay on board to make sure the ship's guns are in working order, so you can't be part of the team."

"Yes, sir."

"Any questions?"

"No, sir."

"OK. Get on it."

"Aye, aye, sir." Williams saluted and left the pilot house.

"All clear to you, Riley?"

"I think so, sir."

For the next seven days we were at sea looking for U-boats and suspicious tramp steamers. We didn't see any. We saw plenty of freighter traffic headed east toward the Florida Straits, and there were fishing boats working the Gulf Stream. Everything looked peaceful, and even the weather cooperated. But we made good use of the time in training the men. We ran drills several times every day, so that the men would know what to do and where to go under different situations. Sailors generally grumble about incessant drilling, but our guys didn't seem to mind. They knew that we weren't very far away from having to use these procedures for real. Sometimes it was a call to go to general quarters—the standard "man your battle stations" drill. Other times it was a drill involving the new small arms team we had put together. In that case, the small arms team ran to the armory, got their weapons, and assembled by the ship's boat, while the rest of the men went to their assignments at the guns.

"Seems like it's working OK," said the captain. "But I sure do wish we had twenty more men, like we're supposed to."

My gang of would-be cutthroats—the small arms team—was made up of five young seamen and a fireman second class named Boyle. Since he was a specialist in the engineering department, he could be excused from the engine room, which was his usual battle station and which meant he was normally not assigned to man any of the topside armament. The other five were relatively new recruits, all young and all eager.

Williams conducted small arms training off the fantail. The deck gang built targets that we hauled behind the ship at about hundred-yard intervals out to three hundred yards, which was about the maximum range we could expect sailors to hit anything. They were flat pieces of plywood mounted on a couple of pallets, and someone painted a life-sized picture of Hitler on the plywood. Every day for half an hour, the small arms team took turns peppering the target with Thompson submachine guns and M1 rifles. At a hundred and two hundred yards, the M1s and Thompsons made a splintered mess of the target. And with the M1s we could hit the target at three hundred yards with some regularity. Then we'd bring the target in to about twenty-five yards, and we'd blast away with the Colt 45 pistols. We got so that we could hit something at that range, though not often—a forty-five automatic is best when the target is standing in front of you. We wanted to be sure that each man was familiar with each of the weapons. We also tried out the twelve-gauge shotguns, and I had to remind the men not to shoot at the gulls or the albatross that seemed to follow us wherever we went.

"Bad luck, men," I said. That was enough. Sailors are superstitious as a rule.

The men took to the training easily and enjoyed it, and we had to build a new target after every session. After a week of this we had burned up quite a bit of ammunition, and I felt confident that if we got into a firefight, the men could give a good account of themselves. We didn't have enough grenades to practice with, but Williams gave us all stern lectures on what to do and what not to do, and then each of us got to pull a pin and throw one over the side. The explosions were impressive.

The men named themselves Fitzy and the Fubars. This was, of course, a breach of proper respect for an officer, so all the men liked it. The captain, former enlisted man that he was, winked at this, because he knew it was good for morale. I have to admit, I kind of liked it, too. The men didn't start calling me Fitzy, though, not to my face. They knew where the lines were and were willing to observe them, mainly because I didn't make any kind of fuss about it.

After about the third day, when we had finished our small arms training, Boyle came up to me and said, "We've been wondering, Mister Fitzhugh, if the Fubars could grow mustaches. Sort of as a special badge."

"Aren't you guys ugly enough already?"

"Yes, sir, but we figure it would add to the general impression of badass-ness. We're not talking about pansy mustaches like that skinny caterpillar on Errol Flynn. We're talking bushy. We're gonna shave our heads, too. We figure the captain won't mind, seeing as he wears a mustache, too. And he looks like two eyes and a nose peeping over a hedge. I say that respectfully, sir."

"Well, Boyle, you have put your finger on the difference between a sailor and a skipper. But you're probably right. I'll run it by the captain. I don't think he'll mind. But what are the ladies in Havana going to say when you show up looking like Genghis Khan and his in-laws?"

"Well, sir, they're all virgins and don't know any better. Besides, they only really love us for our peso-nality. That kind of love never dies."

"You're a philosopher, Boyle."

"Yes, sir. I know."

On the fourth day of steaming, we were about thirty-five miles northeast of Havana. The masthead lookout yelled down, "Contact off the port bow, sir! Looks like a fishing boat of some kind."

I was on watch on the bridge, and the captain was in his usual place, sitting in his chair on the side of the pilot house. We went out to the wing of the bridge to get a better look. Through binoculars I could see something white floating about two thousand yards ahead. The contrast of the whiteness against the startling blue of the sea made the contact, whatever it was, stand out sharply. The sea was calm that day, so there were no whitecaps. If there had been, we might have missed it.

"Let's take a look," the captain said.

"Come left to three four zero," I said.

As we got closer we could see a boat that was half sunk. Only the bow and the front part of the little pilot house were above water. The bow pointed upward like a man trying to stay afloat and keep his nose above water. White gulls were circling above the wreck.

"What're those birds doing, Captain?" I said.

"Fishing, I suppose. There's probably a school of bait fish in the shadows of the hull. Lower the boat and go on over and see what happened. I don't think there could be anyone trapped in that pilot house, but it's worth checking."

We lowered our whaleboat and motored over to the wreck. There was still a small section of the after part of the wreck attached to the pilot house, but most of it was gone. There wasn't much doubt what happened. The bow and pilot house were torn up and splintered. On the bow I could read the name of the boat in faded black paint—*Doris*.

"Put us alongside," I said to Reynolds, the coxswain. "I want to go aboard."

"Be careful, sir," he said. "That wreck could break apart or sink once it feels your weight. Doesn't seem like there's much keeping it afloat, and you don't want to be trapped in that pilot house when she goes down."

"That crossed my mind, Reynolds."

We grappled onto the gunwale of the boat, and I stepped on board. The wreck sagged under me and shifted slightly. I looked through the cabin door, or where the door used to be. What was left of it hung by one hinge. The few instruments and the radio in the cabin were smashed, and all the windows were shattered. A worn-out and cheap life vest was floating in the wash that was sloshing around the cabin deck. The water was about up to my knees. There was blood spattered all over the interior of the cabin. It had dried into a dark brown and black, but there was no doubt what it was. There was some other stuff stuck to the walls, too. A few onions were floating next to the debris from the splintered woodwork. The only thing that was undamaged was a calendar advertising Lone Star beer. A smiling cowgirl said it tasted good. I looked into the V-berth below the cabin, but there was nothing there except some old clothes floating and more onions. No bodies. But on the shelf above the boat's broken wheel there was the ship's log. I looked at it. The last entry was three days ago and said simply, "1535, Sub surfacing."

I took the log and went back to the whaleboat.

"Looks like someone shot the shit out that boat, sir," said Reynolds.

"Not much doubt about who that might have been," I said. "Let's go."

We went back to the ship.

"Seems like the bastards have arrived," said the captain.

"Yes, sir. Lots of dried blood and brains, but no bodies."

"The sharks took care of that, I imagine. See any around?"

"No, sir. According to the log entry, it happened three days ago. I suppose the wreck could have drifted quite a distance in the current."

"Yep. Gulf Stream runs about four knots. Three days at that speed? Could have happened off New Orleans for all we know. Any idea what they were doing?"

"I don't know, sir. Must have been Americans, though. Name on the bow was *Doris* and the log's in English. Maybe they were carrying onions. There were quite a few floating around inside. I didn't see any fishing gear, but the whole after section of the boat was gone, so it's hard to say."

"Yep. That boat, what's left of it anyway, reminds me of my old man's oyster boat on the Chesapeake. A lot of them have that little cabin all the way forward and that high-pitched bow. Kind of pretty in their way. Lots of afterdeck for stowing gear. I always liked the look of these boats, though I didn't like working on 'em."

"I thought your father was from Kentucky, sir."

"He was till the sheriff chased him out. He landed on the Eastern Shore of Maryland and started a crabbing business. Did OK. Well, that's a real shame about the *Doris*. Can you imagine what it was like for those fellas there? Here they were, putt-putting along on a sunny day, minding their own business and looking forward to getting back to wherever they came from and having a cold beer and a cuddle, when all of a sudden a giant black iron monster comes rising out of the sea, looking like something from a bad dream. It'd be enough to make you swallow your cud. But after a second or two you'd figure out what it was and probably think it was one of ours out for a Sunday cruise, and then you'd see their hatches open and men come running out on deck, and maybe you'd give them a wave, and it wasn't until they manned their guns and pointed them at you that you realized it was the end of days for you. I wonder how many were on board. Probably no more than three."

"Not much of a victory for Fritz."

"No. But I don't suppose it cost him much, either. Probably thought it was a good chance to exercise his guns."

"Deck gun?"

"I doubt it. They probably used their version of a twenty-millimeter. I'm told those things will fire upwards of a couple hundred rounds a minute. A couple of bursts and that's all, folks. Well, that's first blood in the Gulf, I reckon."

"I wonder why they bothered."

"Yep. Makes you think, doesn't it? Well, that wreck's a hazard to navigation, so we'll back off and give the gun crew a chance to sink her. Make sure the sonar boys are awake. It's possible that U-boat's around somewhere. I doubt it, what with this current, but like the old man said to his girlfriend, you never know."

"If this happened three days ago, I wonder why we haven't heard of anything else happening. No other messages about attacks or sinkings."

"Yes. It is a little strange. Maybe the Krauts're having some technical problems. Or maybe they hit a target that sank too fast to send any SOS. That's probably more like it. A torpedo that hits amidships can blow a lot of freighters in half. Sink 'em while the morning coffee is still cooling off. Maybe the first we'll hear of it is when someone's reported overdue. A merchant skipper is an independent cuss. Likes sailing alone, like I said. But I expect most of them'll change their minds about that before this war gets much older."

We passed the word for general quarters and pulled away to about five hundred yards, parallel to the wreck. I stayed on the bridge, because I was general quarters OOD. The three-inch gun crew removed the tompions that plugged and protected the opening of the barrel and stood by to load. Shells came up the lift beside the gun, sent up from the magazine several decks below the water line. Williams sat in the gunner's seat and cranked the wheels that raised and lowered the barrel and swung it side to side. He got the target lined up in his sights. The loaders shoved a shell into the breech and stood back. The shell looked like a giant bullet with a brass casing. At the captain's orders Williams fired, and a great cloud of orange flame and gray smoke accompanied the blast of noise. The first shot landed close enough to cover the wreck with spray, and the next hit it squarely and blew it out of the water. It exploded in a shower of splinters and foam. That brought a cheer, even though every man knew that five hundred yards was virtually point-blank for a naval gun.

"Good shooting, Williams," said the captain over the loudspeaker. "Secure from general quarters. We'll send a message to Key West about the *Doris.* Somewhere, someone's wondering about 'em. Damned shame. Let's hope they were dead before the sharks got to 'em. Let's turn around, Riley. I want to take a look at the coastline."

"Aye, aye, sir. Right full rudder! Come to course one eight zero."

The helmsman repeated the order and we headed south, back to the coast of Cuba.

Chapter Ten

For the next four days we steamed slowly eastward following along the Cuban coastline from Cayo Piedras del Norte, where the offshore islands and keys start in earnest. Each night we circled back and retraced our steps, so that in the morning we would be back where we left off and could continue on the next leg east. We also thought we might get lucky and run across an enemy steamer or U-boat loading or unloading in the darkness. But we never did. Our course followed the edge of the Old Bahama Channel, and each day we continued our slow investigation of mile after mile of empty-looking islands. There were dozens of places where we could have entered small bahias and fishing channels, if we had a flat-bottomed boat. Many of these places were little more than mudflats that were almost exposed at low tide. But there was no real need to inspect these backwaters. They were far too shallow even at high tide and, as importantly, they tended to be too far from the offshore deep water to make any kind of supply by ship's boats practical. What's more, the charts for these places were suspect, because every storm season the hurricanes rearranged these flats and the channels through them. You could see between some of the keys that local fishermen had stuck rude channel markers, nothing more than stakes in the mud, proof that the channel was only as permanent as the next storm.

Other keys had reefs protecting them, so that there were breakers splashing over the rocks and coral. Most reefs had openings where there were no breakers, but only rollers washing through and not breaking until they reached the beaches. The scene was an artist's dream of blue water and surf and white beaches, and behind the beaches were jungles of green palm trees and pines. Other keys were nothing more than tangles of mangroves that showed their brown roots at low tide. And in the trees and mangroves were flocks of white ibises roosting, others wading in the flats. There were constant gulls, of course. They followed in the wake of the ship, white and gray with yellow beaks. And it was easy to see where the deep water ended and the shoaling began. The deep blue of the channel gave way sharply to the light blues and greens of the shallows and to the brown and dark green of the flats, where the mud and marl were stirred up by bottom-feeding fish, hunting crabs.

"Good fishing in those flats," said Captain Ford. "Bonefish and redfish will both give you a hell of a run. They take off like a scalded cat, once you hook 'em. They don't care for the taste of a hook."

"I've never eaten bonefish, or redfish for that matter," I said.

"Only the natives will eat a bonefish. Cleaning 'em's more trouble than it's worth. I just toss 'em back. But redfish grilled over a charcoal fire's worth having. I once caught a redfish by casting just behind a stingray. They like to follow rays, because as the ray flaps his wings he stirs up food from the bottom. Makes life easy for the redfish. It's an old trick a fella taught me. Worth remembering."

There must have been hundreds of islands, some nothing more than clumps of mangroves, others solid ground, jungle covered and choked with coconut palms and now and then with a hundred-foot hill in the interior, such as it was. The sun had been brilliant, until the fourth day when the clouds rolled in and the air was thick with humidity. That afternoon there was a cloudburst and a deluge of rain that reduced visibility down to a few dozen yards and made us move out toward the center of the Bahama Channel to avoid the danger of running aground. When the rain left as quickly as it came, there was steam rising from our decks from evaporation as we went in close to the shallows again. Most days there was enough wind so that the mosquitoes and sand flies didn't bother leaving the jungle to pester us.

"A fella once told me that a swarm of Cuban mosquitoes could bleed a man to death," said the captain. "Seems unlikely. That fella was known to be a teller of tall tales, but I guess it's possible. If I was going to test the theory, I'd ask for volunteers, rather than do it myself."

One morning we saw a flock of pink flamingos. They took off with surprising ease considering how big a bird they were. They flew with their long necks outstretched and their legs stretching out behind.

"There's a sight you don't see every day," said the captain, admiringly. "You know, Riley, there are people willing to pay twenty dollars a day to cruise these waters, and here we are getting paid to do it." Talking to him during those watches on the bridge, I understood that I'd never known anyone so completely at ease and in his element as Captain Ford. I forget the Greek who talked about happiness being a combination of form and function. Doesn't matter. But Captain Ford was the embodiment of that idea. Despite his responsibilities, or maybe because of them, he was a happy man. And the *Nameless* was a happy ship as a result, not just because the skipper was usually in a good mood, but also and more importantly because he knew what he was doing. That is the primary source of contentment to sailors. They can tolerate almost anything, as long as they believe in the Old Man. And they were proud of the *Nameless* and kept her in perfect shape. They did the extras that they could have avoided. If she hadn't been painted haze gray, she would have sparkled.

The captain was on the bridge almost constantly during the day, although the three watch standers took their regular four-hour turns at OOD. He sat in his chair and surveyed the shoreline with his binoculars. Other times he would go to the chart table and study the charts of this northern coast of Cuba and the water to the north, all the way to Key West and the Florida mainland.

On the morning of the fifth day, it was time to think about heading back to Key West to refuel and have a discussion with the base commander about what we'd learned and what to do next.

The day was overcast and the air heavy with rain that was coming. The sea that had been so beautifully blue was gray now, and you could hardly see the horizon because the sea and the sky were essentially the same color. We were rolling and pitching a bit, just enough to be enjoyable and to throw our white bow waves into the air and sometimes over the bow of the ship. The dolphins were in the bow wave again, and here and there we'd flush some flying fish. Schools of them would break the surface and glide twenty or thirty yards before splashing down. It was spring, and the temperatures were mild. It was a good time to be at sea. And I remembered my friend Bunny and the book he recommended—*The Wind in the Willows*. There truly was nothing finer than just messing about in boats. Or in our case, ships. It was easy to forget that we were at war.

But Captain Ford didn't forget. The U-boats were constantly on his mind.

"I can't decide whether I'd rather be us or a U-boat commander," the captain said to me as we headed northwest toward Key West. We had checked the entire length of eastern Cuba and found nothing. "We both have problems, and they're caused by the same thing. Most of that damned water in and around those keys is too shallow to float a cigar butt, let alone the

Nameless. If we're gonna locate and destroy an enemy supply dump, someone's gonna have to tell us where it is, first. We'll never find it cruising up and down the coast like we've been doing. We can't get inside those barrier islands except in just a few places, which is probably just the kind of place a clever agent would avoid—for that very reason."

"The U-boat will have the same problem, though, Captain."

"That's why I wouldn't want to be him, either. Any child could look at the chart and see what his problems are and how he has to go about solving 'em. We know damned well the U-boats're coming right down the Atlantic coast in the Straits of Florida, because that's the deepest water. If they try weaving through the Bahamas it's trickier, and in most places they'll lose their one great advantage, 'cause the water's too shallow to submerge to any depth. Even when they're submerged the water's so clear around there that they can be spotted from the air. So they'll stay in the Florida Straits even though it means bucking a four-knot current. They'll come at night so they can run on the surface and make better time and recharge their batteries. But then, if they're coming down here to rendezvous with a Cuban supply base, they'll have to follow the same channel we've been following." The captain was referring to the Old Bahamas Channel that runs along the Cuban north shore. "It's pretty damned narrow," he said. "But that's the only deep water, and that's where the supply freighter will have to go, too. So all that means that the supply ship and the U-boats will all have to do their work at night, like we figured. Anchor out and use small boats in and out for loading and unloading."

"Seems like a lot of trouble, Captain. Why not just rendezvous with a supply ship somewhere out at sea?"

"Good question. I wonder about that, too. Must be something more to it, though I can't think what it might be. Maybe local politics. What'd they call the Cuban Nazis?"

"Falangists."

"Maybe it has something to do with them, for some reason."

"Maybe the Germans are hoping that the local boys can take over the country. Get Cuba to change sides. Or at least go neutral. Or maybe the local boys are anxious to do the Nazis a favor, so that when they win the war, Adolf will reward them."

"Maybe. I just ain't devious enough to be a politician, or to think like one. But I'm pretty damned sure we can't afford to be wasting time cruising up and down this coastline, bird watching. It's a waste of time and resources. So your buddies in the FBI better catch hold of someone who knows where these dumps are, or gonna be, and ask him nicely to tell us. Either that or we have to get lucky and run across the supply ship. He's got to travel the deep water too, so there's at least a chance of finding him. And he can't submerge . . . not till we get finished with him, anyway."

"Do you figure that supply ship will be armed?"

"Well, if I was a German supply ship going into harm's way, as the saying goes, I'd want to have something more than a flare gun in my pocket. Wouldn't you?"

"Yes, sir."

"We'd better assume they will have some kind of serious deck guns."

"Yes, sir."

"So, if we can't get lucky or don't sweat the information out of some Cuban, we'll have to do things the old-fashioned way—cruise around looking and waiting till we see a periscope or somebody else spots a U-boat and calls us for help. The problem with that is, a lot of the time the guy calling for help is in the process of sinking, and we get there just in time to pick up the survivors, if there are any. I wish to hell we had more planes to do the scouting. We're starting to use blimps, too, though. That should help some."

"I'm not sure I'd want to be floating along in a big target like that."

"Doesn't appeal to me much, either. But you know those things can cover a lot of territory. Fellow told me they can patrol a couple thousand square miles every twelve-hour watch. And from their altitude they can spot a U-boat that's submerged, even seventy or so feet down. Drop a depth charge or two and *auf wiedersehen*, Fritz. Like I said, that's the reason the U-boats like coming down the Florida Straits instead of sneaking through the Bahamas. Water's deeper. Their lookout spots a blimp lumbering along and the captain yells 'Dive!' and they disappear into a couple hundred feet of water and take a turn right or left, and by the time the blimp starts dropping depth charges the U-boat's gone. But blimps're a hell of a lot better than nothing. The thing is, we just don't have enough of them or bombers or anything else now. We're gonna get there sooner rather than later. But there's the devil to pay in the meantime."

"Do you speak German, Captain? You said *auf wiedersehen*."

"A bit. I can order a beer and say 'how much?' and 'goodbye' in thirteen or fourteen different languages, including Mandarin. That's all a sailor needs, pretty much."

I had to smile at that. I could tell he was waiting for the straight line.

"How do you say beer in Mandarin, Captain?"

"Beer."

The next morning the weather had cleared. I had the four to eight watch. It was my favorite of all the watches, even though it meant getting up at three thirty. But there was nothing quite like being at sea and watching a black or starry night turn into morning. In the darkness you could still see the whiteness of the bow wave, and from the wing of the bridge you could look down and see the sparkling phosphorescence of the Gulf Stream. At around six thirty you could start to smell the bacon frying and the coffee brewing in the mess deck, and by the time you were relieved, you were hungrier for breakfast than you ever could be ashore. You got a start on it when the steward brought you coffee to the bridge, and it was fresh and laced with milk and sugar. And you drank that and watched the light beginning to appear and then the sun slowly coming up and turning the morning gray, the same color as the sea and almost the same color as your ship, and then rising above the horizon and casting an orange shaft on the surface of the water, and you really did feel you wouldn't want to be anywhere else in the world at that moment. The air was still cool and smelled as fresh as it would all day. And around seven the quartermaster would sing out, "Captain's on the bridge, sir," and you turned around and saluted and said, "Good morning, sir," and told him the course and speed and whether there were any contacts. He'd check our position at the chart table and then settle into his chair and light a cigar and breathe out a plume of smoke, which was his way of expressing complete satisfaction. And you could understand how he felt and you thought that—aside from being in bed with a beautiful woman or, better yet, being in love with her, too—being the skipper of a Navy ship, or any ship, was just about the pinnacle of a man's desires. And then I smiled to think that the boys back in Hollywood would probably think I'd gone native. Maybe. Maybe I had. I just know how I felt out there in the clean mornings at sea. I didn't even have to tell myself that I was doing something that needed doing, something that was worthwhile. That was true, but it wasn't part of the feeling.

The harbor at Key West was busier now than it had been for years. Fishing boats, of course, were coming and going in the harbor as always, and there was an increased naval presence, though not to the level we needed and would get to, later in the war. When we arrived, there was a destroyer in port. It was an old four piper left over from the last war. It had escaped being sent to the Brits, so far, at any rate. Merchant ships were moored in the harbor, because there wasn't enough room for them all to come alongside the docks. The Navy was just beginning to organize convoys. The merchant skippers weren't yet convinced of the need for them, but they were starting to listen, as reports about U-boat sightings had started rolling in.

As we wound our way toward our dock in the Naval Station, the captain was shaking his head over how things had changed and grown.

"Used to be Key West was nothing more than a haven for fishermen who were just barely getting by and rum runners who were doing pretty well, if they didn't get caught. Some of the fishermen decided just getting by was no way to live, so they started making ends meet by smuggling illegals. There's a bartender at a beer joint on Duval Street who says he lost his left arm in a shootout with smugglers. Says they tried to double-cross him. He's not shy about telling that story to wide-eyed sailors and the occasional tourist. Other times he says a shark bit it off."

"You'd think he'd remember which way it was," I said.

"Yes, you would. If you run into a one-armed bartender, don't ask him how he lost his flipper. He's liable to tell you things that may not be true and take a long time doing it."

"It's a wicked world, Captain."

"That's a fact, though I hear it's getting less wicked in Key West. The bad old days are pretty much gone. Kinda sad, really. Pretty soon the town's gonna be almost respectable—for a Navy town, that is. Now with all this building and the Navy growing like it is, some people are starting to call Key West the 'Gibraltar of the South.' Mighty fancy."

"The chamber of commerce trying to attract tourists?"

"I wouldn't doubt it. Ever see the real Gibraltar, Riley."

"No, sir."

"It's something to see, and it looks a lot like Key West, except for a couple of things. There, they have this big mountain and tall cliff in the middle of the island. That cliff is a fortress just bristling with big guns, all pointed out to sea, and it sits right at the point where the Mediterranean goes out to meet the Atlantic. The opening is so narrow, Joe DiMaggio could probably hit one of Bob Feller's fast balls from Gibraltar over to Africa. It couldn't be in a better strategic position if Lord Nelson drew it up, which is why the Brits are there, of course. So," he said, smiling wryly, "there's a lot of similarities to Key West."

By which he meant there weren't any, since Key West sits all alone at the tail end of a bunch of sand pancakes they call keys and guards the Straits of Florida, which are easily ninety miles wide.

"And as you can see if you look around," he said, "we're kind of short on mountains and cliffs, not to mention Barbary apes, and there ain't enough big guns here to worry a nervous cat. Otherwise Key West's almost identical to Gibraltar."

"Captain, I'm beginning to think you have a taste for irony."

"Yep. Tastes good. Yessir, Key West is changing. There's even talk about closing the whorehouses. A lot of the decent folks are against it, though."

"Really? Seems kinda funny. You'd think they'd be the ones leading the campaign."

"You would, but they ain't. They say with all the new sailors and soldiers coming to town there'll be an epidemic of rape and rapine visited upon the town virgins, if the whorehouses are closed. That shows good practical sense and knowledge of human nature. Doesn't reflect well on the Navy, though. The fact is, the Navy, in the person of the station commander, is the one that wants 'em shut down. He's afraid with all the new sailors coming there'll be an epidemic of the clap—Key West has been sort of famous for it in days gone by. The Navy's always been hard on the boys who come down with it. The usual punishment is restriction for ninety days. No liberty. Guess what effect that has on the men."

"They don't care for it, I suppose."

"More to the point, when they get it, they don't report it. Which just makes it worse. Pretty soon the guy's flat on his back or can't take a leak without wanting to jump overboard from the pain. A sailor with a severe case of the clap is useless, until he gets it treated. The Navy's right in the sense that it can damage the readiness of a ship, but it's dead wrong in punishing the boys for catching it. As long as there are sportin' women in a port, and there always will be, some of the boys are gonna get it, and that's as true a law of nature as gravity. So on this ship, there will be no punishment for anyone who reports to sick bay and gets treatment. That's my policy and therefore that's your policy, and I want the men to know it. To hell with the Navy's official Book. It's just flat-out wrong. But for God's sake don't put anything in writing, or the Navy will have my ass. Just have a quiet meeting with the chiefs and have them tell the men—and have them tell them why. And tell 'em why the policy is strictly for the *Nameless* and therefore not for talking about. They'll understand."

"Yes, sir. It makes sense."

"I know."

"And maybe they'll be more willing to use some protection."

"Maybe. Sick bay's got a supply. I remember there was one old bordello called Alice's Plantation. Might still be here. Alice used to advertise that her girls got monthly inspections, but if you didn't believe it, she also had a big glass bowl in her living room that was filled with Trojans. You could help yourself."

"That was considerate."

"Oh, she wasn't a philosopher or Samaritan. She was just protecting her investments. A girl down with the clap's no use to herself or to Alice. And a sailor who comes down with something is not likely to come back, if there're other choices, which there always are. And what's more, he ain't likely to say anything good about the place he got it. Bad word of mouth is bad for business and spreads faster than the clap when the fleet's in."

"Adam Smith said self-interest results in benefits to society as a whole."

"Smart fella. Yes, Alice was quite an operator. Made all her girls dress in white and talk in deep southern accents just like Scarlett O'Hara and say 'Fiddle dee dee' instead of what they usually say."

"What was the point of that?"

"Gave the place style and tone. But one of the girls got herself murdered. Strangled with her own skivvies, they said. Never did catch who did it, or if they did, I didn't hear about it. Anyway, that gave the business a bad name for a while. Probably had a hand in starting all this talk of reform. So things surely are changing."

He trained his binoculars on the city docks. "It appears there's something going on in town. Lots of people gathering around what looks like some folks in a lifeboat. I'll bet I know what this is about."

I looked that way, too, and saw half a dozen ragged looking men and one woman struggling to climb out of a weather-beaten lifeboat. A crowd of people gathered round them offering bottles of water, and they were drinking it as though they hadn't had water for days. And, as it turned out, they hadn't, for they were survivors of a U-boat attack—the first of many who would arrive in Key West. But as we came to learn in the coming months, survivors were in the minority, a very small minority. Many victims of the U-boats, if not most, never reached any safe haven. If they were not killed in the explosion of their ship or incinerated in the fires, they were drowned trying to swim away as their ship sank and created a vortex that sucked them down with it. Or, if they did manage to abandon ship, they were machine-gunned while they swam or while they tried to pull away in the lifeboats. Almost all the attacks in these early days were made by U-boats on the surface. Their gun crews were on deck and in position to fire on any survivors. Whether that happened or not depended entirely on the U-boat captain. Some few refrained and were content to sink the ship and sometimes even allowed the merchant crews to lower their boats and row away before opening fire. Or, if the lifeboats were smashed in the explosions, they let survivors swim away, leaving them to the sharks and knowing that, even if the sharks didn't get them, exhaustion would. The odds of being picked up by other vessels were small. Even if the merchant was able to radio his position as he was going down, it took time for a friendly ship to get to the scene, and it didn't take much time at all for shocked and exhausted people to drown. All U-boat captains had carte blanche for any manner of killing they chose. Their commander, Admiral Donitz, had ordered U-boat crews to "be harsh." That covered a multitude of choices. And captains were well aware of Donitz's obvious dictum that *how* a merchant sailor was killed didn't much matter. What mattered was *that* he was killed and would never sail on another ship. Only a few U-boat captains allowed survivors to row away. And that was in the early days of the war. Later, things changed, and the decision to leave no survivors became pretty much unanimous.

As I said, we learned all this officially much later. But we learned some of it firsthand from the evidence of our eyes and the reports of those few who did survive.

"Looks like the *Doris* wasn't the only casualty," said the captain, as we glided past the city docks and headed for our Naval Station slip. "I imagine the CO will have something to say about all this. And I imagine we'll be going out again as soon as we refuel. See about getting us topped off, will you Riley? I'll go on over to headquarters and see what they have in mind for us. And send Williams over to Supply, so that we can replace that small arms ammo your team shot up. We may need it."

"How about the two three-inch shells, Captain?"

"Yep. Better to have too many than not enough. Like they used to say in the old west, when you're fighting Comanches, either bring enough bullets or bring a toupee."

Chapter Eleven

It was late in the afternoon when the captain got back from Gulf Sea Frontier headquarters. The GSF commander wanted us to go back out hunting the U-boat or boats that had sunk the survivors' ship.

"She was a grain carrier from Galveston," said the captain. "They hit her about smack-dab in the middle of the Gulf, about a hundred and fifty miles due west. She was on her way to Miami. The woman we saw was the skipper's wife. He didn't make it. That cargo made a hell of an explosion and fire, apparently."

"Was it torpedoed, Captain?"

"No. The bastards surfaced and opened up with their deck gun. Those things are bigger than our three-inch gun. About an inch bigger, in some cases. And they can get off fifteen rounds a minute, if they're well handled. Something to think about. Wouldn't take much to blow a few holes in a merchantman's hull. Didn't take much in this case, for sure. A couple of shots and she blew up, burned like a torch, and then rolled over and died. The lifeboat that got away was just lucky. They started lowering away when they saw the U-boat surfacing. Said they saw a big white swastika painted on the conning tower. So they knew what was coming. Even so, most of the crew went down with the ship. The boys belowdecks and in the engine room didn't have much of a chance. That's usually the way."

"Must've been horrible, being trapped like that." Very early on I had understood that a ship, beautiful though she may be, especially in profile and in motion, was also a machine made out of steel and iron and organized into metal compartments that contained other machines. The ship and nearly everything in it was hard and unforgiving. You learned that every day when the ship took a steep roll and threw you off balance and against the steel bulkheads or onto the steel deck. You had a deeper sense of the impermanence and vulnerability of flesh. Especially yours. The idea of being trapped in those compartments was not something to dwell on. It was the paradox of the mariner, for the thing that he thought beautiful and in some cases even loved was also potentially an inescapable trap. And although the steel and iron wouldn't burn, the paint on the decks and bulkheads would, and so too the electrical systems and wiring strung along the overheads, fires that would give off poisonous fumes and smoke. And of course the cargo would burn and the fuel oil and the ammunition, worst of all. So the ship would become an inferno until the very moment that she slid beneath the surface and went plunging to the bottom, which in some cases was thousands of feet below. And then I thought, it was the same for men in a submarine, only worse, because they were well and truly trapped and had no hope of swimming away.

"Yep, that's usually the way," Captain Ford said again, as much to himself as to me. "My very first assignment as a brand-new seaman was on a cruiser. She was the old, and I do mean old, *Chattanooga*. And my first general quarters station was in the ship's magazine, five decks down. Now and then it made me think what might happen to me, if we ever sprung a leak or had a fire. The only way out was a steep ladder up to a hatch that was dogged down to maintain watertight integrity. Now and then it made a sixteen-year-old kid wish he hadn't been so anxious to leave home."

So we were underway again late that afternoon. The ancient four piper got underway too, even though she was having engine troubles. We were assigned to different patrol sectors. The four piper stayed closer to Key West because of her habit of breaking down. We were sent to the sector due west of the base and just north of Havana, where there had been reports of a U-boat sighting. We didn't know how reliable those reports were. They had been sent by message from the embassy in Havana to Key West. And they were a couple of days old.

"Useful as teeth on a chicken," said Captain Ford. "But we do know Jerry's around somewhere. Maybe we'll get lucky. Tell the lookouts to be especially alert. The chances are good that the U-boat will surface once it gets dark. He'll need to recharge his batteries. It'll be hard to see a black conning tower, and he sure as hell won't be showing any lights. But there'll be a moon tonight, and that black shape just might show up against the moonlight on the water. Tell the boys this is for real. Have Bosun Wheatley double-check the depth charges. We might be rolling a few off the stern before this night's over. Also, tell Williams to double-check the deck gun. If that sub's on the surface, we might end up in a shooting match. If he's got any sense he'll run away and hide in the depths, but he may not have any sense. Anybody who'd volunteer to go to sea in one of those coffins has got to be a little nuts to start with."

"Aye, aye, sir."

"There's also the fact that sinking a fast anti-sub ship like the *Nameless* would tempt any U-boat skipper."

Tom Wheatley, known as Bosun Wheatley, was a W4 warrant officer in charge of the deck department. I might have mentioned before that warrant officers were specialists in their disciplines, and although junior to all commissioned officers, including green ensigns like myself, they had wardroom privileges and were highly respected professionals. Wheatley was also one of the OOD watch standers, because of our shortage of commissioned officers. But during general quarters his station was on the afterdeck in charge of the depth charges. There were two racks of them on the fantail. In action against a U-boat, the crew would roll the depth charges off the stern. There were also two mechanisms on each side of the ship that fired the "ashcans" off to the side. Taken all together the *Nameless* could put a hell of a lot of explosive force into the water and make life very difficult for a submerged U-boat. The depth charges didn't have to hit the boat or land right beside it. The shock waves of the underwater explosions could be lethal—could buckle the outer shell of the U-boat. Close enough was good enough. An explosion thirty feet away would blow a hole in the U-boat's pressure hull and send her to the bottom. Explosions farther away could damage all sorts of fittings and instruments inside the boat and weaken the hull so that the pressure of the sea would do the rest. The irony was that as the U-boat dived to what she thought was safety, the increasing pressure of the water became her undoing, once she was damaged. That's what we hoped for, anyway. The depth charges could be set to explode at different depths, and as they rested on their sides in their racks like so many fifty-gallon drums, their firing mechanisms were on safe. As we went into action, the men would set the ordered depth and switch off the safety. Then, in the case of the stern racks, gravity would roll them over the side, as the men released them, one by one.

I went back to the fantail, figuring I might find Wheatley. He had a way of anticipating the captain's ideas.

"It's a pretty evening, Tom," I said.

"Evening, Riley. Yep. I've seen worse."

"The skipper thinks we might have some action tonight. He wanted me to check with you to make sure the depth charges are squared away and ready to go."

"Yes. I figured. Model T has been to the ballpark and back a time or two, so when he gets a whiff of something in the air, there's probably something to it. So I've already done it."

"Have you known the captain a long time, Tom?"

"Yeah, we go back a ways. We were shipmates more than once. The Navy was smaller in the old days, for obvious reasons, and guys seemed to bump into one another pretty regular. He knows his business, I'll tell you that. His old man was a waterman on the Chesapeake, and he's spent more time afloat than ashore for all his forty years or so. His old man started working him early on. Yep, he's a nice fella and a good man. No one you'd want to cross, of course, but he's not all that different from most men, when it comes to that. Had a wife and kid for a while. Little boy, I believe. But the Navy's hard on family life, and she went off somewhere with the kid."

"This ship kind of reminds me of a book I read once—Men Without Women."

"Yep. That applies to more than a few of us. I expect it bothers him some, but he never has said anything about it. Not to me anyway, and I've known him a long time. But that's the way he is. He's friendly, and he likes to tell a story, but you'll never know what's really going on. Lot of men are like that, though. It's not unusual."

Wheatley was a tall, spare man. He'd been in the Navy so long his tattoos had lost their definition and had become vague blue blotches on his forearms. He was about to retire when the tensions started to grow, so he decided to stay. The Navy had been his home for all his adult life, and he was not about to leave it when it was in peril. Like the captain, he wore his hat without the stiffening wire grommet, so that the fabric flopped down on the sides, and like the captain his insignia was embroidered, not metal. It was the sign of an old China hand, for you had those insignias made for you in Hong Kong or Shanghai or in Subic Bay, in the Philippines. Wheatley was as brown as an old leather boot and wrinkled as much by cigarette smoke as by the sun and years. He was a man you could depend on, and I knew we were lucky to have him on the Nameless.

"I admire that embroidered insignia on your hat, Tom," I said.

"Yep. Had some made in Yokosuka, after the war. The last one, that is. Seems funny now that they're the enemy. The Japanese, I mean. I spent a fair amount of time and money in bars in Yoko. I guess those girls were lying, when they said they loved us."

"I wonder how long I'll have to wait, until I can get one like that."

"A while yet, I would say. When the gold on your braid starts to turn a little green, you can start thinking about it."

"I understand. I'm not anywhere near salty enough."

"Well, saltiness is a thing that has to be acquired over time. But, you know, in wartime things get speeded up. And down here in the tropics the humidity gets to gold braid faster than the weather up north. By the time you get your silver bar, your gold braid might be green enough."

"I look forward to it."

"You don't want to rush into it, though. It'd raise the wrong kind of smiles among the men. That'd be a shame, seeing as how you've made a good start with them."

"I appreciate that, Tom. And I understand. Have you seen Williams?"

"He's forward at the gun mount. He figured he'd better check things, too."

"Thank you."

"You're welcome."

I went forward, and Williams was there fussing over the deck gun, replacing the canvas covering over the breach and firing mechanism.

"Everything in good shape, Williams?"

"Yes, sir. I heard that U-boat sank the freighter with its deck gun, so I figured we ought to be ready."

"Thank you, Williams. Are the small arms in good shape, too? I don't think there'll be any action of that kind, but you never know."

"Yes, sir. I checked 'em myself before we left port. And I replaced the ammo we shot up and talked the Supply boys into giving us a few extra grenades. I lied a little about how many we used up."

"Good. It's never wrong to lie to Base Supply."

"No, sir. That's a fact. Besides, they expect it. A priest don't expect you to come to confession just to say you didn't do nothing."

I had to think about that for a second.

"A supply clerk is kind of like a priest, is that it?"

"Yes, sir. They both sit in little cubicles and listen to your sad stories and when you're finished, they do their dispensations. Give you what you came for, usually."

"I never thought of it that way, Williams. Are you a Catholic?"

"No, sir. But I was married to one once, so I know how it works. She went to confession every week, just like clockwork. She always had lots to confess, which is kinda why we split up."

I went to my room and lay down on the lower bunk. It was nine o'clock at night—2100 in Navy time, and I had the four to eight watch coming up.

The room was only big enough to accommodate bunk beds and two metal cabinets and two metal chairs. The cabinets each had drawers and a small closet and a fold-down desk that opened to give you a platform for writing. Behind that was a safe, a small fluorescent light, and some shelves for papers and a few books. I generally left the desk open and kept my forty-five in the safe. Lying there in my bunk, it occurred to me that I should be writing some letters to the folks back home. It was the only way to get any mail in return, and I was well aware that I never got anything. Ironically, the only home I had was Hollywood. And Hollywood was not really home—not to me or to anyone, for that matter. It was only a palm-studded magnet for transient dreamers and illusion merchants who came and went like audiences at a matinee. And what about that girl who had said, "What about me?" She may have gotten over being angry. But that would be a mistake. That chapter was best left in the past. I realized I was having a common reaction among sailors—regret over a woman who was left behind. In separation and distance, she—whoever she was—gradually acquired some virtues that weren't so obvious in person. I thought of one of my men, a middle-aged second class quartermaster who liked to talk during watches, if you gave him any encouragement. And one night during the midwatch, I asked him if he was married, and he said he used to be. "I had this girl in high school, and all the time I was deployed at sea I thought about her and thought about her some more, even though in school we didn't get along all the time. But I liked her, and the more I thought about her, the more I liked her. So when I got home I asked her if she wanted to get married. To tell you the truth, sir, I was afraid she'd maybe get away, so I asked her and she said OK. And I'd been ordered to shore duty, so I figured things could work out. But then after we got married, I was kind of surprised that she was there all the time. Always sort of around. You know?"

"You were surprised about that?"

"Yes, sir. It sounds kinda dumb, I guess. It's the kind of thing you *should* know in advance and the kind of thing you *do* know in your head but that you don't *really* know until you see it day after day. There she was, every day. Then after a year or so I put in for sea duty again, and I shipped out, so it was her turn to be surprised, 'cause I wasn't there at all. So she took up with the mailman. She said he was reliable, and I wasn't. You could see her point, I guess. It's funny though. These days I kinda miss her."

"Because she's not there?"

"Yes, sir. That's about the size of it."

You can learn a lot listening to sailors, I thought. Then I thought about that woman I had met at the Floridita. Martha. She was a writer. Maybe she'd like having a pen pal. Might be interesting. I'd give her a call when we got to Havana the next time, and maybe get to know her a little better. That would be a good thing in itself, even if no letters came of it. Something else might.

And I fell asleep trying to remember exactly what she looked like.

At three thirty the messenger woke me from a pleasant dream of blonds in black dresses. I went up to relieve the watch on the bridge.

"Anything happening, Chief?" I asked the OOD. He was the chief quartermaster who, along with me and Bosun Wheatley, stood OOD.

"No, sir." He gave me our course and speed, and I checked our position and surveyed the sea in all directions for contacts. There were a couple of merchantmen hull down and heading east. You could see their masthead and range lights just barely above the horizon, but that was all. "It's been quiet."

So I relieved the watch and sent the messenger for coffee. It would be old, and it would be a couple of hours before the galley fired up and started some fresh. But it would be better than nothing.

When the morning light was just beginning and the sky was turning gray, there was a shout from one of the lookouts. He sounded excited.

"Contact bearing three three zero, relative! Could be a conning tower!"

I looked in the direction indicated and saw nothing. The sea was a little disturbed that morning, and we were rolling and pitching moderately. That made it harder to focus the glasses, and for a few moments all I could see was the tops of the waves and some scatterings of whitecaps. But then I got a glimpse of something. It was a shape, just barely visible, and in the choppy water it would appear and then disappear. It was hard to make out just what it was, but it could be a U-boat conning tower. Captain Ford's standing orders were that he was to be called in the event of suspicious contacts.

"Go call the captain, Smithers," I said to the messenger. "Tell him we have an unidentified contact."

In another moment the captain was in the pilot house in his bathrobe.

"Captain's on the bridge!" yelled the quartermaster.

"What's up, Riley?"

"Funny-looking shape bearing three three zero relative, Captain. Can't make out what it is."

"Let's get a little closer."

"General quarters, sir?"

"No. We'll hold off, until we're sure what we're looking at. No sense waking everybody up."

We turned toward the contact and increased speed. We closed the gap quickly and the contact became clearer.

"Looks like a sail of some sort, Captain."

"Yep. I think I recognize that boat. The sail's been patched a time or two. Kind of distinctive. Let's slow down."

In another few minutes we were looking down at an ancient fisherman in his skiff.

"I know this old boy," the captain said. "Used to hang around the terraces at Cojimar and tell fish stories. Probably still does. He was the one who told me that story about the fisherman who was dragged out to sea and never came back."

The captain leaned over the wing of the bridge.

"Olla, *Viejo!*" he said.

"Olla, Capitan. How is it with you?"

"Well, Viejo, very well. You're a long way out."

"Well, Capitan, you must go where the fish are. They have their own ideas about things. If you wait for them to come to you, you will soon be rolling cigars or sweeping the streets."

"You are wise beyond your years."

"No, Capitan. I am wise because of them."

"Have you seen any strange ships? Submarines?"

"No, Capitan. I saw thick smoke, as if from a serious fire, last evening. It was to the south. But a long way from here. I could not see what was burning."

"Could it have been a ship?"

"Who can say, Capitan? Maybe. Why not? But it might also have been a fire in the Oriente. They often burn the jungle to clear the land for sugar and tobacco."

"Do you need anything? Water? Food?"

"No thank you, Capitan. Send me a big fish. Otherwise, I am the picture of satisfaction."

"Well, Viejo, take care of yourself. There's more than sharks out hunting these days."

"Sharks are enough excitement for me, Capitan. I am too old for new adventures."

"*Buena suerte*, Santiago."

"And to you, Capitan."

We got underway again and left the old fisherman in our wake.

"How'd you get to know that old boy, Captain?"

"Santiago? Oh, we go back a ways. When I did my second hitch, I was stationed in Key West, which wasn't much of a place then. Life in the Navy was pretty dull. The Coast Guard were the busy boys, 'cause those were the days of Prohibition. So when my Navy hitch was up, I walked across the street and joined the Coasties, which meant I got to spend a lot of time chasing down rum runners and smugglers of illegals. Lively times! And naturally we spent a fair amount of time in and around Cuba, since that's where a lot of the booze was coming from. Got so I liked the country, and the people, too. When I had any leave, I'd take it there. I met that old boy in those days. He was fishing out of Cojimar, same as now. He was also running some booze now and then. Nothing grand. If he moved a case or two, it was a lot for him. I imagine he's still using that same skiff from those days. He was harmless. We left him alone in exchange for some product."

"Fresh fish?"

"Of course."

"But you came back to the Navy afterwards."

"Simple. The Navy offered me a commission, and the Coast Guard didn't. I wasn't tall enough, you see. You have to be at least six feet to be a Coast Guard officer. That way, when your ship sinks, you can wade ashore." He smiled, genially. "That's an old Navy joke. Coast Guard boys don't think it's very funny, though. Well, I'm going to go and get dressed. Carry on."

"Aye, aye, sir."

Chapter Twelve

Half an hour later the captain was in his chair on the bridge with a fresh cup of coffee and his morning cigar. He was obviously enjoying both. As usual, his expression suggested he was expecting something interesting or ridiculous to appear, expressly for his enjoyment. Whatever it might be, he was open and ready for it.

"Have you noticed that some things are best after you've had a few, but other things are best the first time?" he said to me. "The first cup of coffee, the first cigar, and the first cold beer are the best ones of the day."

"How about a woman's first kiss in the morning?" I said.

"Depends on whether she's brushed her teeth or not," said the captain. "Of course, that goes both ways. I once knew this woman in old Key West. She was as pretty as the sunrise. And she liked her cuddle first thing in the morning. That was OK by me. But after a night of bourbon and cigars, I wasn't what you'd call a fragrant petunia, and she said so, too. Said my breath could buckle the knees on a sawhorse. Well, I can take a compliment as well as the next man. But I could also see her point. She couldn't abide me till after I'd been up awhile and done what needed doing. Then it was all right. I always kind of liked her. It didn't last, of course. But things of that nature generally don't."

"What ever happened to her?"

"She moved away. Her husband got transferred to some place upstate, and she went up there so it'd be easier to see him on visiting days."

That started me thinking about Martha Gellhorn for some reason. I wondered when we'd be stopping in Havana again. And I wondered what she would say, if I called her. I wondered if she really looked as good as I seemed to remember. My memory was a little fuzzy on the details. Time would tell, I guess. Or not. These are the kinds of things you think about on watch, when the weather's fine and there aren't any contacts to worry about, and there's nothing to do but make sure the helmsman stays on course. There are lots of hours like that on the bridge of a ship.

The captain got up from his chair, still puffing on his cigar, and stretched sort of languorously. Then he strolled out to the starboard wing of the bridge. He tossed his cigar butt into the water, then picked up a smoke pot, which was a wooden device about the size of a fire extinguisher, pulled the pin and threw it over the side. Then he looked at me and grinned evilly.

"Man overboard," he said, calmly. It was a drill.

"Right full rudder!" I yelled. "All ahead full!" The helmsman answered as he spun the wheel, and the quartermaster moved the indicator on the engine order telegraph.

The *Nameless* began her pivoting, sliding turn. The stern pulled away from the "man" in the water so that the ship's screws wouldn't suck him in, chew him to shreds, or drown him, while the bow swung right, and I watched the compass spinning. Our heading had been 270, and as we turned the compass spun to 280, 290, 300, and when it hit 330 I shouted, "Shift your rudder," and the helmsman spun the wheel back full to the left, and we started turning in the opposite direction. As we turned we could see the smoking indicator that was floating astern. We swung all the way toward the reciprocal of the course we had been on. "Come to course 090," I said, and the helmsman, experienced sailor that he was, gradually eased the wheel as we approached 090. When we were steadied up on 090, I said, "All stop." Then "all back full," and we could feel the ship shuddering as the screws reversed and dug into the water. Then, after a few seconds, when the *Nameless* had lost almost all her forward motion, I said, "All stop," and we glided to a stop beside the marker that was still emitting a white plume of smoke. If there really had been a sailor overboard we would have been able to throw him a line and pull him aboard without having to lower a boat to retrieve him.

"Neatly done, Riley. They teach you that maneuver in training?"

"We studied it, Captain. And tried it out once, in the Yard Patrol Craft. It seemed like a good thing to remember."

"Good thing it was just a smoke pot. Look at those nasty little bastards."

The marker was floating in the middle of a flotilla of Portuguese man-of-war jellyfish. They floated by means of their inflated, translucent bladders and spread their evil-looking dark tentacles for yards across and below the surface of the water.

"Now, what do you suppose the Almighty had in mind when he designed those miserable critters?" said the captain. "He must've had an off day, that day. Either that, or he was in a really bad mood."

The captain left the wing of the bridge for a minute and went back to his room. He returned with his thirty-eight revolver and fired four shots at the jellyfish bladders. He popped two of them.

"Pretty good shooting, Captain."

"Not too bad. I hate those damned things. Got stung once. It's a hard thing to forget. You know those damned tentacles can still sting you even after the critter dies, and even after they break off they float away on their own? I don't know how long that venom can survive. But it reminds me of some other things that last longer than they should."

I wondered what he meant by that; it could cover a lot of stories, but I didn't ask him.

"Maybe that's what the Almighty had in mind—he figured they'd make a good metaphor."

The captain looked at me and grinned.

"Damn! Maybe that's it. I'll bet you're right. Well, thanks, Riley. You've answered a question that's been bothering me for a while. Up till now I was starting to doubt whether the Almighty knew what he was doing, or if maybe he was just being ornery. I see now that these things have been sent for our benefit, and I'm gonna go right back to my cabin and look up 'metaphor.'"

But I knew he wouldn't have to do that. His aw-shucks manner was a cover, and a good one, for a lot of things.

He fired two more shots and popped two more jellyfish and then went back and sat in his chair. A sailor from the radio room came into the pilot house.

"Message from GSF, sir," he said, handing it to Captain Ford.

"Hmm. Interesting. Well, Riley, seems like your friends in J. Edgar Hoover-ville may have earned their money. GSF is ordering us to Havana for a conference with ONI about an enemy fuel dump."

"They found one?"

"They found something. Let's go see what it is. Set a course for the Floridita."

"Aye, aye, sir."

Late that afternoon Captain Ford and I were meeting with the ONI and the FBI, including Bill Patterson, at their conference room in the embassy. The subject of the meeting was a place called Cayo Hermosa.

Cayo Hermosa was the name of a jungle-covered key stuck at the end of a deep bay, or *bahia*, and tucked behind some barrier islands that were mountainous and uninhabited. It wasn't marked on the chart; it was little more than a postage stamp. A local fisherman, who got blown into Havana by a strong east wind, mentioned something about people building houses or huts on what had always been a deserted cayo. He said the local name for it was Hermosa. It was more than a hundred miles to the east. The Havana cops were slow to bump the information up to the army, and the army was slow to tell the Cuban navy, but the navy was quick to understand the possible significance and notified the embassy and the ONI. Air reconnaissance couldn't confirm anything other than some vague activity. But they were able to take photos and bring back a good visual idea of the opening into the bahia and the tiny cayo at the end of it. On that basis the FBI and Cuban intelligence services both thought it could be the long-rumored U-boat refueling station. The *Nameless* was being sent to check on it. If it turned out to be what people thought it was, our orders were to destroy it.

"It would be helpful, though," the ONI had said, "if you could capture one or two of the people. They're probably all Cuban Falangists, but it would be especially good if there's a German in the woodpile, so to speak. If there is, try not to kill him."

"How do we recognize him, sir?" said the captain, smiling.

"He'll be the one with the monocle. But, first things first. Destroy what's there. At the very least that will prevent them from using the same spot again, and I have to say, it is a very good place for this kind of thing. Perfect, really. Completely hidden and deep water. A U-boat and a merchant ship could just barely squeeze through the opening, but once through, they're in a very good anchorage. That's what the fisherman says, anyway. And air photos seem to confirm it. We're extremely lucky someone reported it. That fisherman happened to sail in there, and the people on shore drove him away and threatened him. So it seemed to him, and it seems to us, plenty suspicious. Especially since we've been getting all these reports about just this sort of thing."

We spent the rest of the meeting discussing a plan for the attack. There was nothing complicated about it. Because it was at the end of a deep-water bahia, it would be simple enough to sail right up to it and blast it with our deck gun. The only wrinkle involved first making sure that this was what it seemed to be and not a bunch of harmless villagers slapping together some new huts, or missionaries putting up a health care center for lepers or syphilitics.

"We checked with the Archbishop," said the ONI, "and he says the Church is not building anything out there, so we're pretty sure it's not a

Catholic summer camp. We think we're on solid ground. Still, we need to be sure before we start shooting."

When he said "we," I thought of the old joke about the Lone Ranger and Tonto.

"Could it be some rebels?" said the captain.

"Could be. In this country, yes, it could be."

"What do we do about them?"

"Nothing, I guess. But use your own judgment. No one in this government is going to complain if you accidentally shoot some commies. And knowing those boys, they could be working with the Krauts. Hitler and Stalin signed a treaty, after all. So play it the way you see it. We'll back you. If you make a mistake, just be sure it isn't a big one."

"Which would be what, for example?" said the captain.

"Blowing up a casino under construction."

That brought a laugh and an end to the meeting.

As we were leaving the conference room, Captain Ford said to me, "Everything ready for this shindig, Riley?"

"Yes, sir. It seems pretty straightforward."

"That's the way I see it, too. I suppose it's kind of funny we never saw the entrance to that deep-water bahia. But on the chart it looks like there's nothing there. And the entrance is mighty narrow. Easy to miss from the sea."

"I was thinking, though, we might want to make sure the bahia is as deep as they said. It would be a hell of a place to run aground."

"Most places are. But I agree with you. In fact, I sort of thought of that, myself."

"I'm not surprised, Skipper."

"But I like the way you think. Anyway, now that we have the coordinates and the photos, we should be able to locate the place. We'll see what's what, when we get there."

"Yes, sir."

"Well, as the bride said to the bridegroom on the night before the wedding, all will be revealed tomorrow. You can take the rest of the night off, if you want to. We'll get underway at 0700. There'll be time on the way there to discuss any last-minute questions. All right?"

"Yes, sir."

"Well then, good night."

"Good night, Captain."

Later, Bill Patterson and I were sitting in his office.

"Your skipper seems like a good guy," said Bill.

"One of the best. I lucked out with this assignment."

"What do you think of the information we gave you?"

"Sounds legit to me. We'll find out in the next day or so, I suppose."

"Well, don't forget to take your ankle piece when you go ashore." By which he meant the thirty-eight snub-nosed pistol I sometimes carried strapped to my ankle. I picked up that trick from the cops.

"Ah. I left that in L.A. Gave it to Kowalski as a souvenir." Kowalski was a lieutenant in the L.A. homicide department. He and I had worked on a few cases together.

"I wouldn't have done that," said Bill. "He might plant it on a suspect to make a police shooting look like self-defense. Then they'll trace it back to you."

"First of all, he's a friend of mine and wouldn't do that, and second, the cops don't do such things. It gets too expensive and they can get the same result with a cheap switchblade. Besides, the gun wasn't registered to me and the serial number was filed off."

"Impressive. Who was your supplier?"

"I'll never tell. Besides I don't need it now. I have an almost new forty-five, and the Navy won't ask for it back until the war's over."

"Can you hit anything with it?"

"Depends what it is. And if it'll hold still while I'm shooting."

"Well, like you said, I guess we'll find out. So—I call that a good day's work. Care for another round of *boliche* and Hatuey?"

"I might. But I want to make a phone call first."

"You mean I'm second choice."

"By a long stretch."

"OK. I'll give you a minute. I have to hit the head."

Bill left for the men's room, and I dialed the number Martha Gellhorn had given me.

"Hello?"

"Hello. Martha?"

"Yes."

"This is Riley Fitzhugh. We met a week or so ago in the Floridita."

"Yes! I remember you." She sounded agreeably pleased to hear from me. "The good-looking sailor I was flirting with. Where are you?"

"Right now I'm at the embassy."

"You looking for a date?"

That was one way to put it, I thought. "Actually, yes. I am."

"Good. Me too. How about if I meet you at the Floridita in an hour? I'll be the blond in a black dress, in case you forgot what I look like."

I knew that was too easy an opening for a compliment, and I knew that she would know that too. I didn't know much about her, but I was pretty sure she'd have little or no patience for the obvious, in anything. So I passed on it.

"One hour? Good."

"See you there." She hung up.

Bill came back.

"Do you have a good book?" I said.

"Got lucky, eh?"

"Not officially. But I do have a date with a tall, willowy blond lady."

"Better than a tall, willowy blond guy. Is this the famous author's wife?"

"Maybe."

"Maybe, my ass. Well, you're nimble enough to dodge flying bestsellers, so as PG Wodehouse might say, 'Heaven speed your wooing.' I'll see you when you get back from Cayo Hermosa. Good luck with that, by the way. Or should I say good luck with that . . . too."

Chapter Thirteen

As a way of checking the lay of the Floridita's land, I sat down on the end barstool and leaned against the wall. I assumed that if the famous writer who sat there was expected, I'd be warned away. But no one said anything. Constante was the bartender again, and he seemed to remember me. He smiled in a friendly and professional manner.

"Hello, senor. Welcome back. Did you have any luck?"

"Luck?"

"The last time I overheard you telling a lady you were an officer in the Navy, and there have been reports of German submarines in our waters. I naturally assumed you were out looking for them, so I wonder if you had any luck finding them."

"You are well informed, Constante."

"It is impossible in this business not to hear things. It is, however, not at all difficult to say nothing about what one hears. Or sees, for that matter."

He smiled in a way that might be considered conspiratorial. Or might not.

"You would make a perfect secret agent, then," I said.

"Oh, no, senor. That is too dangerous. And besides, in this country we are already well supplied with such people. Single and double agents of all kinds. On the other hand, good bartenders, especially those who are artists, are rare. I count myself among them. Will you have a daiquiri, senor? A double?"

"Why not."

Precisely at seven she walked through the door. She was smiling and seemed genuinely glad to see me. Or, at the very least, glad to be out and about.

"Hello," I said. "You're right on time."

"You're a Navy man. I assumed you'd approve of that. Hello, Constante. I'll have one of those, too."

She sat down next to me and lit a Chesterfield. That was too bad, because I liked the perfume she was wearing, and the smoke got in the way.

"Do you want one of these?" she said, offering me the pack.

"No, thanks. I don't smoke."

"Oh, dear. Does that mean I'll have to refrain when you're around?"

"No. I don't mind."

"Some people say it's bad for you. I don't care. I like it."

She was wearing the same black dress, or another that looked a lot like it. She knew, of course, that the color suited her and displayed her blond hair and tanned face and neck to advantage. She wore no jewelry at all. No rings. And I was happy to see that my memories of her as being beautiful were not very far off. Maybe my imagination had added a little something here and there, but not much. Then I realized that it was a different black dress. This one was cut quite a bit lower in the front than the one she wore last time.

"Constante was just telling me that he's not a spy, but that he's good at not repeating what he sees and hears in here."

"It's a good thing," she said. How many meanings or suggestions were in that little comment? There was room for a few.

"Have you had dinner?" she asked, when the drinks had come.

"No. I was thinking you might want to have it with me."

"That's a coincidence," she said. "I was thinking the same thing."

"Good! I don't know many places in town, though. So you'll have to choose."

"I have a better idea. How would you like to come out to the farm? I mean we call it a farm. It isn't really. I'm not much of a cook, but I can throw something together. And it's quieter. I imagine you'd like a little quiet after being at sea for a week or so."

Actually there were few things quieter than the bridge of a Navy ship underway, during a midnight watch, at least—just the hiss and splash of the bow wave and the steady hum of the power plant that you don't even notice after a while. When you're the officer of the deck, you set the tone for conversation. If you don't talk, no one does, except to respond to orders. You could easily have four hours of virtual silence. But she wouldn't know that, and I thought it was nice of her to think I'd need a little peace and quiet.

"I'd like that," I said. "Is it far?"

"Oh, no. Ten miles, more or less, out in the country. Afterwards I can drop you at your ship. What time do you have to be back?"

"The captain gave me the night off. So . . . no time in particular."

"Good. Let's go. We can take the drinks with us."

"What about the glasses?"

"Don't worry. Constante won't care. He's used to us. We always bring them back. Put these on my tab, will you please, Constante?"

"Si, Marty."

On the way, in the car, she said, "I guess you know who I meant when I said 'we' back there."

"Yes. Constante told me you were married to Ernest Hemingway. I assume you meant him."

"Yes. Have you read any of his stuff?"

"Yes. The most recent thing about Spain. I thought it was very good."

"Most people did. It certainly sold well, thank God. What did you think of all that 'obscenity this' and 'obscenity that?'"

"It took some getting used to, but it was obvious what the characters were actually supposed to be saying, and after a while I liked the way he did it. I used to work in L.A. crime scene, and now I'm in the Navy, so you can't shock me with language. After a while you don't even notice it. But in a book, on the printed page, too much of it either gets in the way or becomes dull. The way he did it got the point across and made it seem like a foreign language, too."

"I suppose you'd like to meet him." There was just a barest tinge of sourness in her tone.

"Why do you say that?"

"Why? You surprise me. People turn up at the farm all the time hoping for an autograph or an interview. It's getting so that even *he* doesn't like it. Which is saying something."

"Well, I guess maybe I'm getting jaded. I'm not starstruck. I've never asked anyone for an autograph in my life. When you work in Hollywood for a while, you get immune to stars of any kind."

I didn't mention that one of my best friends out there was a writer who had, at one time, at least, been far more well-known than Hemingway. And now he was writing travelogues and going out with a virtually illiterate advice columnist. *Sic transit gloria*—and pretty damned fast. So celebrity was not something I got too excited about.

But I'm not sure she believed me. She was looking at me skeptically.

"Seriously," I said. "It's not a pose. I know how publicity works. And I've known people who are good at generating it for themselves. But as the saying goes, they're just folks. When they drink too much, they get hangovers, like anyone else."

"Is that another way of saying they put their pants on one leg at a time?"

"I suppose so. If your husband's around some time, well then, sure, I'd be happy to meet him. But if not, that's OK too."

She smiled and seemed pleased about that.

The road out to her house left the city behind pretty quickly and wound through patches of tropical forest interspersed here and there with some hardscrabble farms, shacks, and hovels, all with sagging porches. Various animals—dogs, chickens, and pigs, mostly—were lounging in littered yards.

"Not exactly the high-rent district," she said. "Not too long ago, there was a ragged couple who were sort of camped out along this road. They were there day after day, looking pathetic. I made the mistake one day of making some comment about them being poor and hungry, and Ernest said, 'If you're such a bleeding heart, why don't you give them some money?' So I gave them twenty dollars, and the next day they were still there, still looking poor and hungry and no better off. But they'd bought a dog with the money."

"What's the moral?"

"Got me. Nothing makes much sense. Maybe that's the moral."

"Maybe it's simpler than that. Maybe they just always wanted a dog," I said, and she laughed.

"Good! And I made their dreams come true!"

"And they probably had nineteen dollars and ninety cents left over."

The house was only a mile or so away now, on the other side of a little village, which was not picturesque in its poverty.

"We found the house a couple of years ago, and it was more or less a wreck. But we put a lot of work into it and a fair amount of money, so I think you'll be surprised."

I was. We pulled into the well-tended gravel driveway with tropical plants on both sides and a huge ceiba tree almost in the center, so that the driveway split to go around it on both sides. The driveway ended at some stone steps that led to a large, one-story white house. Over to the side was a swimming pool and a tennis court. The house had long windows on all the walls, and there was a huge terrace overlooking the pool and smaller stone patio beside it. At the end of the pool was an arbor with flowering plants twined around the beams. There was a table under the arbor, a perfect place for morning coffee, or for writing letters. Or some sort of book.

It was just coming on dusk and you could see the lights of the city in the distance. The house was on a hill and had a view in all directions.

"Welcome to Finca Vigia. That means Lookout Farm. You can interpret 'Lookout' any way you want to. One word or two."

"'Lookout Farm.' What do you grow here?"

"All sorts of things. Egos. Freeloaders. Cats. Come on in. I'll show you around."

"It looks like you've had a bumper crop of cats." There were at least a dozen wandering around. A few came over to say hello.

"Cats! God. There must be a full regiment. Do they bother you? Are you allergic, or something?"

"Not at all. In fact I'm usually pretty popular with them. Dogs, cats, and babies all seem to like me."

"Really? Well there are some dogs around here, too, but no babies, thank God."

The main room seemed to run the length of the house. It was really very handsome—high ceiling, white walls, and bookshelves here and there, as you'd expect. There were a couple of mounted heads of African animals that I couldn't quite identify. Distant cousins of the deer family, I supposed. Long, tapered horns and large, dark eyes. And there was a supremely ugly head of a Cape buffalo. On another wall there was a large bullfight poster. The furniture, though, seemed straight out of an English country house—sofas and overstuffed chairs upholstered in flowered patterns. The floor was Spanish tile and highly polished. It was all neat and well ordered. There was nothing overdone, and nothing that suggested a disordered, bohemian style. It was very civilized.

"This is really nice," I said, sincerely.

"Do you like it?"

"Yes. Truly."

"Would your Hollywood friends approve?"

"Yes, certainly. But 99 percent of them would have had to buy the heads on the wall. And the books would have come from an interior decorator, bought by the yard. Did you shoot any of these former critters?"

"No. They were before my time. I only recently got into shooting. You can imagine why, I'll bet. But it's only game birds and live pigeons. I'm surprisingly good at it."

"Why surprisingly?"

"I didn't think I'd like it. It's wicked, of course. But I do like it. Gary Cooper and his wife are pals of ours. I imagine he's one of the few hunters out in Hollywood. We went duck hunting with them in Sun Valley. They're going to make a movie out of *For Whom the Bell Tolls*, and I think he's going to star in it."

"He'll be good. I met him once or twice. Nice fella."

"Let's see what's in the kitchen. There's always some cold stuff. Chicken salad or poached salmon and mayonnaise. And cucumbers. OK with you?"

"Sure."

"Do you know what Doctor Johnson said about cucumbers?"

"No, but I'll bet you do."

"He said, 'A cucumber should be well-sliced, dressed with pepper and vinegar, and then thrown out.' He's always good for a pithy quote. It's the cook's day off. In fact, all the help is off tonight. So you're at my mercy. Would you like a glass of wine? There's a couple of bottles of Tavel in the fridge. Do you like rosé? Ernest thinks it goes well with some things."

I was pretty sure she didn't know that I knew what she was talking about. So I think she was making a joke to herself. But I had learned what he said about Tavel from a jolly French gangster who had a romantic streak. It was, Hemingway said, the wine that goes best with love.

"Speaking of your husband, where is he?"

"Oh, he's out on his boat looking for phantom German submarines. He and his crew of cronies. It's just an excuse to go drinking with his buddies. He likes to play captain of the ship, going into harm's way. You know? Open the wine, would you?"

She got out two icy-cold bottles of Tavel. As I uncorked them, I wondered whether I should tell her about the shattered fishing boat and the sunken merchantman and the survivors in Key West—whether I should tell her that her husband actually *was* in harm's way. Whether he knew it or not probably didn't matter much. After all, a fact isn't dependent on your awareness of it. But I had the feeling he knew what was happening out there, in the Gulf. He was well connected with the people at the embassy, and if he had not told Martha what was going on, maybe he had a good reason. Maybe if she knew, she wouldn't be so dismissive. Not that he needed or would appreciate my being an apologist or advocate. And not that I was in the mood to be either one. I suppose if I'd been a better person, I would have mentioned it. But I wasn't. Besides, it really wasn't any of my business. And just what was my business, I wondered? Well, I had a feeling that would become clear before the evening was much older. I was looking forward to finding out.

She got out a couple of plates and dished out some cold salmon and capers and a dab of mayonnaise on each. And despite Dr. Johnson, some sliced cucumbers on the side, along with some crusty rolls.

"It's impossible to get decent bread in this country. I lived in France for a while so of course I'm spoiled when it comes to bread. I'm not sure salmon goes with rosé wine. Do you care?"

"Not in the least."

"Let's sit on the floor in the living room. OK? Grab a couple of glasses from the shelf, there."

We arranged the plates and glasses and silverware on a coffee table and spread some cushions on the floor across from each other.

"Do you like popular music? We just got some new records."

"Some of it, yes."

She put a record on the phonograph. It was somebody singing "What'll I Do When You Are Far Away." It made me smile to hear it.

"Bring back memories?" she said. "I can recognize a wistful look when I see it."

"A few."

"Was she married?"

I thought it was kind of a funny question, under the circumstances.

"Are you really interested? Or are you teasing?"

"Yes. I'm interested."

"Well then, yes. She was—is—the wife of a big-time producer. She's also the girlfriend of a gangster, no less."

"Busy girl."

"Yes. She always told me not to fall in love with her, because she had too much on her plate already."

"Good advice. Did you follow it?"

"Pretty much. Wistful look notwithstanding. That was more nostalgia than romance."

"Yes. They are very different things."

"She's a good friend, and I like her. We used to have lunch every week or so, sometimes at her beach house in Malibu. Sometimes at the Polo Lounge."

"And then bed afterwards?"

"Usually before. Sometimes after, too."

"A friend for a lover! How wonderful. You know the French have an expression for that—*une amie amoureuse*. They would, of course. It means 'lover-friend, friend-lover.' I think it's a lovely idea. I lived in Paris for a while. There was a man there. He was married. We started as friends, too, but it didn't end that way. You know how those things go."

"I guess I do."

"I'll bet. Have you gone to bed with many movie stars?"

"Hardly any."

She looked at me out of the corner of her eyes and smiled slyly.

"I like that, Riley Fitzhugh. 'Hardly any.' That's neatly put. Conveys exactly the right impression. And leaves so much room for interpretation. Allows for a little mystery."

"Well, you're a writer, so you would know about that."

She looked at me and smiled again, this time with surprising sweetness, and without any nuance or irony.

"Yes, I am," she said.

As I came to know, there was no better compliment you could give her than calling her a writer, except of course to say that you liked her work and recognized its quality. It was the most important thing to her. She was good and she knew it, and she had been working at it pretty successfully for just about ten years—long before she met Hemingway. When she married him a couple of years ago, she was already an established journalist and had written some fiction, too. She'd even been on the cover of *The Saturday Review*. She didn't want to be known as the wife of a famous writer; she wanted to be known for herself. I only glimpsed all this that night, but I understood it thoroughly, as time passed. It wasn't very complicated.

"So no serious love affairs?" she said. "Only *amies amoureuses?*"

"I didn't say that. I was out there six years, after all."

"So, yes. Anything current?"

"No."

"Really?"

"Yes. Really. The last woman I was involved with was shocked and hurt when I told her I was joining the Navy. She apparently had ideas and plans that I wasn't aware of. I was really surprised that she cared enough to react that way. I had no idea."

"Are you usually that obtuse?"

"Not usually. No."

"You weren't really being a heartless bastard, then."

"I didn't think so, but she seems to have. She left out the 'heartless' part. She got over it fast enough, though. The next week I saw her going down the Pacific Highway in a convertible, laughing with some actor I knew."

"How funny."

"I thought so, too."

"OK. Now it's your turn. You can ask me."

I looked at her for a moment. Her face and neck were a little flushed. It could have been from the wine, I suppose.

"I'm not sure I want to," I said.

"To ask or to know?"

"Either. Both. The fact is, I'm happy with a little mystery."

The truth was I really didn't want to know too much. I might start feeling guilty or something that would spoil what was going on. Because it was obvious that something was going on. She wasn't being at all coy about her signals. Her honesty—or was it frankness—was unusual and therefore appealing. Or more accurately, charming. Or more accurately, alluring. Plus the fact that she looked really great.

"Mystery. Yes. I like that, too. You have a way of saying the right things," she said. "How's the salmon?"

"Delicious. So is the wine."

"Do you know what Ernest says about Tavel?"

"Yes. I do."

That got a reaction; she seemed surprised and a little off balance, somehow.

"You must read a lot," she said, after a moment.

"I do. I'd like to read your stuff."

"Truly? Or are you just saying the right thing again. And it *is* the right thing, of course."

"No. Truly. I'm interested."

"That could mean several different things."

"Yes. Or all of them."

We finished the supper and drank both bottles of wine and talked. And became friends.

When we finished the last of the Tavel, she lit up a Chesterfield, glanced at me, and then stubbed it out.

"Want to go for a swim?" she said. "It's a perfect night for it."

"Yes."

We went out to the patio beside the pool. It was dark now, but the moon was almost full. She looked at me for a second and then slid her dress off. That was all she had on. Then she stood there in the silvery light. Waiting for me, I guess. I didn't hurry, but I didn't dally, either.

"Um. I'm flattered," she said.

"Are you sure you want to swim?"

"Yes. Come on. The water will take care of that. And I'm sure it'll come back quickly enough."

We stepped in the water down the pool steps, and when we were about waist deep she came into my arms and kissed me.

"Oh," she said. "That's nice."

"Not that I'm complaining," I said, "but why is this happening?"

She shivered a little. The water wasn't cold, so it wasn't that.

"God, I don't know. But it is. And I knew it would. Did you?"

"No. But knowing and wanting are different things."

"The right thing again," she said, softly.

An hour later we lay in the big bed with the moonlight still coming through the window. It was the only light, but I could see her well enough. Her hair was still damp from the pool.

"That was lovely," she said, stretching languorously.

"I'm glad. I wasn't sure about that."

"You couldn't tell?"

"As I said, I wasn't sure." For a moment at the end, her body arched and went rigid as though in a spasm and she uttered a quiet moan, almost a sigh, and then relaxed. But that was all. Nothing dramatic.

"Well, it was," she said. "But my climaxes tend to be little ones, and even they don't come that often. So the earth didn't move, as the famous line goes. But it never does. Never has anyway. Nothing ever 'shattering,' like the kind you read about. How about you? Did the earth move?"

"No, it stayed put. But the bed moved."

She laughed.

"Yes, well, that's good enough for me, too. Shall I tell you a secret? The truth is, I don't much like sex. The act, I mean."

"Really? You could have fooled me."

"Well, I mean as a general rule. A lot of the time I just wish whoever it is would get it over with. But not tonight. I liked tonight. Yes. I liked tonight. And I'm not just saying that for your benefit."

"Enough to want it to happen again?"

"Tonight or some other time in the future?"

"Yes."

"Well then, yes. Yes to both. 'She said, yes.' Do you know that line?"

"Molly Bloom."

"Bravo. Let me ask you something—do you think I need a pillow under my ass?"

"Whatever for?"

"Just thought I'd ask. It's been suggested."

"Whatever for?"

"Thank you, darling. Do you like endearments?"

"Sure."

"Good. Mostly what I like is tenderness, afterwards. I've always thought of the sex part as a prelude to that. That sex part is something for the man, mostly, followed by something for me, mostly. Seems like a fair deal. But most of the time the guy wants to get up and get on with things, and the second part never happens."

Thankfully, she left it at that. I didn't want any information about her married life. Or anything about other 'guys.' Or about who said she needed a pillow under her ass, although that wasn't hard to guess.

"Not tonight, though," she said. "You seem happy to stay. And be tender with me."

"I am."

"Is it just because you want to do it again?"

"No. Not just that. I like this part, too."

"You have lovely hands. All sunburnt from being at sea."

"And you are elegant and tawny and tanned all over."

"I like to sunbath and swim naked. It feels wonderful. I've been told I'm like a lion on a beach."

"Very apt. Golden. Lithe. Beautiful to watch moving."

"Thank you, darling Riley. It's been . . . awhile since anyone has spoken to me quite that way."

"I don't need to know about that."

"Yes. You're right. We won't talk about that again. Speaking of swimming, want to jump in the pool and cool off?"

"Yes. But first tell me something."

"Anything, almost."

"How am I supposed to think about this?"

"Oh, don't think. It spoils things. But come back. As often as you can. As often as we can manage it, I mean. All right? Promise?"

"Of course. I wonder, though, if you'd do me a favor."

"Sure. I'll bet I know what it is. I don't mind that sort of thing."

"I don't mean that. I mean, would you write to me now and then? To the ship. It would be fun to get letters from you. You could tell me what you're doing and thinking about and working on."

"Really? Are you serious? How sweet. Yes. Of course I will. I'd love to. I like writing letters. I'll be your sweetheart at home, like in the movies. But you must write back to me."

"How would that work?"

"I have a personal post office box in Havana. You could write to me there."

"OK. I'd like that."

"Good. I'll be the sweetheart you left behind when you marched away, and I'll promise I won't sit under the apple tree with anyone else but you, and you'll promise not to parlez-vous with those naughty French girls, and we'll have a lovely imaginary, parallel life like in some movie. What fun. Deal?"

"Deal."

So that's how that started.

Chapter Fourteen

The next morning, as we were getting the *Nameless* ready to get underway, Bill Patterson drove up in his embassy car.

"Got a minute?" he said.

"Sure. What's up?"

"We got a report last night that the thing on Cayo Hermosa just might be a rebel camp."

"What's that mean?"

"I don't know. But I thought you ought to know. ONI did, too. He sent me to tell the captain."

"I'll tell him, but I don't see how that changes much. If they are rebels, they could still be helping the Krauts."

"The enemy of my enemy is my friend. Yes. It's quite possible."

"Cayo Hermosa sounds like it's the ideal spot for all sorts of mischief. The way I see it, our only real worry is if they're a bunch of harmless fishermen or a Baptist Bible camp—which seems unlikely, given the way they treated that old guy who reported them."

"I agree. But I guess it only means you'll need to measure three times before you cut, instead of the usual two."

"OK."

"So . . . about last night. Are you in love?"

"What good would that do me?"

"Uh huh. Answering a question with a question. Very significant."

"I just have a new friend. That's all."

"I understand. Well, good luck on Hermosa."

We got underway at 0700, as planned. I told the captain about Patterson's information.

"I agree. I don't see how it changes things too much," he said. "Although, if they are rebels and if they aren't in any way helping Fritz, we'll leave them alone. Let the Cuban government worry about their own litter of unwanted cats. I'm not risking my men and my ship for Batista. Besides, once they know we're on to them, they'll probably pack up and find some other place to open their shop."

"There's still the problem of deciding who they are, though, Captain."

"I know. We'll just have to play it by ear. Let's hope there's a guy there wearing a monocle or those leather shorts. What are they called?"

"Lederhosen?"

"Right. Or better yet, let's hope there's a U-boat parked alongside the gas pumps saying 'Fill 'er up.'"

"How do you say 'fill 'er up' in German, Captain?"

"Same way as Mandarin."

We steamed east into the sunrise. The weather was good, again, and the visibility perfect. The sea was calm, almost flat. The sunlight was glaring off the surface. This would be a good day to get sunburnt, if you wanted to. We could see several merchant ships traveling east, too, toward Florida. One or two of the ships had only their masts or upper works showing. You had to look hard to see they were there, although their dark smoke hovered above them, for there was no wind that day.

"Makes you wonder how the ancients ever thought the earth was flat," said the captain as he watched the freighters with his binoculars. "You can understand the Russians or people who lived far away from the sea and were stuck out on the steppes, which are flatter than Olive Oyl. But the Greeks and those old boys were seafarers, and if there's one thing a sailor understands, it's the horizon and the notion of a ship being hull down. Curious. It's always bothered me. Ever bother you?"

"It does now, Captain."

"Reminds me of the problem Galileo had—trying to convince the ignorant of something he figured was obvious. Got in trouble for it, though. You know the Church finally made him confess that the sun moved around the earth, when he knew damned well it was the other way around. And do you know what he said when he caved in? 'Eppur si muove.' Which is Italian for 'And yet, it moves.' Probably said it under his breath, so the cardinals wouldn't stick him on a hot griddle."

"Meaning—believe what you want, but the facts are the facts."

"Yep. Wouldn't hurt some of our folks to learn that little bit of Italian."

"That one of your fourteen ordering languages, Captain?"

"Yep."

"So how do you order a beer in Italian?"

"Same way as Mandarin."

It was after noon when the *Nameless* reached the chart coordinates of the barrier island that almost blocked the narrow entrance into the deep-water bahia—the bahia that we hoped was deep water, that is. That same island completely hid Cayo Hermosa, which was directly behind it.

The plan was to send me and the Fubars in the whaleboat to the seaward side of the barrier island. We'd land and then climb the hill in the center of the island, so that we could look down on Hermosa. With luck, we'd be able to see something that would tell us what was going on. And with luck, the water in the bahia would give us some clue about how deep it was. We knew it wasn't a bonefish flat from the fisherman's report, but the *Nameless* drew ten and a half feet of water. We'd need to be confident there was more than that before we poked our nose into and through that narrow opening.

Fortunately there was no reef to manage. And the surf was not too strong, so we should have no trouble getting the whaleboat to the beach of the barrier island.

"I could go by myself, Captain. Maybe take one man with a walkie-talkie."

"I know. But it'll give your gang some experience. Good team building in case we really need 'em sometime. Besides, it's possible you'll run into something and be glad you have 'em along."

I got the Fubars together on the quarterdeck as the deck crew lowered the whaleboat. Most of them had gotten a good start on their mustaches, although one of them, a blond kid named Smithers, wouldn't be able to grow anything but fuzz for the next twenty years. But all of them had followed through with shaving their heads. They had all drawn their weapons from the armory, either M1s or Tommy guns, and the forty-five sidearms they wore on web belts with canteens. They also each had two grenades in their pockets. I had my forty-five and an M1 and binoculars. We were all wearing our gray battle station helmets. Boyle, my second in command, also carried a walkie-talkie.

"Guys, we're going to look for a suspected U-boat fuel dump. We don't know if it's really there or just a bunch of villagers. But something's on a little key just on the other side of that hill. We're going to land and climb it and take a look. And we're going to climb quietly so as not to disturb any siestas. OK? Any questions?"

"What do we do in case someone starts shooting?"

"Well, if they're shooting at us, shoot back, but don't shoot first. We're not going there to do much more than look. If there are people there at all, they could just be fishermen. Or they could be Cubans manning a fuel dump as a favor to Adolf. They could even be Kraut sailors dropped off by a U-boat. They could be commie rebels making exploding cigars. They could be the Andrews Sisters, sunbathing. Our job is just to try and find out what's there and report back to the ship. And if they're the bad guys, we're gonna take them out with the guns of *Nameless*, assuming we can get in there. If not, we go to plan B."

"What's plan B, boss?"

"The one that comes after plan A."

"I think the Andrews Sisters stink. I say we take them out, too," said Reynolds.

Reynolds was the ship's unofficial music critic. He had played trumpet in a band before the war and claimed he was the model for the song "Boogie Woogie Bugle Boy." He was down on the Andrews Sisters, because their version made it about the army. No one believed him, but everyone agreed he could play the trumpet pretty well. He'd sometimes sit in with the combos playing in the bars of Duval Street.

"I like 'em, but they ain't much to look at," said Otto, a twenty-year-old signalman.

"I don't think they're so bad," said Smithers. "It all depends how long you been at sea."

"You could say that about anything," said Boyle, my second-in-command.

"All right, guys," I said. "Save the debate for the gin joints. Make sure your weapons are not loaded before you board the whaleboat. Let's go."

We clambered into the whaleboat and headed for shore. The *Nameless* got underway. The plan was for her to lie off and cruise within easy visual distance, and wait until we returned to the beach and the whaleboat. There was a U-boat around somewhere, and there was no sense giving him a stationary target.

We were only five hundred yards or so off the beach and had no trouble running through the mild surf and up onto the gently sloping white beach. There was a sea breeze blowing, and I hoped it was enough to keep the mosquitoes and sand flies at bay. We pulled the whaleboat up onto the beach, took a look around at the jungle we were going to struggle through, and realized the life of a pirate had its drawbacks.

"Let's go," I said. "No talking from here on, unless there's an emergency. Remember, we can get as much information by listening, as watching."

We started straight up the middle of the hill. The jungle was thick, but we didn't need to cut our way, which was lucky. A couple of the men had brought machetes but we didn't need them. It took us a good ten minutes to push our way through the undergrowth to the top of the hill. We went in single file. The ground was slippery because of the humidity and the constant shade of the overhanging trees and palms. By the time we reached the top we were all soaked from sweat and moisture from the bushes.

The view from the top was disappointing. We couldn't see anything, because the trees on the reverse slope were as thick and high as the ones on the way up. We listened and could hear men's voices and the sounds of hammers and saws.

I looked around for a tree that I could climb. There was a huge pine with branches that started about ten feet up. Above that thick branches stuck out on all sides. It would do.

"Guys," I whispered. "Give me a hand up to that branch."

Smithers and Boyle grabbed each end of an M1 and held it between them for me to step on.

"That rifle unloaded, Boyle?"

"Yes, sir. Breech is open. I double-checked."

"OK. Hoist me up."

I stepped on the M1 and balanced myself while the two men lifted me up so that I could grab the first branch. The branch was rough and sticky, but I pulled myself up and stood there. I still couldn't see much. I climbed up several more branches like a bear after a beehive, and about twenty feet up I got above the trees that were on the reverse slope of the hill.

There it was. At the end of the bahia. On the little island were four shacks, all covered over with palm fronds as a kind of thatch. The buildings were made from plywood that hadn't begun to weather. Some men were painting the walls of the largest building, painting it green so it would blend in and be virtually invisible from the air. I assumed they'd get around to painting the others, too. I counted eight men working at various construction jobs. Over to the side of the buildings was a large black tarpaulin covering some lumpy-looking shapes that could easily have been fifty-gallon drums. Or shipping crates. Or both. One of the smaller shacks had an antenna snaking up the side and into the tree next to it. Perfect camouflage for a radio antenna.

There wasn't much of a clearing. They had left as many trees and bushes in place as possible. There were no roads or even visible paths, anywhere. The water in the bahia was dark blue all the way to the sandy beach of Cayo Hermosa. That didn't mean that it was necessarily deep enough for the *Nameless*. But it could be. Certainly, it was not a flat or a tide pool.

There was a large flat-bottom boat, much like an assault landing craft, pulled up on the beach and covered over with a camouflage netting. It could be used to ferry supplies to vessels anchored outside. That could have indicated that the bahia was too shallow for a deep draft vessel. Or maybe it was deep enough at high tide but too shallow at low, so they needed the flat-bottomed boat as a backup.

I turned the binoculars on the men working and studied each one. I was hoping for a blond guy with a scar on his cheek—one of those dueling scars that the young German aristocrats considered the height of fashion and went through actual sword duels to acquire. They wore masks to protect their eyes. But no one could blame them for that. They still tried to slash each other viciously. But there were no blonds, no scars. No monocles. No lederhosen, either. All the men were dark skinned, but that could have been from expo-sure. It didn't take long to get a tan in this country, and absurdly I had a sud-den vision of Martha's body, tanned and tawny, like the lions on the beach. 'A fine time for that sort of thing,' I thought. 'But as random thoughts go, I've had worse.' I could hear the men talking to each other, and the rhythms of their speech were definitely Spanish.

And then a shirtless man wearing only shorts and combat boots stepped out of the shack with the antenna. There was a little dog with him, scam-pering around. A black-and-tan dachshund. The man had dark hair like the rest, but, unlike most of the workers, he had identification disks on a cord around his neck. Dog tags, but not like ours. His were larger disks. He said something to one of the workers. And the rhythms of his speech were defi-nitely not Spanish. I couldn't hear what he was saying, but he was obviously the man in charge. And at the end of his speech to his subordinate, he said, clearly, almost shouted—"*Schnell.*" To which the other man said, "*Jawohl.*" And saluted. Kriegsmarine, I thought. None of that "Heil Hitler" for them. We had been told that the professional German navy wasn't all that keen on Der Fuhrer. Not that it mattered much. People said the same thing about the German regular army, too, and that didn't slow them down. When the subordinate turned in my direction, I could see that he was wearing dog tags, too. The man in charge turned around and went back into the radio shack. He stopped at the door and called the dog—"Fritz!" Well, that figured.

I worked my way down the tree to the lower branch, and Smithers and Boyle raised the rifle for me to step on and lowered me down.

The men gathered around me.

"What'd you see, sir?" they said, whispering.

"Krauts," I said.

"How many?"

"Only a couple. And half a dozen Cubans. Let's go. Quietly."

"Any vessels? U-boats?"

"No. Nothing big. Just a flat-bottomed boat."

We went back down the hill the way we came and shoved the whaleboat into the water.

"Home, Jeeves," I said, and we headed straight out to sea where the *Nameless* was coming back to us with her bow wave indicating she wasn't wasting time.

When we were back on board, I told the men to return their weapons to the armory and go back to their normal duties.

"Wasn't much of a raid," said Boyle. "But we got the job done, right, sir?"

"That's right. Good work, guys. Carry on."

I went to the bridge and told the captain what we saw.

"Our orders are to destroy it," he said. "But that doesn't make any sense, now that I think about it and now that we've seen the setup. Those guys aren't going anywhere. Seems to me pretty obvious that they're in a trap. No roads in or out, no transport. They're apparently sitting on a load of fuel that would blow them to Munich, if we put just one shell into that tarp. They're stuck. We can knock them out any time we want. But as long as they think they're safe, they'll use their radio to talk to their freighter and, even better, to call their U-boats. Do you know the German word for cheese, Riley?"

"The same as Mandarin, Captain?"

"Nope. It's *Käse*. And the way I see it they're the *Käse* in the trap, and we'd be damned fools to blow that place now, before the rats arrive in *das boot*."

"I agree, Captain."

"What do you think about the water depth in that bahia?"

"It's hard to say. It's definitely not a shallow flat. And if the supply freighter or a U-boat plan to go in there, the *Nameless* surely could. Of course, they could lie offshore at night and send their boats in for loading or off-loading, if it's too shallow. They'll know which it is, and we can take our cue from them. But I don't think we'll need to go in there all the way, Captain. The position of that island is straight down the end of the bahia, no more than eight hundred or a thousand yards."

"A straight shot, you say?"

"Yes, sir. We won't need to do anything more than push our bow through the channel entrance far enough to unmask the three-inch. We couldn't miss from that range. Two or three shells into the fuel dump will do the job, and then we can back out again to avoid the flying body parts. And if there's a U-boat tied up alongside, or a merchant ship, they'll be broadside to us. Unmissable."

"On the way in we can send a boat ahead of us to take soundings, just to make sure of the depth in the entrance. If we can get the *Nameless* all the way in, we can unmask the forties and the twenties and really raise hell with 'em. If the vessels are anchored offshore running boats in and out, we can deal with them first. The cheese in the trap won't be going anywhere."

He turned to the messenger. "Have Sparks come to the bridge."

Sparks was the nickname of our highest-rated radioman, petty officer second class Edwards.

"Aye, aye, sir."

"This guy, Sparks," said the captain to me, "is a genuine whiz kid with radios and what have you. Builds his own for a hobby. Plus, he reported to the ship after finishing an advanced training course. I have an idea he can be useful."

A minute later Sparks came to the bridge. He was a skinny redhead, no more than twenty-one. The tropical sun had turned him bright pink.

"Yes, sir?"

"Sparks, remember that story you were telling me about the Brits and how they developed a portable radio transmitter and receiver for their spies to use in Europe?"

"Yes, sir. They call it the Paraset, because they plan to drop them by parachute. They're about the size of a suitcase. It can send and receive Morse code. No voice transmissions, sir."

"It seems to me that I heard you got hold of the plans for one of those."

"Not really, sir. Those are top secret and the Brits won't share. But in my last training class they explained how they worked, and they aren't too complicated, sir. I figured it out, after a few tries, and drew up my own set of plans. I checked them with our instructor, and he said they looked pretty good."

"And it seems to me I heard you were building one in your spare time. Is that true, Sparks?"

"Yes, sir. But only in my spare time, Captain."

"I'm surprised you have any spare time, Sparks, what with us being short-handed."

"It's my hobby, Captain. I like doing it."

"Understood. Now, is your radio operational?"

"It works, sir. It isn't perfect yet. But it works."

"What's the power source?"

"Well, a real Paraset comes with a power cord that's adaptable for European current. But it can run on a car battery. In a pinch, sir."

"What's yours run on?"

"A car battery, sir."

"Where'd you get one? Buy it?"

"Well, no, sir. Not exactly. There was an army MP jeep . . ."

"Just sitting there? Not being useful?"

"Yes, sir."

"So you borrowed it?"

"Just the battery, sir."

"Do you believe that the army and the navy are on the same side, Sparks?"

"Only part of the time, sir. And army MPs aren't on anyone's side, Captain. Especially sailors. It's a well-known fact, sir."

"Yes. I've heard that, too. How would you like to try out your radio with a little real-life spying?"

"I'd like that, Captain. Yes, sir."

"Well, here's what I'm thinking of. You tell me whether you can do it and whether your radio will work. On the other side of that barrier island is a German fueling station for U-boats. That narrow channel there is the only way in or out. Now there are two kinds of vessels that are going to show up—supply freighters dropping off drums of fuel and food and what not. And U-boats looking to take on the stuff. The *Nameless* aims to trap all these birds and sink the vessels and blow up the station. But we've got two problems—there's no place for us to hide except over the horizon, and those enemy vessels will be coming at night. Those two factors bump up against each other. When we're that far off, we might miss them coming in. They sure as hell won't be showing any lights. But if we're hanging around too close, it will certainly scare them away. The U-boat will submerge and the freighter will keep on going, pretending he's an honest merchantman."

"I get it, Captain. But if there's a man ashore watching, he can signal you with the radio whenever an enemy ship shows up."

"That's it, Sparks. Want to be a secret agent?"

"Yes, sir."

"Good. Pick someone to go with you. We don't want you to get lonely."

"Well, sir, we're a little shorthanded in the radio shack. As it is, we'll have to go on port and starboard watches, if I'm going ashore. We'll need my guys here to receive messages."

"I understand. But the man who goes with you doesn't need to be able to send Morse code. All we need is for someone who can spell you, keeping watch. Take anyone you like."

"Yes, sir."

"Why not take one of the, uh, Fubars, Captain," I said. "Seaman Otto will probably be glad to volunteer."

"OK with you, Sparks?"

"Yes, sir. We're pals."

"One question, Sparks," I said. "Both of your radiomen can read and send Morse code, but can they operate your new gizmo?"

"No, sir. But I could teach them in fifteen minutes. Nothing to it for an experienced radioman."

"Well then, Skipper," I said. "Maybe we should rotate the three radiomen. Twenty-four hours on, forty-eight off."

"That work for you, Sparks?"

"Yes, sir. I think the other guys would like it."

"OK. One signalman, one Fubar, every twenty-four hours. The *Nameless* will drop you off tonight at full dark and pick you up tomorrow night, same time. Between now and then get the other two up to speed on your gizmo and think about what you'll need. We can sneak in tight along the shoreline to the west in case the Krauts decide to put a lookout on the barrier island. We'll drop you off a quarter of a mile west of the entrance to the bahia. That'll give you a good view of whoever's coming and going, but keep you out of view. OK, Sparks?"

"Yes, sir."

Chapter Fifteen

"All right, Chief," said the captain. The quartermaster chief, Russo, was standing watch as officer of the deck. "Let's clear out of here, pronto. Head north for the horizon."

"Aye, aye, sir," said the chief. "Left full rudder. All ahead full. Come to course zero zero zero."

"Riley," said the captain. "Let's you and me have a cup of coffee in the wardroom."

A few moments later we were sitting opposite each other in the *Nameless*'s modest wardroom. The steward brought us coffee and some Oreo Cookies.

"Dammit all, Blake," the captain said to the steward. "Do you know *any-one* who can eat an Oreo without a glass of milk?"

"I can, sir."

"That may account for your humble station in life. How long have you been in the Navy?"

"Six years, Captain."

"What made you join?"

"Well, Captain, I came home from work early one day and found my wife in bed with Parson Phillips. It taught me a lesson."

"I'll bite. What was the lesson?"

"Just that Parson Phillips was right when he said that man was a sinful creature. And that went for women, too, though he never said that, exactly."

"So he was proving his own point. Living the Word. With your wife assisting."

"Yes, sir."

"I call that an admirable lack of hypocrisy." The captain wore his usual expression—a sympathetic but joyful appreciation of absurdity. He was a connoisseur of the ridiculous, but could cover it up well enough, when he wanted to. "So what did you do, Blake?"

"Well, when I walked in on them, I didn't say nothing. We hadn't been getting along, anyway."

"You and Parson Phillips?"

"No, sir. We always got along good. I was a deacon. I meant me and my wife. I just turned around and walked out. I was just as glad to be shut of the whole thing. Didn't bother to say so long or good luck. When I walked out the door, I turned right, and the Navy recruiting office was the first one I come to. They asked me what I could do, and I said not that much. So here I am. If I'd a turned left when I turned right, I could be in the army. Or working in a gas station. The Esso had an opening."

"'The Turn Not Taken.' Sounds like a country song," said the captain. "Or a poem."

"Yes, sir. I'm glad I didn't go left. I like the Navy."

"I'm pleased to hear it. The army's loss is our gain. But if it ain't too much trouble, how about finding me a glass of milk."

"Me, too, Blake, if you please," I said.

"Yes, sir."

Captain Ford looked at me and grinned.

"Wouldn't trade this job for anything. No, sir. Not even for two nights with Betty Grable. So, let's get down to business. We need to think about the different ways this thing might go. Possible scenarios, I think they're called out there where you come from. You've seen the setup on that island. How do you see this thing playing out?"

"Well, sir, it seems we have to plan for two different situations. Either the water in the bahia is deep enough for U-boats and merchants to go all the way in, or it isn't, in which case they'll anchor as close as possible to the channel entrance and use boats."

"I suppose they could actually go into the channel and anchor there. That would reduce or even eliminate their nighttime silhouette. They'd blend in with the islands."

"Yes, sir. I hadn't thought of that."

"Keep going."

"Well, sir, it seemed like there was a lot of stuff under that tarp. Whether crates or fuel drums, I couldn't tell. But it looks like a freighter has already been there and dropped off more than just a few guys and some building materials."

"So the next most likely visitor will be a U-boat, rather than a freighter."

"That'd be my guess, sir."

"Mine, too. Which is lucky for us, because the U-boat is our number one priority, for a lot of obvious reasons. Priority number two is the station, because when that's gone the next freighter, which may not arrive for days or weeks, has nowhere to go when it gets here. Nothing to do."

"And if there's a freighter in the area when we open fire, the station will surely send signal that they're under attack. So the freighter would almost certainly turn around and run."

"OK. Let's assume the U-boat comes. If he anchors offshore, and if he's got any sense, he'll man his topside guns while the boats run back and forth. Did you say there was one landing craft–type boat beached at the station?"

"Yes, sir. It's just a guess, but it could be that at high tide there's enough water but not enough at low tide, so they'll use that flat-bottomed boat as a backup."

"Possible. When we're finished here we'll check the tide tables for the next couple of weeks. That may give us some clues. Anyway, if they can't get in there for whatever reason, they'll be using that boat primarily, running it back and forth. Those things can carry a good load of supplies, so they won't have to make many trips. It would be good to hit them when the supply craft is alongside or just coming, and they're distracted. But with us having to travel some to get there, the timing will be difficult."

"Life would be much simpler if it were in the daytime. We could call for an airstrike."

"That's why they'll do it all at night. We need to think in terms of 'gun-fight at the Hermosa corral.' In the dark."

"In that case we need to hope the water in the bahia is deep enough to let them go all the way in. They could be broadside to us when they tie up at the beach, and I doubt they'll be manning their deck gun when they're tucked in like that. Even if they are, we can stick the nose of the *Nameless* into that channel and put a half a dozen shots into them before they can respond. We'll have surprise on our side."

"Probably. Unless they're smart enough to post a lookout with a signal light up on that barrier island hill. But that's a chance we'll have to take. That's what they say in the movies, right?"

"Right, sir."

"On the other hand, if the U-boat anchors in the channel because the bay water's too shallow to go all the way in, their only big weapon will be their stern torpedo tubes, which means we'll need to come at them at an oblique angle. We can blow off their conning tower. That should disable them. It will certainly put their machine guns out of business. Then we can put a few holes in their hull."

"Yes, sir."

"Now . . . suppose a U-boat doesn't show up, but a freighter does."

"Well, we can at least sink the freighter, wherever she anchors—while she's busy unloading—and then blow up the station."

"It'd be a shame to miss out on the U-boat, but it'd also be a good day's work, considering. At the very least we'll be depriving the U-boat of fuel."

"Well, sir, it's possible we could knock out the station and knock out their radio, so that a U-boat just coming into the Gulf might not know the station has been destroyed. A shot into that radio shack would do the trick, although the timing would be tough. They'd probably start sending messages as soon as we showed up and started shooting."

"That's a thought. Or, I should say, that's a thought that bears thinking about."

Just then the bridge messenger knocked on the door.

"Message from the OOD, sir. We've sunk Cuba." By which he meant that Cuba had disappeared below the horizon.

"Very well. I'll be there in a minute."

"Yes, sir," said the messenger and left.

"We'll do some figure eights out here until it gets dark, and then we'll go back in and drop off Sparks and Otto. Then we'll see what we shall see. Make sure Sparks and Otto are up to speed on what they need to do—and what they don't need to do, which is, primarily, not get seen. If somebody spots them wandering around collecting seashells in a pail, the whole deal falls apart. OK?"

"Aye, aye, sir."

Sparks and Otto didn't need much in the way of help or instruction. They would be ready to go with their equipment, weapons, water, and some food. The only thing I suggested was that they take some bug repellent. There was no telling how long the sea breeze would hold, and the mosquitoes would be a problem if the wind dropped.

"Maybe we should take some mosquito netting, sir," said Otto.

"Good idea."

"Have you got the other men from the radio shack up to speed on your gizmo, Sparks?"

"Yes, sir. There's nothing to it, really."

"Good work."

I went to the bridge for the 1600 to 2000 watch. The captain was in his chair and looking at something through his binoculars.

"Appears to be a sport fishing boat," he said. "Looks to be about forty feet or so. Maybe not quite."

I looked through my binoculars and saw the contact. It was a dark-hulled boat with her outriggers extended. She was going along at a slow trolling speed. In the middle of the Gulf Stream, she was doing exactly what a sport fisherman would do.

"Want to check it out, Captain?" I said.

"We've got time. Let's see what he's up to. I have a feeling I know, but let's be sure."

I had a feeling I knew, too. We turned and headed for the boat, which was about two miles away and heading east.

A few minutes later we were alongside the fishing boat, the *Pilar*. There was a man standing on what might be called the flying bridge, but was actually just the roof of the cabin where there was a steering wheel and controls for speed and forward or reverse, but not much else. The man was burly and heavily bearded, and he wore a fishing hat with a long black bill, khaki shorts, and no shirt or shoes. Martha's husband. He pulled his boat alongside and put his engines in neutral. I had ordered "all stop."

Captain Ford and I went out to the wing of the bridge for a chat.

"Hello, Skipper," said the captain. "How's the fishing?"

"Not so bad. How are you, Captain?" He was smiling and seemed happy to see us. Three or four of his buddies were standing outside the cabin beside the fighting chair, looking up and grinning. "See any Krauts?"

"No. You?"

"No, sir. It's been quiet as a Sunday morning whorehouse."

"Well, personally, I wouldn't know about such things, but I'll take your word for it. Where're you headed?"

"They asked me to set up a base camp in Confites and hang around there for a while. See if any U-boats try to sneak through the Mayaguana Passage, instead of coming down the Florida Straits."

The Mayaguana Passage was a deep-water route through the Bahamas. Confites was a little cayo toward the eastern end of Cuba almost a hundred miles from Cayo Hermosa. Captain Ford was pleased to hear that. The last thing he wanted was for some civilians to get mixed up in our plans by accident.

"What are you supposed to do if you see one?"

Hemingway smiled slyly.

"I'm supposed to call Key West, which I will do. But I've got an idea about maybe getting close enough to lob some grenades into their conning tower. The embassy in Havana fixed us up with some grenades and a couple of Tommy guns."

The captain looked at me and grinned, as if to say—Here speaks a lunatic. Maybe we should humor him. But he doesn't seem dangerous.

"Well, that sounds like a plan. I ain't sure it's a good one, but it's definitely a plan."

Hemingway laughed. He had a deep, booming sort of laugh that went along with his baritone speaking voice. He was plainly enjoying himself.

"You sound like the ONI. When I told him my idea, he just laughed. But I figure we'll have the element of surprise going for us. No one will think we'd try something like that."

"You're right about that. No one would. But just in case you can't get close enough, how about you give us a call, too, when you contact Key West. They'd just send us the message afterwards, and it would save a little time if you contact us directly. Our call sign is Astrolight."

"Trying to steal our glory, eh, Captain?"

"No. You're welcome to it. But a word of advice—call us. We've got a job to do, too, and we're equipped to do it." By which the captain was suggesting that Hemingway and his buddies were definitely *not* equipped to do it.

"I will, Captain. I promise."

"Seen much of Honest Lil lately?"

"Now and then. She's lost some weight, but she still doesn't need a pillow under her ass."

"Good to know. Well, good hunting."

"Same to you."

The *Pilar* pulled away and continued on her way east. The captain turned to me. "OK, Riley, let's head back to Hermosa. Take it slow. We don't need to get there till dark."

We headed south.

"Funny fella," said the captain as he watched the fishing boat pulling away. "I've run into him a time or two over the years in Havana and Key West. Always the life of the party in whatever bar we were in. He writes books, I believe. Ever hear of him?"

"Yes, sir. I've read a couple of his novels. He's good. His last one was a bestseller."

"Made lots of money?"

"I think so."

"That's good. His widow will be well provided for. Do you figure he's crazy or just showing off?"

"Hard to say, Captain. Hard to say."

"Well, I'll say this for him and his buddies—another bunch of eyes keeping watch can't hurt and might help, even if they are amateurs with dreams of glory. Long as they remember to call us if they see anything, they'll be doing something worth doing. You know as well as I do that no U-boat commander's gonna let him get close enough to toss grenades into his lap."

"No, sir. It's more likely the *Pilar* will end up like the *Doris*."

"Yep. Too bad. It's a handsome boat. Well, maybe they'll get lucky and never see anything, except at a distance."

It wasn't hard to imagine the *Pilar* as a splintered wreck. It was a little harder to sort out what I would think about it, if it happened.

Chapter Sixteen

The light was beginning to fade as we approached the coast.

"We'll drop Sparks and Otto about a quarter of a mile west of the channel entrance," said the captain. "We'll darken ship going in. No sense taking any chances."

"Aye, aye, sir. Messenger. Find Bosun Wheatley. Tell him we'll darken ship."

It was better not to use the ship's intercom. Sound travels a long way over water, and we were trying to be as quiet as possible going in.

"You know," said the captain, "I've been doing a little reading lately. Mostly history. I ain't much interested in novels and such, but I am interested in things that really happened."

I knew by now that this was not just a random thought. It would lead to something, and sooner rather than later.

"I've been reading about the Civil War," he said, "and how telegraph communications made such a difference in the way battles were fought. It didn't make the generals any smarter, but it did give them more information about what the enemy was doing. It also tied the politicians and the political generals back in Washington in tighter with the men in the field. That part wasn't so good. There's nothing like a politician's courage when he's a hundred miles away from the enemy. Give him a map and a telegraph, and he can get mighty aggressive and brave and can come up with all sorts of bright strategic and tactical ideas. But as a general rule, having the telegraph was better than wandering around wondering which end was up."

"Yes, sir. Somebody once said the best weapon a soldier has is a radio."

"Who said that?"

"I forget."

"Well, it makes sense. The same thing happened out west during the Indian wars. Once the army got the telegraph stretched out on the plains, the cavalry and the civilians could pass the word along about where the Indians were and what they were up to. Cramped the Indians' style, more than a little. But it didn't take them long to figure out what was going on. After all, those telephone poles out on the empty plains stuck out like a boy's first woody. And the Indians learned pretty quick what those wires could do and that they were a danger, because they were one hell of a lot better than smoke signals or mirror flashes. So you know what they did?"

"Cut the wire."

"Yep. The only trouble was, the army could repair the lines pretty damned quick. A couple of riders could find the breaks and they'd be back in business in no time. So you know what those pesky redskins did next? They started cutting the wires, but then tying the pieces back together with a piece of rawhide, so that the wires looked whole and the repair crews couldn't find the breaks. But the connection was broken. An inch of rawhide will stop an electric message dead. Pretty smart, don't you think?"

"Pretty smart."

"I think so, too."

There followed a few minutes of silence as we watched the sun setting.

"You know, Captain," I said, finally, as if something just dawned on me. "That story gives me an idea."

"Really? What is it?"

"How about if someone sneaks into that camp on Hermosa and cuts the line to the antenna and then hides the place it was cut with some mud or something. That way they won't be able to contact either a freighter or a U-boat and warn them away. I may be wrong, but I don't think they'll even know they aren't transmitting. The lights on the radio will flash and they'll hear the dots and dashes or their own voices, but nothing will be going out."

The captain looked at me with only slightly exaggerated "wild surmise."

"Why, that's right smart, Riley."

"Thank you, sir."

"Wish I'd of thought of it, myself. Yes, sir. That kind of creative thinking'll look good on your fitness report. Got any ideas about who should go?"

"I figure I should take the Fubars in. They can stand guard on the perimeter, and I can sneak in there and cut the antenna wire. If something happens the guys can cover me. There aren't that many of them—a couple of Germans and a half dozen Cubans. And we'd have the element of surprise."

"Just like that Hemingway fella?"

"I hope not like that."

"Hmm. Well, that's a mighty interesting idea. When do you think we should do this Indian trick?"

"Just before we attack the station, Captain. Until then, we probably want to leave their communications intact. That way their customers won't be alarmed when they try to call in and can't get through."

"Makes sense. Well sir, we'll just put that idea in the back pocket until the time comes to bring it out and dust it off. I'm mighty glad you thought of it, Riley. Good work."

"Thank you, Captain. By the way, have you ever heard the story of the fox and the hedgehog?"

"Don't believe so."

"It goes, the fox knows many things, but the hedgehog knows only one big thing."

"What's the one big thing?"

"He knows to roll up in a ball when danger threatens."

"That a fact? Well, personally, I'd rather be a fox."

"Yes, sir. That's what I figured."

He sat back and smiled to himself.

"You know," he said a few minutes later, "speaking of hedgehogs, we're due to get a new anti-sub weapon called just that—a hedgehog. The thing throws a wide pattern of bombs that explode on contact with a U-boat. Kind of like an old pepper-pot pistol but with something like twenty-four different bombs per load. They say they can fire a couple of hundred yards ahead. I figure they'll be a good addition to our bag of tricks. Kind of funny that you mentioned the hedgehog just a minute ago. Ever see one in the wild?"

"No, sir. I don't think they live around here. Or anywhere in the States."

"Kind of too bad. Reminds me of a politician I knew. I forget which party he was from. Doesn't really matter. If you asked him what the hell he thought he was doing, he'd smile, roll into a ball, and say nothing, till you got tired of waiting for an answer and went away."

Around an hour before midnight, we were in position just off the coast, only a couple of hundred yards from the beach and safely west of the channel into Hermosa. I went down to the quarterdeck to see Sparks and Otto off. They were going to row an inflatable boat in to shore and keep it there, pulled up on the beach and hidden in the trees.

"You men have everything you need?"

"Yes, sir. Radio, battery, water, chow, weapons, bug repellent, mosquito net, waterproofs, flashlights."

They were dressed all in black and wore black knitted watch caps.

"Well, you look the part, anyway," I said.

The messages they would send were simple enough, and Sparks had shown Otto how to send them, just in case. They were to send a single letter—F for freighter, and U for U-boat. That was all. They were to keep sending until we acknowledged the transmission by sending R, for Roger. The object was to keep it as simple as possible and not ask Sparks's homemade radio to do too much. And there was the added possibility, although slight I hoped, that Otto might have to transmit, in which case, the simpler the better. If no enemy vessel showed up, they were to send nothing. They were not to check in, except in an emergency. There was no way of telling what the Germans might pick up on their radio, and there was no need at all for periodic reports. As a precaution they were to tune in to the frequency every four hours, starting at midnight, to see if there were any messages from us. But they were not to stay on for more than a minute or so.

The two men loaded their gear in the raft and set off for shore.

"We'll be back tomorrow night, same time, same station," I said.

"This episode of Sparks and the Handsome Fubar is brought to you by Wheaties, the Breakfast of Champions," said Otto, in a stage whisper.

They paddled off in the darkness, leaving me grinning.

And I thought of the captain's remark in the wardroom. I had to agree with him. Right now, I wouldn't trade this job for anything. Not even for two nights with Betty Grable. But what about Martha Gellhorn? Luckily for me, when it came to Martha, I wouldn't be forced to choose. At least, that's the way it looked right now. Of course, I was pretty sure there was no long-term future in it. But is there a long-term future in anything?

Chapter Seventeen

We followed the same routine for the next four nights. We'd steam in the Gulf Stream looking for U-boats during the day, pick up the radio team and drop off replacements every night, and then return to patrolling in our as-signed sector. We never saw a periscope or a conning tower. We never had any contacts on sonar. There were merchantmen on the horizon heading east in the Florida Strait, but none coming along the coast of Cuba. When Sparks was not ashore, he was on watch in the radio shack. He was trying to pick up signals from the Germans on Hermosa, but they were not trans-mitting or receiving, so far as we could tell. Either that or they were on a frequency Sparks hadn't discovered yet. As it was, everything was quiet. Searching frequencies was a hit-or-miss proposition, because you had to be dialing past just at the time that they were transmitting. It was a chance in a thousand, as long as they were not talkative. And they weren't. We were also listening on HF-DF, but there were no U-boats transmitting within our thirty-mile radius.

We knew that the U-boats would be traveling on the surface at night. They had to recharge their batteries by running their diesel engines. But even on the surface, the hull and the conning tower of a U-boat didn't create much of a silhouette, especially at a distance and especially on a moonless night, or after the moon had set. The stars were some help, but not much. On nights when there was cloud cover, we could have collided with the U-boat before we saw it. It would have been a great help if we'd had our radar installed, but we were still standing in line for that. Other larger ships, ships with names, had a higher priority.

On the fourth night I had the midwatch. We were in the process of recovering the men from the Hermosa watch and sending their relief to the beach. The men came alongside in the rubber raft and were climbing back aboard. The relief team was standing by, ready to go. I was standing on the port wing of the bridge, when Sparks came rushing in from the radio shack.

"SOS, sir! A freighter under attack from a U-boat!"

"Did he give his position?"

"Yes, sir. Here it is." He handed me the coordinates on a scrap of paper.

I went to the chart table to check. The ship under attack was sixty miles to the west, about twenty miles northeast of Havana. Our top speed was just over twenty knots, so we were three hours away. A long time.

"Stay on it, Sparks. Tell them we're coming. Messenger, call the captain."

"Aye, aye, sir."

The relief team was about to climb into the rubber raft when I signaled to them to stop.

"Get that raft aboard, men. We'll skip the watch ashore tonight. There's an emergency."

"What about the radio and gear, sir? We left it ashore."

"It's hidden, isn't it?"

"Yes, sir. Under the waterproof and in the trees."

"Good. We'll be coming back."

As soon as I saw that all the men and the boat were aboard, I stepped back in the pilot house and ordered, "All engines ahead full! Come to course two eight five."

"All ahead full. Come to course two eight five, aye, aye, sir," said the helmsman.

The captain came in his bathrobe.

"What's up, Riley?"

"SOS, sir. Merchant under attack from a U-boat. Sixty miles. They radioed their position, almost due west of here."

"Did they report their status?"

"No, sir. Not yet. No word on whether they're damaged, or how badly. I thought it best not to send the relief radio team ashore. I figured we might be gone awhile. We recovered the men and the boat."

"Yes. Good."

In the pilot house we could hear the reports coming in, but they were in Morse code—three dots, three dashes, three dots. SOS. Then the message became more extensive, a wild mixture of dots and dashes.

Sparks came back a minute later.

"Sir, they've been hit by a torpedo amidships and are sinking. They're on fire and are breaking up. Casualties are heavy."

"Did they say who they are?"

"Yes, sir. The *Esso Galveston*."

"Tanker," said the captain. "Fires. Poor bastards."

He got on the phone to the engine room.

"Chief, can you give us three hours of flank speed without blowing something."

"Yes, sir. She can take it. She won't like it. But she can take it."

"All right, Riley. Crank her up."

"All ahead flank," I ordered. The quartermaster moved the engine order telegraph to indicate flank, which was our topmost speed. It put the greatest strain on the engines, but it would give us another two knots, and these were the times you used it.

The *Nameless* started to shudder a bit as she picked up speed and her body reacted to the increased stress. There was a moderate sea so we began to pitch and throw our bow wave in dramatic fashion. It looked like surf in a storm. If it wasn't so serious a matter, it would have been beautiful to see.

"Carry on, Riley. I'm gonna get dressed. Messenger, go tell Blake to bring us all some coffee. It's gonna be a long night."

"Aye, aye, sir."

In two hours we could see a red glow on the horizon. It wasn't the first light of morning. It was a ship on fire.

"Red skies in morning, sailors take warning. Trouble is, it isn't morning," said the captain. When the captain dropped his folksy habit of saying "ain't," you knew he was in a serious mood.

We were still an hour away, and as we drew closer to the inferno, minute by minute, the fire seemed to diminish so that by the time we reached the scene, it had burned itself out. The torpedoed oiler had sunk, but her cargo was spread over the sea in all directions for hundreds of yards. Oil—some of it smoking—floated in huge patches, undulating in slow motion on the surface, like blankets of tar spread haphazardly as far as you could see. I remembered reading that Ben Franklin experimented with pouring oil on troubled waters. He was astonished at how it spread and smoothed a roiled surface. But this was not what Franklin had in mind. The mind of an eighteenth-century scientist could not possibly imagine modern war, either on land or at sea. On the other hand, someone like Franklin would not have been surprised by this kind of savagery. He knew what men could be.

"Turn on the spotlights," the captain ordered to the signalman on the flying bridge just above the pilot house. "Scan the area. Look for survivors.

Call Bosun Wheatley to the bridge." Then he said to no one in particular, "God, what a mess."

There were giant puddles of crude oil that had separated from the mass and had escaped the fire. Thick black smoke hovered over the area, for there was no wind, and the stench of the fire was thick. The air was like an oily fog. You could taste it, and the smell got in your nostrils and stayed there. There were no lifeboats to be seen anywhere. None upright, that is. We could see one lifeboat capsized and barely floating. It was splintered and riddled with bullet holes.

"Plain to see what happened to that lifeboat," said the captain.

We couldn't see anyone clinging to wreckage, though there was plenty of that scattered everywhere. Mattresses and clothing, papers of all kind, crates of supplies, mostly split and broken, empty cans and trash they hadn't got around to dumping yet, broken furniture like chairs and sofas and tables, and, absurdly, even a Ping-Pong table and a toilet seat—all the detritus of shipboard life, most of it floating obscenely in the thick oil. It was as though some evil genie had grabbed the ship and torn it apart in his hands, then scattered the contents out on the sea. And in a way, of course, that's pretty much what happened. The scene lent itself to metaphors.

It was impossible to tell how far the oil had spread across the surface of the sea. It was too dark.

Tom Wheatley appeared a few moments later. He was as calm as you could want. He'd seen this sort of thing before, in another war.

"Tom, lower the whaleboat and take a couple of men with you. Look for survivors, but for God sakes don't venture too far into those oil slicks if they're still smoking or if you see any sparks. A puff of wind and the fire could start up again."

"What if we see a survivor in there, Captain?"

"Get him if you can. But your primary responsibility is to the men with you."

"That'll be a hard decision, Captain."

"I know, Tom."

"What about bodies?"

"Can't take the time for that now. That U-boat may be around here somewhere, and we don't want to be sitting here like a duck in a cattail swamp. Take a signal light with you. We're gonna take a look around for the U-boat. Maybe we can pick him up on sonar. But we'll stay in visual range of you. Signal us if you find too many men to carry in the whaleboat, and we'll come and get you. I kind of doubt you will, from the looks of things."

"Aye, aye, sir."

"Riley, if that son of a bitchin' U-boat is still around and with us lit up like a Christmas tree, let's not make it easy for him. Crank her up to ahead one-third and let's take a look around. It wouldn't hurt to do some zigzags while we're looking. Stay out of the oil. That U-boat will be doing the same if he's still around. He won't want to stick his periscope into the slicks or wreckage. Remind the sonar boys, this isn't a drill."

"Aye, aye, sir." The sonar men had been on it since we got word of the attack, although our flank speed getting here meant we had almost no chance of getting a good signal. But I passed the word back to their listening station that we were in the area and would be going slower now—better chance of picking up a contact. And a better chance of being attacked.

We began to circle the scene of the wreck, all the while focusing the spotlight on the oil slicks and the debris, looking for bobbing heads or waving arms. Bosun Wheatley and the two seamen in the whaleboat were using their flashlights to scan the wreckage, too. The sonar operator was sending his pings off into the depths, but he was getting nothing useful in return. We made a full circuit of the oil slick and then another, even wider, but still there was no returning echo on sonar.

We searched almost an hour and saw nothing but wreckage. We watched Wheatley in the whaleboat moving carefully through the debris and in and out of the massive puddles of oil. Now and then they would stop and examine some blackened shape in the water. Then let it slide back into the water. Dead bodies, one after another. Burned and blackened, they didn't look much like men, and they were hard to distinguish from the ship's debris. Finally we saw Wheatley stop beside some floating wooden crates. His two sailors leaned over the side and fastened the boat hook to a blackened body in the oil and pulled it toward the boat. They examined it for a second or two and then lifted the body over the side and into the boat.

"Looks like he found someone alive," said the captain.

We circled back toward the whaleboat, and when we were alongside the captain yelled down from the port wing of the bridge.

"What's up, Tom?"

"We found one man, sir. He's in bad shape. Burned and covered in oil. Swallowed some, too, maybe. I hope not."

Our hospital corpsman, like all Navy corpsmen, was known as "Doc." He was our closest thing to a medical man, even though he only had to shave once a week. He was at the railing as the sailors on deck lifted the water-logged body of the survivor onto the quarterdeck. Doc started to administer some treatment—stripping the man of his oil-covered life jacket, cleaning some of the oil off his face and hands, and examining his burns. The man was barely conscious.

"Anybody else out there, Tom?" said the captain.

"None that we could see, Captain. But I can't be sure. I'd like to take another look around. It's pretty goddamned black out there. Heads are hard to see and there's no one waving at us. No sounds. But there might still be some survivors. I'll tell you what is out there, though—a couple of dozen dead bodies. We've checked the ones we could find, to make sure."

"OK. Keep at it. We'll do the same. OK, Riley, let's go around again. Doc?" the captain shouted down to the quarterdeck. "What do you think?"

"He's bad, Captain. But he's alive. He might have a chance if we could get him to a hospital. I won't know how serious the burns are till I get him to sickbay and get his clothes off."

"Very well. Carry on. Damn it all, Riley," said the captain. "That gives us a lousy choice."

"Yes, sir. It does."

"But we've got to keep looking until we're sure there's no one still alive in that water. We'll have some light here shortly. That'll help. Let's hope that fella can hold out till we can get him to Havana. But we can't leave here till we're pretty certain there's no one else floating around out there half dead. One hell of a mess. Goddamn Krauts."

We searched for the rest of the darkness, and when dawn started breaking I thought of Homer's repeated references to "Dawn with her rosy fingers." But Dawn's rosy fingers would be covered with thick black oil and smoky film this morning. Maybe it was an absurd time to be thinking of poetry, but on the other hand, when it came to war, old Homer knew a thing or two. And when we recovered the whaleboat and made ready to head south to Havana, we were pretty sure the blackened, burned, and oil-covered bodies we left behind were all past caring whether they were left behind or not.

"Do you think the Cubans or someone will send something to collect the bodies, captain?"

"I dunno. And I don't know if sharks like the taste of oil." He took his hat off and rubbed his hand though his white hair. He looked tired. "Seems like there's lots I don't know, Riley."

"Well, sir, knowing and being able to make sense of it are different things."

He looked at me and smiled, wanly.

"Yeah. You're right. Let's go."

We radioed ahead to have an ambulance waiting for us at the dock. There was a small crowd waiting there when we arrived—people from the embassy, the naval liaison, and the Cuban officers who had visited the ship.

"I'll talk to these folks, Riley," he said. "You check on all the departments and make sure we're ready to get underway again as soon as possible."

"Aye, aye, sir."

"I wish we could stay awhile. It's been a few long nights. But we have all the more reason to get back to Hermosa. That son of a bitch could be in there right this minute, getting topped off on fuel. I kind of doubt it. He's allergic to daylight. But you never know. I tell you one thing, though, this time we're going to blow hell out of Hermosa. The bastards have got me in the mood to start a few fires."

"Yes, sir."

He was right, of course. We had to get underway as soon as possible. But I wished we could have stayed a little longer, too.

Chapter Eighteen

In another hour, we were on our way east, back toward Hermosa. We wouldn't be going back at flank speed. There was no sense stressing the engines. It would be another story if we knew the enemy was there, but we didn't. So I figured I had a couple of hours to get some sleep. I was about to stretch out on my bunk when the yeoman who handled the ship's mail knocked on the outside of my doorway, next to the curtain across the opening.

"Got some mail for you, Mr. Fitzhugh," he said. "We got a bagful from Key West. A PBY flew it in."

"That was nice of them," I said.

"They were coming here anyway, sir. Got a letter for you."

"Thanks, Elliott."

Elliott was a yeoman third class and the captain's secretary. Everyone called him "TS." Most of the guys didn't know why and thought it meant something obscene. It might have, actually. His real name was Eddie.

The letter had no return address, but it smelled good.

Darling Riley,

I am sitting under the apple tree and thinking of you. There is no one here with me. I promised that, remember? Are you being true to me and not fooling around with those naughty French girls in Gay Paree? I know you are. I knew you would be true when you left and gave me your Eagle Scout badge. I won't tell you where I wear it, but I will say sometimes it pokes.

For my sins, which I suppose must include you (though I don't really think so), I am starting another novel. I have to do something other than feed the cats. I remember you said they liked you. Dogs, too. And babies, if I remember correctly. I am Oh for Three with all those critters, I'm afraid. The first two avoid me, and I avoid the third.

Do you think of that night we had together? What a dopey question. Of course, you do. I do. And I get quite warm all over. It surprises me when that happens. I don't do anything about it, but I think about it—doing something, that is—which is something new for me. "What'll I do when you are far away . . ." etc.

Come as soon as you can. (Oh, dear.) I mean—come and see me as soon as you can, and we'll have a swim and drink Tavel and compare suntans. I'll be surprised if you don't have tan lines, and you'll be surprised if I do. I'll give the servants the night off, again.

I loved our night together.

Marty

I had to smile when she said she'd give the servants the night off "again." That suggested significant premeditation on her part the last time. And she would know, I think, that I would take it that way. She was a writer and knew how words worked. I also smiled about the Eagle Scout badge. In real life I never made it past Cub Scouts. But she wasn't talking about real life.

I turned out the light and lay down on the bunk, still smiling and wondering where she put that imaginary badge and also thinking that her letter was at least a partial antidote to images of an oily sea littered with smoldering trash and blackened bodies. It gave me a much better image to sleep with. I closed my eyes and passed out.

The rain came that afternoon during my watch. It was the very definition of a tropical storm, and the torrents reduced our visibility to almost nothing. We cut our speed to all ahead slow and turned on our running lights in the hopes they'd be seen by any wandering merchantman. We sounded our horn periodically, as stipulated in the nautical Rules of the Road. Whether the noise would scare away or attract our enemies was something we couldn't worry about. The safety of the ship was the first concern. People quote Thucydides as saying a collision at sea will ruin your day. I don't know if he actually wrote that, but it is nonetheless true. On the other hand, I think any of us who'd seen the results of that tanker sinking would have been happy to ram the U-boat that did it. Or any U-boat, for that matter. We'd get a broken and bloody nose, but they'd go to the bottom. We'd take that trade, collision or not. Ramming was a tactic older than the Greeks, and it was still part of our repertoire. A broken bow in exchange for a sunken U-boat was a good exchange—a pawn for a queen.

Because of the storm, we had no way of checking our position. Once again, if we'd had radar we could have scoped the coastline and picked out landmarks. But we didn't. We plotted by dead reckoning, which is nothing more than drawing a line on the chart reflecting your compass course and ordered speed. Dead reckoning is only somewhat accurate when there is no current and no wind and nothing in the sea or weather that can affect the ship's course and speed—a situation that almost never occurs at sea, and certainly wasn't the case today. "All Ahead Standard" on your engine order telegraph may say you're going fifteen knots at so many RPMs of the screws, but you could be going a lot slower "over the ground" because of sea conditions. That afternoon there was a good twenty-five knots of wind from the northeast, and gusts higher than that—enough wind to drive the rain almost sideways, and more than enough to buffet the *Nameless* in the same direction. Either wind or seas could affect our course and speed, and together they were more than doubly bad. Both threw us off the line that we drew on our chart. We knew that the fixes we plotted reflected only wishful thinking and where we should be according to our course and speed, but not where we were. They were about as accurate as a game of pin the tail on the donkey. And the moderate seas caused the slender and slightly built *Nameless* to pitch and roll enough to make us all a little uncomfortable. A battleship or a carrier would plow right through those seas without much motion. But we resembled a cork more than a dreadnaught, and we were taking thirty-degree rolls. When you're knocked off balance and thrown against a bulkhead, you learn again the eternal lesson that steel is unforgiving. "Hard" does not begin to describe it.

"Remind me, Riley," said the captain. "Did I say one time that tourists pay twenty dollars a day to sail these waters, and here we are getting paid to do it?"

"Yes, sir," I shouted to make myself heard over the wind.

"I thought so."

We thought we should be just off the barrier island and the Hermosa channel, but we couldn't see the coast and we didn't dare go too close for fear of the shallows. The lookouts were posted at their stations in foul-weather gear. They were drenched and dripping manfully, but they couldn't see any more than we could in the pilot house. We stationed a lookout in the masthead, but he might just as well have been in a phone booth. The way we were pitching and rolling and the fact that he was so high up gave him a serious ride back and forth, side to side. With every roll he'd be looking down at the gray sea only to be whipped upright and back over the other side. He had almost no chance of seeing anything. Holding on was about the best he could do. Everything was gray, except for the whitecaps the wind created, and there were plenty of them. With each pitch of the ship the bow splashed down and sent cascades of water off to the sides and a cloud of spindrift over the wings of the bridge and against the windows of the pilot house. We couldn't see anything through the windows, so the captain went out to the starboard wing of the bridge and I took the port. Visibility wasn't much better in the open. It was all we could do to keep the lenses in our binoculars clear. The wind was howling—that's how they always describe it, and for good reason. And it was making the wires on our rigging vibrate and whine like violin strings—Jack Benny's violin, that is. Nothing you enjoyed listening to. The day was altogether a son of a bitch.

It wasn't cold, but when you're soaked through your foul-weather gear, you get a clammy feeling that makes you think you'd rather stand watch in your skivvies. On the other hand, I figured this was a great day to improve the overall saltiness of my officer's hat. I had long before removed the stiffening grommet so that the sides flopped down elegantly, and I had tied it on my head with a length of line. It was getting a thorough soaking in rain and seawater. I might still be a rookie, but at this rate I'd look a lot less like one, which is half the battle—the battle in your own head where you fight against the voice that whispers that you really don't know what you're doing, and everybody knows it. That voice was getting weaker and less frequent as the days and weeks went by, but it still chimed in now and then. A salty hat would help banish it even further.

For safety's sake we veered northeast, farther out into the Bahama Straits. Our fathometer showed that we had plenty of water under the keel, and we briefly considered using that as a navigational tool by going in closer and comparing depths on the chart to readings on the fathometer. But that was a fool's gambit. The shallow water off the Cuban coast was always just an estimate on the charts, and it was constantly changing because of hurricanes and just the normal cussedness of shoaling and sands. Going in too close and relying on the accuracy of the Cuban soundings was an invitation to run aground. Running aground on a sandy or muddy bottom was one thing. You could usually reverse your engines and back off, if you hadn't been going too fast when you hit. But running onto a coral or rocky reef was something quite different. Things got broken. In the old sailing days a captain's worst fear was being driven onto a lee shore by the wind and seas—onto reefs and rocks and shallows battered by surf. It usually meant the death of the ship, and the crew as well. You had to admire and even marvel at those old sailors who bet their lives on their skill at harnessing the wind. But sometimes, on days like this, even skill didn't help. I was mighty glad we didn't have *that* problem.

Toward the end of my watch the clouds started to break up and the wind dropped to comfortable levels. The sun came out now and then behind the shifting clouds. The chief quartermaster was BF Russo. He was my relief, and just before he took over, he was able to take a sunline and figure our latitude. That line drawn over our dead reckoning line on the chart gave us some clue about where we were, but it was only a clue. We couldn't be sure how far to the east we'd come.

I went to my room and reread the letter, thinking that it really was fun to get mail. Then I started thinking about Martha, again. In fact, I started thinking hard about her. This whole thing was certainly not a good idea and could only end badly, right? Of course. The only question was—how badly and in what way? But even so, I was looking forward to seeing her again and drinking more Tavel and doing all the rest of it. Some writer once said that the sign of an intelligent man was the ability to hold two conflicting ideas in the mind at the same time and still function. I always thought that almost anyone could do that, and almost everyone did it, all the time. And it was more a sign of indecision or confusion than intelligence. I decided to follow Martha's advice and not think about it at all. That is, not think about the *situation* and just think about her. After all, she had said we had a parallel, imaginary world to live in, and that was a good place to be right now. I liked it. And though it was only a temporary place, I asked myself, what wasn't? The music always ends. All the more reason to listen carefully while it's playing. *"What'll I do when you are far away . . ."*

Then I fell asleep and dozed for another two hours before dinner. I didn't dream about blonds with no suntan lines. I didn't dream about anything. I was too tired. Besides, the sea was calming down and the rolling and pitching didn't bother me. In fact, it was kind of restful, like being on a porch swing.

I woke up and went to the wardroom for dinner. The captain was still on the bridge, so I was by myself.

"What's for chow, Blake?"

"Frankfurters and beans, sir."

"That the best you can do?"

He looked hurt.

"Yes, sir. To be honest, Mr. Fitzhugh, I've always thought franks and beans was pretty good as food." Then he brightened up. "And I made a pan of cornbread."

I don't know why that pleased him so much. It wasn't much of a surprise. Blake made cornbread every night. It was getting so that I could actually eat it. Being from Maryland's Eastern Shore, the captain was a southerner of sorts, and he always poured blackstrap molasses on it.

"Kills the taste," he'd say.

"Bring it on, Blake," I said. "Let's get it over with."

I ate quickly and went to the pilot house. Bosun Wheatley had the watch, and the captain was in his chair as usual.

"Cornbread, tonight, Captain."

"That a fact? You know, one of these days Blake is gonna surprise us and give us biscuits for dinner and cornbread for breakfast. It'll take one of those sudden flashes of inspiration, but I believe he's got it in him."

"I don't know, Captain. I'd say he has what they call a foolish consistency."

"Somebody famous once said something about that, if I'm not mistaken."

"Yes, sir. I believe it was Emerson."

"Must have had someone like Blake in mind when he wrote it. What else has Blake rustled up?"

"Franks and beans."

"Sorry to hear it. Good thing we're not paying twenty dollars a day for this cruise."

The wind finally blew the clouds away and then blew itself out, so that by the time it was full dark the stars were out and the moon had risen and the night was perfectly clear and calm. Chief Russo was able to get sextant readings, including a reading on the moon, so that he could work out our position, finally.

"Nice work, Chief," said the captain. "It's not everyone that can shoot the moon and get anything but a tangle of confusion from it."

He was right. I tried it more than once, and I thought I was pretty good at celestial navigation, but my calculations always resembled a paragraph from *Finnegan's Wake*.

"She's unreliable, Captain," said Russo. "I agree. But . . ."

"I know," said the captain. "It's all a matter of knowing how. Well, anyway, we know where we are and what we're doing, which sets us apart from the majority of humans." The captain paused for a minute. "You know, Chief, when I was looking through your service record, I noticed that your first two names are Edgar Allen. Not anything like a BF. Where's that come from?"

Russo looked a little embarrassed.

"It's a nickname, Captain. Stands for Buddy Fucker."

"I figured it was something like that." The captain nodded, his expression all innocent seriousness. "How'd it come about?"

"I once bird-dogged a shipmate's girlfriend. At a USO dance."

The captain smiled benignly. You could almost see him giving thanks to the gods of absurdity. Although Russo was a thoroughly competent seaman and navigator, he was short and fat and going bald. The image of Russo cutting in and jitterbugging away with someone else's girl warmed the captain's heart.

"That explains it," said the captain. "Those USO dances can be regular Roman orgies. They even serve free coffee and donuts. It's a wonder there aren't more riots. What kind of music was playing?"

"Glenn Miller, Captain. 'In the Mood.'"

"Figures. What happened to the girl?"

"My buddy married her."

"So it was a happy ending."

"No, sir. She ran off with a Marine, not long afterwards."

"Seems like the Marine should go by BF, then."

"Well, sir, he wasn't a buddy. The fact is, neither of us knew him."

"But she did."

"Yes, sir. Not at first, though. They met at a Christmas get-together. Toys for Tots. That's a Marine charity, you know. Does good work. And me and my buddy were away on a cruise at the time. That kind of thing happens."

"Yes, it does. But your nickname stuck."

"Yes, sir."

"The nickname stuck, but the girl didn't. Sounds like a country song. Well, that clears up something I'd been wondering about. Nice job fixing our position, Chief."

"Thank you, Captain."

Russo left the bridge.

"I may never see the moon again, without thinking of BF," said the captain.

"Sounds like the first line of a poem, Captain," I said. "Even better than a country song."

"Yes, it does. Moves along right smart." He took a cigar from his pocket and fired it up with his Zippo and took a long, contented drag. "Yes, sir," he said. "Not for two nights with Betty Grable."

It turned out that we were not that far away from Hermosa. We were just about on the proper longitude but were about twenty miles north of the coast, because we had moved farther into the Straits as a precaution against being blown onto the shoals of the Cuban north shore. We could turn south from our current position and be back at Hermosa in about an hour.

"I wonder if Sparks's radio survived the storm."

"Maybe. They stowed it under their waterproofs, Captain."

"Well, I guess we'll find out. Let's go see."

Chapter Nineteen

An hour later we were just west of the channel into Hermosa. It was almost midnight, and I was just about to go off watch.

"Seems pretty quiet around here," said the captain. "But I wonder what's going on in that camp. It's a shame we had to leave to look after that tanker. A Kraut freighter might've snuck into Hermosa when we had our back turned. Maybe even a U-boat. I kinda doubt it, since there doesn't seem to be any light or noise coming from there. But we can't be sure."

This, I knew by now, was kind of like an opening for a straight line.

"Why don't I go take a look, Captain? If nothing's going on, we can put Sparks back on shore. But if someone's in there, there's no sense doing that."

"I believe you're right. I'm sure you know where Custer went wrong."

"Charging in without knowing what's ahead."

"That's about it. Like Sitting Bull said—finding your ass is easier if you use both hands."

"He had a way with words."

"That's a fact. 'Course, it sounds better in the original Sioux."

"Is that one of your seventeen languages, Captain?"

"As a matter of fact, it is."

"So how do you order beer in Sioux? I'm guessing it's the same as Mandarin."

"No. It's more like Italian. Now, I don't see the need to take all the Fubars over to Hermosa. But you might take one along, for company."

"Aye, aye, sir."

I went below and sent for Otto.

"Grab your rifle and gear, Otto. We're going ashore again. Same drill, but just you and me."

"Yes, sir."

"And grab me an M1 and a bandolier, too. Meet me on the quarterdeck in five minutes. We'll take the rubber raft in. No sense lowering the whaleboat. Besides, it'll be quieter."

The darkened ship was slipping slowly eastward along the coast and past the opening to the channel. We'd stop opposite the hill on the barrier island.

I went to my room and grabbed my forty-five, black watch cap, and a dark jacket. Then I stepped across the passageway to the wardroom and called for Blake. He emerged from the galley, sleepy eyed.

"I'm starved, Blake. Can you make me a sandwich to go?"

"To go?"

"To take with me. Wrap it in wax paper. I'm in a hurry."

He thought about things.

"I can open a can of corned beef."

"Never mind. Just give me one of those leftover franks, if you've got any. Put it in a piece of bread and I'll pretend I'm at the ballgame."

"Yes, sir." He seemed doubtful. "But you know a hot dog ain't really a sandwich, officially."

"Don't worry about that, Blake. Just do it."

He was back in less than a minute with the package.

"I guess it's kind of like baloney, being cold like that," he said. "A hot dog's made of the same stuff, more or less."

"Good to know."

I put it in my jacket pocket and went to the quarterdeck. Bosun Wheatley's deck gang had put the inflatable in the water. Otto was in the boat and waiting with the weapons.

"I don't think the surf will give you any problems coming back, sir," said Johnson, the second class bosun mate. "Tide's going out. Might be a little stiff paddling in."

"Thanks, Johnson."

I clambered down into the boat and grabbed a paddle, and Otto and I headed for the beach in the darkness. We could hear the surf, and Johnson was right. It wasn't too noisy, and not too rough. Getting in through the surf wasn't the problem. It was getting out again in a rubber boat with only two men paddling—that could be a problem. But with the tide the way it was, we should be all right for the next hour or so. There was no time to dawdle, though.

It didn't take us long to get to the beach. It was only three hundred yards away, although the outgoing tide added a little to our labors. But we beached the boat in good order and dashed into the nearby jungle. We took our time climbing the slope and working through the bushes and vines along the way. The moist earth and the pine needles made for slippery going. We paused every few yards to listen. There was always the possibility of a posted sentry. We listened hard for the noise of movement, a cough, or a sneeze. We sniffed the air for cigarette smoke. But there was nothing. "Whoever's in charge of security on Hermosa was doing a lousy job," I thought. At least I hoped that was the case. We got to the top and found the big pine tree again.

Otto bent down and I climbed on his shoulders and was able to reach the lowest branch. I pulled myself up on the rough and sticky bark and then climbed the next few branches until I was above the tree line on the reverse slope.

Through the branches in my tree I could see some dim lights below, in the camp. As I pushed through the branches a little more, I realized the light wasn't coming from the camp. There was an old tramp streamer tied up parallel to the shore. A few of its lights were on, and there were two sailors standing watch on the deck. They didn't appear to be armed, and they didn't appear to be paying attention. They were smoking and chatting, obviously at ease. I couldn't make out any words or speech rhythms, so I couldn't tell if they were Germans. It didn't really matter. They were Germans as far as we were concerned, at least for tonight. The ship was small, maybe two hundred feet, but large enough to be an oceangoing merchant. It was nothing anyone would paint a picture of. Rust spots and red lead paint were the principal decorations, and her old black hull was faded and her white superstructure was as dingy as a poor man's extra shirt. Her one funnel used to be red. All in all, the old bucket was a perfect imitation of a harmless tramp. I couldn't see any deck guns on her. That figured. On such a miserable-looking vessel, any sort of visible armament would have given the game away. Their protection lay in her shabbiness. In this light I couldn't read the name or the registry. It was too dirty and faded. There was no flag flying.

The camp itself was quiet. They were not running their generator, so the lights were all off. No one seemed to be up and about. I couldn't be sure, but it seemed that the tarp covering the oil drums was bigger or higher. It appeared that more material had been delivered. More fuel. More food. More ammo. If so, that meant the freighter had already unloaded. Her rigging booms were stowed, which indicated that they were finished doing what they came for. They had come in the dark, unloaded their cargo, and were now resting before getting underway again. And yet there was no sign of preparations to leave. Maybe they'd get underway around four. It would still be dark, and besides, they gave every appearance of being a legitimate merchantman. As soon as they cleared the Hermosa channel, they were safe. They wouldn't need more than fifteen minutes to get out of there. Their papers would say they were empty of cargo and "sailing in ballast." Or maybe they also carried some innocuous cargo. But it was obvious they'd want to leave before first light. They were in danger of being seen by a random aerial reconnaissance if they stayed past dawn. Then their cover would be blown.

I looked at my watch. It was just twelve thirty. We'd have time to do what needed to be done. I climbed back down the tree and hung by two hands from the lowest branch. Otto grabbed my legs and lowered me down.

"Kraut freighter in there," I said.

"Bingo."

"Right. But we've got something to do before we get back to the ship."

I had a pretty good mental picture of the layout. To the left of the barrier hill and at its base was a small saltwater outlet or inlet—no wider than a mountain stream. It separated the barrier island from Hermosa. I figured it wasn't that deep, although that remained to be seen. The lights from the freighter were enough for me to see all the little buildings on Hermosa and recognize the radio shack.

"What's up, sir?"

"We're going to sneak down the east side of this hill. We need to cut that antenna wire at the radio shack. I know where it is, but you'll need to cover me. There's a little stream to cross between the base of this hill and that cayo. You'll stay on this side of it. I'll cross over and sneak around through the jungle behind the radio shack. I don't think anyone will be able to see me. The only watch is on the freighter. The island generator is not running, so if they wake up and start raising hell the only light they'll have is from the freighter and flashlights. They'll be milling around and wondering which way is up, and by that time I hope I'll have cut the antenna and gotten out of there."

"What'll I do?"

There was that phrase again. I had to smile, though I wasn't in an especially happy frame of mind.

"Cover me. But for Godsakes, don't shoot unless you see them standing me against a wall with a blindfold. Last resort. OK?"

"Yes, sir. Ah, do you mind me asking why we're doing this? Just curious, sir."

"In a couple of hours, the *Nameless* is going to come through that channel there to the right and blast the shit out of that freighter and camp. But when she pokes her nose in here and the krauts see her, they'll know they can't fight it out, so the first thing they'll think to do is get on their radio and warn any of their buddies in the area. This is a refueling base, and we don't want the U-boats to know we've flattened it. As long as they think the base is operational, they'll keep coming. It's a mighty fine rat trap. If we cut the antenna wire and they don't realize it, they can try to send messages till Eva kicks the clap. It won't matter."

"Eva?"

"Eva Braun. Adolf's girlfriend."

"I get it, sir. But if we blast the place it won't matter, will it, sir?"

"No. Once that's done. It's the time between when we show up and when they meet their maker that I'm worried about. That might only be a couple of minutes, but it could be fifteen or twenty. It's not likely, but we can't take the chance. OK?"

"Yes, sir."

There was also the dim possibility that there was a U-boat in the area, and if Hermosa called for help the U-boat could come up behind the *Nameless* when we were inside the channel, and then the roles would be reversed in a very bad way. We'd be a prime candidate for a torpedo right up our stern—an unmissable shot right down the channel. But there was no sense getting into that with Otto.

"All right. Let's go. Quietly."

We slid carefully down the hillside on our butts. We didn't want to take the chance of tripping. As they say in the movies, it was too quiet, so any unusual noise might alert the watch on the freighter.

We got to the bottom of the hill and crawled to the stream. Otto took up a position in some bushes where he could see the entire camp. I left my rifle with him and crawled about thirty yards farther "upstream," so that I was hidden from the camp. I carefully stepped into the water. The water was only waist deep, and the bottom was a firm marl and seashell mix. My shoes sank only an inch, if that. I waded slowly across, listening for any noise that might be suddenly unusual. But all was quiet, aside from the normal clanking and discharge of the freighter's bilge pumps.

The other side of the stream was more jungle. I went into it about a yard or so, then turned toward the camp. I didn't want to waste any time, but still I crawled forward. It didn't take long to reach the opening to the camp. The radio shack was the second building after what I assumed was the bunkhouse for the Cubans. I didn't know whether the two Germans were in there with the Cubans or not. Somehow I doubted it. They might well be sacked out in the radio shack.

I crawled another ten yards to get behind the radio shack, but I stayed in the bushes while I studied the side of the building, looking for the wire leading up the side to the antenna. I couldn't see it in the dark. Very cautiously I crawled out of the bushes to the side of the shack. I had a clear and uncomfortable view of the freighter in front of the shack, but I was in the shadows. I could hear the two guards talking now. They were speaking some language I couldn't identify. That was not surprising. Crews of merchant ships generally were a mulligatawny of nationalities. I ran my hand along the wall very gently and kept moving slowly toward the front of the building, feeling for the wire. I wondered if the wily Krauts had strung the wire between the seams of the plywood panels. The bastards were capable of that, but why would they bother? I kept crawling forward and brushing my fingers along the wall. Finally, about three feet from the front of the shack, I felt it. I traced it down to the ground and found the tiny hole where the wire came through the wall of the shack. It was at ground level. I hollowed out a little hole at the base of the building. I got out my knife and cut the wire. Then I covered over the hole to bury where the cut was. I had to make a little mound of dirt also, to make sure the cut was completely hidden. It should be good enough. After all, I thought, it didn't have to stay hidden for long. The way things turned out, I really didn't have to hide it at all. But at the time I guess I was thinking of the Indians and the telegraph.

That done, I started to crawl backward toward the bushes. It seemed to take forever, but it was only a few seconds. When I got in there, I turned around and started to creep back around to the place where I had crossed the little stream.

That's when I heard the growling, low, but not menacing. I looked to my right and saw a pair of eyes looking up at me. It was Fritz, the dachshund. He was wagging his tail.

We stood there for a second, looking at each other. If he started barking like a good German watchdog, he would probably wake the camp. Or at least, it was a possibility. What was the German for "good dog?" The only German I knew came from the captain—how to order beer. But in a moment of inspiration, I remembered my sandwich. Carefully, maintaining friendly eye contact with the dog, I reached in my pocket. The waxed paper was soaked and the bread had dissolved into mush, but the frankfurter was, of course, unscathed. Absurdly, I wondered what the half-life of a wiener was. Then I wondered what a half-life was. Why didn't they just say "the life?" It's odd the things that flash through your mind, uninvited. I pulled the wiener out of my pocket slowly and leaned over and offered it to Fritz. He seemed to smile—dogs smile with their ears—and came over to me and took the hot dog, happily. I knelt down and patted him as he chewed and gulped the wiener and wagged his tail. When he finished, he licked my hand. Fritz had good manners, apparently.

I said nothing, assuming he wouldn't understand English anyway. But I picked him up and cradled him in one arm. He licked my face, and I patted his head and stroked his ears, and we headed for the crossing. He was happy to come along, for as far as he knew there were more wieners where that one came from. And of course he was right about that. We waded the stream carefully, but quickly, and soon found Otto in his hiding place.

"Who's that?" he whispered.

"Fritz," I said, also in a whisper. "He was a political prisoner. Wants to defect. Let's go. Do me a favor and carry my rifle."

"Mission accomplished, sir?"

"Yep."

We got to the inflatable boat and dragged it into the surf. I put Fritz in the boat and Otto and I pushed the boat through the line of breakers and out beyond, where we climbed aboard and started paddling for the dark shape waiting for us three hundred yards away. Fritz put his front paws on the side of the boat and sniffed the breeze, contentedly, ears flapping. In all that time, he hadn't said a word.

"Cute dog," said Otto. "But why'd you bring him?"

"Knowing what I know about what's going to happen to that camp, I couldn't very well leave him." Besides, I thought, I know someone who might like him. Or at least might keep him for me, because I guessed that from now on, Fritz and I would be partners. As I told her—dogs, cats, and babies all like me. And here was living, wiener-eating proof. "Right, Fritz, old boy?" He turned his head and licked my hand. "Smart dog," I said. "Learns English quickly."

"I guess he's not much of a watchdog, though."

"No. Thank God. And good work tonight, Otto. Well done."

"Thank you, sir. But I've been wondering. How'd you know Eva Braun has the clap?"

"Just a guess, Otto. Just a guess."

Chapter Twenty

"Good thing you had that hot dog in your pocket," said the captain.

"I wish I could say I was prepared for it, Captain, but it was just luck. I was never an Eagle Scout." Not in this world, anyway.

We were in the wardroom to discuss the plan of attack. Fritz was napping peacefully in a box that Blake had made for him.

"I've been thinking," said the captain. "How far would you say the top of that hill is from the camp?"

"Straight line? Maybe three hundred yards. Maybe a little more."

"Do you think your boys can hit anything at that distance?"

"It's possible. With M1s. Not the Tommy guns, though."

"No, I agree. Those things throw a lot of lead, but you're better off the closer you are. You didn't happen to see the waterline on that freighter."

"No, sir. It was too dark and their paint was pretty faded and dirty."

"That's OK. If they got in there, I reckon we can, too. All the way, I mean—enough to unmask the forty-millimeters on the afterdeck. There's no need to go in any farther than that, and I will refrain from making the obvious joke. So here's the way I figure it. We'll send you and the Fubars to the hilltop with M1s. From the time you hit the beach, how long will it take you to climb the hill and get in position?"

"Fifteen minutes at most. It's not that far to the top, but we'll need to spread out on the reverse downhill slope to get a clear view of the camp. The view from the very top is obstructed. I had to climb a tree to see. So we'll need a little extra time to find good sight lines."

"OK. We'll give you fifteen minutes from the time we see you hit the beach before we push through the channel. We'll man the three-inch and the forties and not worry about the twenties, since we'll be shorthanded. But I think you boys on the hill will get better shots than we would with the twenties, anyway."

"Yes, sir."

"Now do you think that freighter will be blocking our view of the supply dump?"

"No, sir. The dump's off to the side, on the right as you're looking at the camp. *Nameless* will have a clear shot at it, I'm sure."

"Good. That's the first target. Three-inch and forties together. As soon as we're in the channel and in position, we'll fire up a star shell and turn on the spotlight to illuminate the targets. Then we'll hit the supply dump with Willie Peter."

Willie Peter was Navy slang for white phosphorous. It started a fire that could not be extinguished. It even burned underwater. It would not go out until it had burned itself out. It was very nasty stuff and created thick clouds of white smoke.

"If the supply dump blows the way it might, the blast could take care of the whole shebang. Will you be protected well enough on the hillside in case the whole camp goes up? It could be a hell of an explosion."

"I think so, sir. There are lots of good-sized pines. I'll have the men take cover behind them."

"Good. But you be the judge of that. It could be one gigantic blast, so make sure you and the men are as well protected as possible. And if you think it's better to wait on the seaward side of the hill, that's up to you. You might get there and decide you're closer than you thought."

"Yes, sir."

"The second target will be the freighter. High-explosive shells into the hull. If we blow enough holes in her she'll roll over where she sits. If she tries to get underway and turns toward us with evil intentions, we'll take out the whole bridge and superstructure. You can help from the hillside and discourage anyone in the pilot house in case we miss. But I think it's more'n likely we'll sink her while she's still tied up and broadside to us."

"What are the Fubars' targets?"

"You've got the camp. I figure the freighter will be blocking the view of the ship's guns, so you take care of people in the shacks and anyone running around on the freighter's decks, though that will be secondary. Concentrate at first on the radio shack just in case there's another aerial or something.

Blow the shack to splinters. Seven guys with a clip of thirty-caliber ammo will make anyone in the shack dream of better days."

"I think we'll be able to hit the shack even at three hundred yards."

"Good. Hit that right when you see our star shell go off, because once we fire Willie Peter, the smoke's likely to be thicker than Hell's blocked chimney. Once that happens, do the best you can and shoot anyone you see."

"Aye, aye, sir."

"One more thing. If for some reason we have trouble with the guns, if the three-inch malfunctions—or anything, you'll be responsible for cleaning out that camp. Once the Krauts are all dead, we can go in there with our Zippos and burn anything that's left. I don't think that will be necessary, but it's always good to think of contingencies."

"Yes, sir." That, in a nutshell, was the Navy's chief rule of thumb—imagine what might go wrong and think what to do if it does.

"If one or two manage to scamper off into the jungle, it won't matter. But I'd rather they didn't. And Riley, cutting that wire was good work tonight. Well done."

"Thank you, sir."

"Now let's explain matters to the crew and then see about sending some Krauts to the infernal regions."

I didn't tell the captain that the two watchmen I overheard on the freighter were not Germans. The whole merchant crew might be from anywhere. It wouldn't matter; it didn't matter. As for the Cubans that were helping, well, maybe they were rebels or maybe they were just hired hands. If so, I hoped they were all orphan bachelors. Chances are they weren't, but there was no sense thinking about it.

As I left the wardroom I yelled back at Blake, "You're in charge of Fritz, Blake."

"Yes, sir. We're good buddies already."

That didn't surprise me.

The captain got the key members of the general quarters team—especially the gun captains and crews—together in the mess deck and outlined the plan. I assembled the Fubars on the quarterdeck and told them what we were going to do. They were equipped and ready to go, each with an M1, bandoliers of extra clips, and a couple of grenades each. They wore their dark sweaters and dungarees, their forty-fives and canteens on their belts, and their battle station helmets on their heads. They had all been to the hillside and understood perfectly what I meant when I explained about deploying on the reverse slope and hiding behind thick trees.

"We need to stay in a rough line abreast," I said. "I don't want anyone to get too far forward. There might be a hell of a blast when that fuel dump gets hit, and even if there isn't, I don't want to take the chance of anyone getting shot by one of us just because he's too far in front. Stay within sight of each other. Our first priority is the radio shack. It's the second building from the left as we look at the camp. The captain's going to light up the targets with a star shell and the spotlight, but it'll be dark on the hill, so the Krauts will see our muzzle flashes. I don't think they'll have time to start shooting back, but stay covered anyway. We won't load the rifles until we're all in position on the reverse slope. Any questions?"

"Anyone who's down there is a target, right, sir?"

"That's right. Anyone and everyone in the camp and anyone and everyone on deck of the freighter."

"The Andrews Sisters?" said Reynolds.

"Yes. They'll be the ones in sarongs."

"I wonder what they'll be singing."

"Bei Mir Bist Du Schoen," said Otto.

"Any other questions or smart-ass comments?" I said. "No? All right. Double-check to make sure your rifles are not loaded before you start climbing down to the boat. All set? Let's go."

As we climbed aboard the whaleboat I heard one of the men say, in a mock radio voice, "This episode of Fitzy and the Fubars is brought to you by Trojan Rubbers, the choice of men with dicks." Another voice added, "And favorite of the Andrews Sisters."

I was grinning as I climbed in. And I thought—not for two nights with Betty Grable. But then, as I thought of what could happen ashore, I hedged a little.

As we turned for the beach I could see the *Nameless* start her pivot toward the opening of the channel. They'd go slowly till we hit the beach, and then they'd start in. We didn't waste any time going in. I wasn't too worried about the sound our motor made. There was enough ambient noise coming from the freighter just sitting there on the other side of the hill.

We reached the beach, and I saw the *Nameless* lined up with the channel and ready to start in. We were careful going up the hill, but once again there was no sign of a sentry anywhere. Strange, but there it was. Maybe the German officer in command realized he was undermanned and in a trap and that early warning of an approaching predator would not help in any way; it would only give him time to send messages of warning and farewell. Still, it seemed strange that he did not plan for that.

We reached the top of the hill and then spread out in a line abreast only a yard or two apart and slowly went down the reverse slope. Each man then found a spot behind the trees where he could see the camp. I guessed we were more than three hundred yards away, but not much more.

There was activity in the camp now and on board the freighter. As we figured, they were getting ready to leave. It was 0330 and in another hour or so the night would start to change from black to gray. They were planning to be gone by then.

I looked to my right and then my left and counted the men. All six of them were in view and no one was too far forward.

"Load up," I whispered to the closest man on either side. I could hear the sound of the clips being inserted and the chamber sliding shut. Slick as the click of a Zippo. All set.

I took another look at the camp and especially the supply dump. I didn't think we were too close, but it was really impossible to tell. We didn't know what was under that tarp. If it was fuel and ammunition, we probably would feel the blast. But the men had all found good stout trees to hide behind. As long as the blast didn't uproot them and crush us all, we should be all right. That was no idle thought. I remembered reading about the WWI poet Edward Thomas who was killed by an artillery shell whooshing close by. He didn't have a mark on him. It was the blast that killed him. The force of the air.

I looked toward the opening of the channel. It was no more than six hundred yards away to our right. The night was fairly dark. There were clouds covering most of the stars and the moon had already set. But there was just enough light to see, if you knew what to look for. In a few moments, I could see the bow of the *Nameless* edging into the bahia, and then she gradually emerged like some grande dame entering a ballroom. Elegantly and silently. Unhurriedly. And then I could just barely hear the captain's unmistakable voice say, "All stop." I looked to the freighter and the men on deck getting her ready to leave. They heard it, too.

And the next thing we all heard was "Fire!" And the three-inch gun blasted a star shell into the night sky and the shell exploded over the camp in a brilliant flash of white light and a burning white flare slowly floated toward earth at the same time the *Nameless*'s spotlight flashed on the camp and the night was as bright as day.

"Fire!" I yelled to the men, and seven M1s opened up on the radio shack. At the same moment a German came out of the door yelling, "*Was ist los?*" Then he was spun around and dropped. The bullets tore into the plywood of the shack, and pieces of it were flying everywhere and the roof began to sag and one wall fell over. All seven of us emptied our clips, eight rounds each, and I could hear the ejected clips flying out of the rifles and I shouted, "Reload and fire at will." The men on the freighter were running for different spots to hide and the men in the camp were still trying to come to terms with what was happening. One or two stood still looking toward the hill and the flashes of our rifles, but they were shot down almost immediately. It wasn't our marksmanship, so much, as the volume of fire. This all happened in a matter of seconds. The noise of our rifles was deafening, but the bahia got a whole lot louder as the *Nameless* fired a series of three Willie Peter shells into the supply dump, just a second between each shot, and the whole world suddenly flashed into fantastic white light and smoke.

"Cover your eyes!" I shouted, unnecessarily, for the men were all lying face down hard in the dirt.

A huge cloud of white ostrich plumes sprouted from the dump, followed by another and then a third, and then there was an orange flash of exploding ammunition followed by the red and black smoke and fire of burning fuel. And we felt the wind of the blast come rushing up the hillside and heard the trees and branches breaking and the palm fronds being stripped off, and we all buried our faces in the dirt and felt the wind tearing at our clothes as the blast passed over us. The camp was wreathed in white phosphorous smoke, a noxious fog that covered everything and everyone. I could see the deck of the freighter through the smoke, though. There was no one stirring. But I could see a few bodies.

Then the *Nameless* switched targets and started firing high-explosive shells. She started to pump shots into the freighter. She was firing one a second. Gunner's Mate Williams was sitting in the firing seat cranking the wheels that aimed the gun and firing as the loaders on both sides of the breech shoved shells into the gun as fast as the gun could take them. And each shell slammed into the hull of the freighter, exploding on impact and tearing great holes in the hull, and the forties were firing into the superstructure, smashing the freighter's windows and blowing holes in the dingy white bulkheads. The freighter kept absorbing the punishment, but gradually she started listing to starboard, and as she listed, she exposed the new holes in her sides more and more, and that caused the list to increase so that toward the end she was almost at a forty-five-degree angle, and she was offering her superstructure to the pitiless fire of the *Nameless*'s three-inch gun as well as the forty-millimeters. And finally, after holding at a forty-five-degree angle for a few moments, as if she was trying to decide whether to resist any longer or just give up, she rolled completely on her side and sank at her moorings.

The water wasn't deep enough for her to go all the way beneath the surface, so she lay there on her side, like a beached whale. Then she caught fire and her boilers blew up, and on the hillside we were once again blasted, this time not only from the air but from particles and pieces of the freighter. Metal and wood fragments of all kinds. Fortunately for us, most of the debris flew inland and destroyed what remained of the camp and the surrounding jungle. We only got the scraps. But that was enough.

My guys had all stopped shooting, primarily to grab their helmets and make themselves as small as possible behind the largest trees. The hillside looked like a hurricane had passed over it, and in a sense, one had. Smaller trees were knocked over. Palms were stripped of their fronds. Larger trees had branches torn off and scattered on the ground. The bushes on the hill were stripped away, torn from their roots.

I heard the captain yelling, "Cease fire! Cease fire!" and in a moment the only sound we could hear was the ringing in our ears.

I looked down at where the camp buildings were. There was nothing there. The hurricane had swept it all away. Even the bodies were missing, blown into the jungle by the blast. And the edge of the jungle now was farther away from the waterfront than it had been. Trees were down everywhere. The supply dump was now a huge, smoldering crater. Trash was scattered in the hole and papers were blowing in the breeze, and the white phosphorous smoke and black oily smoke were swirling in spots like mini tornadoes, and in other places it was drifting off to hang in the trees that were left. Small fires were burning everywhere in the jungle as the white phosphorous finished burning itself out, and the fires set from fuel oil or ammunition burned the palms and pines around the camp. Now and then a bullet or two would explode with a pop and some pyrotechnic crates would send rockets shooting wildly. You couldn't really compare the scene to anything you'd ever seen before, because it was like nothing you'd ever seen before. The air smelled terrible, a mixture of phosphorous and burned fuel oil and cordite from exploded ammunition and burning paint from the freighter and who knows what else. We were all coughing, but we were the only ones coughing. Nothing else in the near vicinity was alive.

"Anybody hurt?" I said.

The men all started shifting around where they lay, as if checking to see if they were all still in one piece.

One by one they checked in and reported they were OK. All except Smithers. He was on the end of the line and he was lying on his face, perfectly still. There was a thick branch that had fallen next to him, and when I went to check I saw that the branch had actually fallen on him. It was lying over his left arm.

"Smithers," I said. He groaned.

"I think my arm is broke," he said. "Branch fell on it."

"Can you move it?"

"I don't think so." We helped him sit up, holding his arm against his side.

"We'll make you a sling and get you back to the whaleboat. The arm may be broken. I can't tell, but it's not a compound fracture. There's no bone sticking through the flesh."

We rigged up a sling out of one of the men's shirts and tied Smithers's arm tight against his chest. He didn't like having it done.

"Otto!" I said.

"Yes, sir?"

"You take Smithers back to the whaleboat and run him over to the *Nameless* so Doc can fix him up properly. Then come back for the rest of us. Tell the skipper we're going to keep watch here and see what we can see. If things stop popping and exploding we'll go down to the camp and see if anyone or anything is left."

"Aye, aye, sir. Do you want me to pick you up at the camp or on the seaward side?"

"Seaward side. *Nameless* will be backing out of that channel in a few minutes. If we're not there when you get back, just wait for us."

"Aye, aye, sir. Come on, Smitty. Don't be a pussy."

"Screw you, Otto."

By which I knew Smithers was more or less all right.

Chapter Twenty-One

Captain Ford and I were sitting in the wardroom a couple of hours after the attack. The *Nameless* was anchored just west of the channel entrance to Hermosa. Sparks and one of the Fubars had gone to the beach to check on his radio, and we were waiting for him to return before heading for Key West. Through the wardroom portholes we could see the former camp on Hermosa still smoking. You could have seen the smoke from a long way off.

"It'll be a while before that stuff blows off and all the fires are out. Until then, I don't think there's much chance of a U-boat wandering this way."

"No, sir."

"I considered leaving Sparks and another man here while we go to Key West—if his radio works. But we could be delayed for some reason. I don't want to risk it."

"I think that's wise, sir."

Just then Sparks showed up at the wardroom door. The captain had told him to report as soon as he was back aboard.

"We got the radio, Captain," he said. "It's not working, but I think I can fix it. It's mostly damage from the rain. I need some new parts, but I can get them. The battery is shot, though."

"That's all right, Sparks. There'll be another MP jeep in Key West. Good work."

"Thank you, sir."

"Well, that answers that question," the captain said to me. "Now what's the story with this guy you found—who is he, or what is he?"

"He's a Cuban, sir. One of the Fubars speaks a little Spanish, and he speaks a little English. Between the two we found out he's a rebel and a member of some gang with a fancy-sounding name. I forget what, exactly."

"How in hell did he survive the attack?"

"He was in the latrine. They had built an outhouse pretty far back in the jungle, and he was just sitting there when all hell broke loose. The blast knocked the outhouse over and trapped him until we heard him yelling when we checked the camp. We pulled him out of there. Smelled really bad. We took him down to the beach and threw him in to soak. He was one frightened Cuban. He didn't figure out that if we were going to shoot him, we wouldn't bother about his stench."

"Imagine his surprise. Just sitting there reading *Popular Mechanics* in Spanish and BANG! If he didn't have the runs before, he probably had 'em afterwards. I wonder what we should do with him. Is he hurt anywhere but in his philosophy?"

"Just a few bumps and bruises and splinters. Seems like an OK guy. Used to be a fisherman. He doesn't look very dangerous. Could use a square meal. Kind of scrawny. Said he was working for the Germans just for the money and the chow."

"I guess we should turn him over to the boys in Havana. I reckon they'll stand him against the wall, no questions asked." The captain looked at me for a moment. "What's the matter?"

"I dunno, sir. Maybe we could give that a little more thought. We're not in any hurry."

"Feeling sorta soft-hearted?"

"Maybe. Maybe we did enough for one night. It's not like he's a German or a dangerous character. At least he doesn't seem like it to me. Seems harmless."

"I suppose. He's sure enough been through a lot. Goes to take a peaceful dump and the next thing he knows he's trapped under a pile of outhouse boards and a mound of crap. It's enough to make a fella think he's not all that important in the grand eternal scheme of things."

"Yes, sir. As for being some kind of revolutionary, I doubt he knows the difference between Karl and Groucho. He was so terrified when we found him I thought he was going to die of acute trembling. If he's an example of the rebels, I don't think Batista has much to worry about."

"OK. Well, we're going back to Key West anyway, and we have to take this Jose along regardless of what we do with him afterwards. We'll see about things once we get there. What's Jose's name, anyway?"

"Jose."

He grinned, probably for the first time that day.

"I swear. It just keeps getting better and better. Turn him over to Blake for the trip back to base. Maybe Jose can show Blake how to make decent black beans and rice."

"Yes, sir."

"I guess you didn't find anyone else alive down there."

"No sir. I didn't think it was safe to be crawling around on the inside of the ship, even if we could get in there. There were some huge, jagged holes in the hull. We could look down into the guts of the ship. Mostly twisted metal and girders and wires everywhere. But every space we could see was pretty much filled with water. We walked around on the part of the hull that was above water and banged our rifles on it and shouted. I figured if anyone was trapped, they'd yell or hammer back or something. But there was nothing. I don't see how anyone could have been left alive. I hope not. I mean, I hope we didn't leave anyone trapped in there."

"How about bodies?"

"Nothing. We found some things on shore that might have been parts, but everything was so burned it was hard to tell. We didn't look very hard in the jungle, but I don't think we would have found much. Jose was the only one making any noise. I think the guys on the freighter's deck were blown way off into the water, probably in pieces."

"Sharks and crabs will take care of them soon enough."

"I felt kind of bad looking at that ship, especially after what we saw at the tanker. Really bad, in fact."

"Yes, it's a sad thing to see a ship sink or even just turn turtle and slide into the mud. No sailor likes to see that. You know when the *Bismarck* sank the *Hood*, the Germans watched it from the deck and nobody said a thing. No cheering. Nothing. Fifteen hundred men went down with the *Hood*. Only three survived. Three. 'Course not too long afterwards, it was the *Bismarck*'s turn. No sailor likes to see a ship go down. It's about the saddest thing there is, short of losing one of your folks."

"How about a U-boat skipper? Think they feel that way?"

"Well, I don't know about them. But I imagine the good ones don't feel that happy after they torpedo a ship, not completely happy, anyway. They feel good about doing their job and making a good shot, but not so great about the rest of it. Same as us. Some of 'em anyway. But there are a few real bastards, too. Anyone who'd machine-gun a lifeboat full of people falls into that category."

"I'd say so, too, sir."

"Anyway, Riley, good work tonight. As my old pappy used to say, 'Ya done good.' You and the boys."

"Thank you, sir. I'd say the *Nameless* earned her pay."

"Yes, and a couple of days of liberty. Kinda too bad we're going to Key West instead of Havana."

"Yes, sir. Kinda too bad."

"You know, though, if a fella had a really strong desire to get to Havana for some reason or other, there's a PBY going over there and coming back just about every day. Something to think about."

"That *is* something to think about, Captain."

"In fact, now that I think of it, somebody should brief ONI and the Cuban navy boys about our action this morning. I'll be tied up with our skipper in Key West. Maybe you could handle the Havana folks for me."

I guess I brightened up enough that he noticed.

"Yes, sir, I'd be happy to."

"Ain't surprised. You've always been a willing volunteer." There was not even the slightest flicker of anything in his eyes or expression. Well, maybe just the merest flicker.

Not for the first time it crossed my mind that Captain Ford must be one hell of a poker player. I did wonder how the captain knew about the *Hood* and how the Germans reacted as they watched her sink. Maybe he read about it somewhere. But maybe he just knew.

We pulled into Key West that afternoon. We authorized liberty for two sections. The third section would get started cleaning up and doing routine maintenance. We'd be in port for a few days, anyway, so everyone would get equal amounts of liberty and work. As soon as we were tied up, Doc took Smithers to the base hospital to get his arm taken care of, Sparks went in search of some vacuum tubes for his radio and another battery, and Williams went to the Supply Office to see about replacing the ammunition we shot up. Elliot the yeoman went to headquarters to get the mail. He was back pretty shortly and we had mail call, the sailors' favorite event, after liberty. It revived their spirits almost immediately—they had been a little subdued on the voyage back to Key West. They had seen some things they hadn't ever imagined, both at the torpedoed tanker and especially on Hermosa.

I was stretched out on my bunk thinking that I wouldn't need to answer Martha's letter, because I'd be going to Havana on tomorrow's PBY. I decided to take Fritz with me and ask Martha if she'd take him for me, at least for the time being. I figured one more dog at the Finca Vigia wouldn't matter much.

Chapter Twenty-Two

The next day I flew to Havana in a PBY. I took Fritz with me. He seemed unfazed by the experience. We landed outside the seawall and then taxied in the channel to the harbor and the seaplane section, tied to a mooring, and then took a motor launch to the city wharf. I walked over to the embassy and tied Fritz to a bush outside the front entrance. He lay down in the shade and seemed content. He was a mellow dog if there ever was one. Then I met with the ONI and the two officers of the Cuban navy and gave them the outline of the action yesterday morning. They were all pleased and impressed. It was the first combat action of the war in the Gulf, so far.

"You say there were some Cuban nationals working with the Germans?" This from the Cuban captain. His sidekick was as quiet and saturnine as usual. But watchful."

"Yes. They were doing the construction work on the camp. I only saw two Germans in the camp. But there may have been more."

"What was the registry of the freighter?" said the ONI.

"Liberian." Neither Captain Ford nor I had given much thought to that. But I had noticed the lettering on the stern when we checked the camp. It was not surprising that the ship was not registered to any belligerent countries.

"Figures," he said.

"Is the ship a total loss?"

"Yes, sir. Not worth salvaging for scrap. I mean, I think the expense would outweigh what you could get for it."

I went on to describe the details of the attack, bit by bit, and the three officers nodded in appreciation.

"Well, done, Mr. Fitzhugh. Please tell Captain Ford that I said so, although I will certainly follow it up with a personal message. And Washington will hear of this action, of course."

"Thank you, sir."

"And were there no survivors at all?" This came from the quiet Cuban.

"No one who was unhurt, sir. There was one Cuban who was very badly wounded. We took him on board our ship. He's in Key West now, but I don't think he's going to survive. He was buried under debris in the attack. Our corpsman said he was as good as finished. I didn't check on him before I came here, though."

"If he dies, it will save us the trouble of shooting him, but it would have been nice to be able to question him."

That's more or less what I figured.

"He couldn't talk when we found him, sir. I'd be surprised if he isn't dead already. If you'll pardon a Yankee vulgarity, he was really in deep shit."

"Oh, well. So much for that gang of rebels. Thank you, Mr. Fitzhugh. You have done your Cuban ally a service."

"Thank you, sir."

"I think that does it, Riley," said the ONI. "We'll look forward to Captain Ford's written report, but I'm sure we have the gist of the story. What are your plans for the evening?"

"I'm not sure, sir. I need to make a call."

"Of course. Use Bill Patterson's office. He's off somewhere doing something."

"I wonder if I could borrow a car for the evening. Maybe a jeep."

"Sure. I'll give you a chit. Just show it at the motor pool."

I walked down the corridor to Bill's office. It was just four o'clock. Sixteen hundred, Navy time. I dialed Martha's number, having first decided what I would say if her husband answered. I assumed he was still on Confites, a couple of hundred miles away. But husbands could be unpredictable. I had to smile at the thought that I had some experience in these matters. I asked myself if I felt the slightest bit guilty about any of this. I answered myself that I didn't. Really? No, really. I had other things to feel guilty about, maybe, but meeting my *amie amoureuse* wasn't one of them. Not as far as I was concerned, anyway. Most husbands wouldn't like it, of course, but as the old Spanish saying goes, what the eyes do not see, the heart does not feel. With his extensive knowledge of Spain, Hemingway would be familiar with that point of view.

She answered on the second ring.

"Marty, it's Riley."

"Riley! Where are you?"

"Here in town. I came for a meeting."

"When did you get here?"

"An hour ago."

"How long will you be here?"

"At least until tomorrow. Maybe longer."

"I wish I'd have known. I would have had something nice delivered."

"I just found out myself, this morning in Key West. I came by the PBY."

"Can you get hold of a car?"

"Yes. A jeep."

"Good. My car is on the blink. Otherwise I would come for you. Can you find the house? Do you remember the road to take?"

"Yes. I'm a navigator, you know. I notice landmarks."

"Yes, darling. I remember. Besides, there aren't really any turns. When you see the ragged couple with the dog, keep going straight. Give me an hour?"

"Perfect. Will you be the one in the black dress?"

"I'll be the one in something. But let me think about what it'll be."

I wondered if this was the day the servants had off. I couldn't remember. Well, we would see soon enough.

I went downstairs and got Fritz. He was still napping under the tree but woke up and wagged his tail when I called his name.

"We've got a little time to kill, buddy. What do you say we stop in at the Floridita and have a drink?"

This time I didn't sit at the end of the bar. There were a few other people in there. They looked up when I walked in then went back to their drinks—it was the same in any bar. I had Fritz on a leash, of sorts.

"Hello, senor. Welcome again," said Constante. "You have a new friend."

"Yes. He's a prisoner of war."

"A German dog, yes? I wonder why they breed them so long and low. Some would say they look ridiculous."

"I'm told they were bred that way to go down into holes after badgers and drag them out."

"This is true? They must have great courage, then, despite their appearance. A badger is a serious animal. They can be formidable."

"Appearances are often deceiving, Constante. You know that, I'm sure."

"Of course. I myself, though I am short and fat now, was once tall and elegant and a famous matador. I killed many bulls with great style, and I loved many women—and was loved by even more—also with great style. Do you believe that, senor?"

"Why not?"

"*Bueno.* Daiquiri, senor?"

"Si. Por favor."

He made me a double and placed it before me. He was apparently in a mood to talk.

"Did you have any luck this trip, senor?"

"Luck?"

"Well, there is talk about some action to the east. Some sort of military camp was destroyed. Some say it was a U-boat that bombarded the camp. Why, no one explains. Others say it was an accident. Some amateur rebels handling explosives carelessly. I tend to believe that story. Poorly trained rebels blowing themselves up. Most of them are peasants, so it's no wonder they are uninformed about weapons. They should stick to machetes. They are safer."

"Really? When did this happen?"

"Yesterday, senor."

"Word travels fast."

"Yes. As I told you the last time, this country is well supplied with spies and informants. Our friend who sits at the end of the bar, himself, has a group of his friends who go around asking questions and learning things. He calls them the Crook Factory."

"Funny name."

"Yes. He has a famous sense of humor."

"So it would seem."

"There are many other such groups, though. Most of them are political in some way or other. But of course they notice other things as well."

"They must be very observant."

"Yes. And they have friends who have friends, and that is the way information travels so quickly."

"I see."

"Are you by any chance meeting anyone tonight?"

"No. Unless I get lucky. Why do you ask?" Yes, Constante, why *do* you ask?

"Oh, I thought you might be seeing Marty here tonight."

"Marty?"

"The great man's beautiful wife." He nodded toward the empty stool at the end of the bar.

"You mean Martha? Martha Hemingway?"

He looked at me as if trying to decide if I was playing the ingénue, but I was good at not showing anything, which is one way to describe one of the things I was good at.

"Yes," he said. "But she goes by her own last name, usually. She prefers it that way. He does not like it so much, but a husband sometimes must make compromises."

"Why, no, I don't know her that well at all. She seemed like a nice lady, though. A writer, I think she said."

"Yes. She is a serious person. Would you care for another drink, senor?"

"No, thank you. But since I seem to have become something of a regular here, maybe you should call me Riley. That is my first name."

"Ah. Thank you, Riley. I am always pleased to make a new friend."

I'll bet, I thought, as I left with Fritz. I'll just bet you are. And then I thought that when Bill Patterson came back from wherever he was, I'd have a word with him about the bartender at the Floridita. I don't think Constante could tell that I was lying about Martha. I had a lot of practice asking and answering questions with an innocent expression, the way card hustlers say, "Is this the game they call poker? I've always wanted to learn. Do you mind if I play?" And I'd talked to more than my share of cops. And starlets. Keeping an open, straight face helps with both of them. So, yes, I could pass for a member of the Boy Scouts' choir, when I needed to. But Constante's questions made me wonder—about him and about the Crook Factory. What the eyes do not see the heart does not feel—true enough—but when there were many sets of eyes on the lookout, the heart might be at greater risk. And just exactly whose hearts were we talking about?

Chapter Twenty-Three

She was waiting outside the house, by the pool. She was wearing black shorts and a sleeveless black top. The shorts showed off her tanned legs nicely. Of course, she knew that. I took it as a compliment.

I pulled up in the jeep. It didn't have a top or doors. Fritz was on the seat next to me. She walked over, adding a little something to her walk, and she was smiling in a certain way. She was being playful, of course, and she knew that, too. How much was real, how much was irony? The more sophisticated the woman, the blurrier the line. Sometimes there was no line at all.

"Hello, darling," she said. "Who's your friend?"

"Another dog for your crew, if you don't mind watching him for me for a little while."

"Why not? Where'd he come from?"

"It's a long story. But I'll tell you. Anyone around?"

"Just me. The servants were delighted to get an unexpected night off. So you're at my mercy once again."

I got out of the jeep and put my arms around her carefully and kissed her very seriously, and afterwards she smiled a little breathlessly and said, "My goodness. You weren't gone *that* long."

"No. But I was thinking about you."

"Anything in particular?"

"I was thinking, 'Other women cloy the appetites they feed; she makes hungry where she most satisfies.'"

She stared at me.

"My God. Shakespeare? Are you serious?"

"Almost."

"I like it, I must say. I must be a pushover."

"You don't really think that."

"I didn't before. Now I'm not so sure. I didn't realize you were so literary."

"I read a lot."

"Tell the truth. Have you ever used that line before?"

"No. I've never met anyone who made it seem appropriate." So said the member of the Boy Scout choir.

She looked at me with a large measure of skepticism and just a faint bit of wistfulness. Or was it wishfulness?

"Liar," she said, softly.

But the truth was, I hadn't used it more than once or twice. That was almost the same as never. Wasn't it? And in those cases, I hadn't really meant it. Here, I wasn't so sure. There was definitely something about her . . .

"What's in the basket and duffle?"

"A surprise. Do you feel like taking a drive? There's a place I know on the south coast, almost a straight shot from here. It's only about thirty miles, and the road is not too bad."

"Sounds good."

"When do you have to be back?"

"No set time. I should head to Key West tomorrow or the next day, but I'm sort of on official business, so there's no firm schedule. The ship is going to be in port for a couple of days. I think so, anyway."

"OK. Good. Shall we leave the dog here? The others will look after him. The other dogs, I mean. They're all very friendly. There's plenty of fresh water in the bowls."

"Sure. Come on, Fritz."

He jumped out of the jeep and ran over to sniff one of the mutts that was watching the scene. No fight erupted, so I figured leaving him would be OK. He was going to have to get used to the place sometime, anyway.

We drove south for about an hour. Martha was wearing a white silk scarf to keep her hair from blowing. She had put the basket and the duffle in the back.

The two-lane road was pitted and potholed, but we were able to go along at about twenty miles an hour, for the most part. The road went through hills and tropical forests with only a hardscrabble village here and there. Ragged people sat on their dingy porches and stared at us as we drove by. They were blacks, mostly.

"What must it be like to be one of these people?" she said. "I mean, have you ever wondered how it must be to have been born dirt poor or ugly or stupid or deformed or diseased or any of the awful things so many people have to endure? Have you?"

Actually, I had now and then. I mean, who hasn't?

"Occasionally," I said. "Once I helped out a panhandler on Hollywood Boulevard. I gave him twenty bucks because he said he needed a dog."

"Oh, I see. You're a soft-hearted philanthropist. Did you really vote for Roosevelt?"

"Didn't everyone?" Bill Patterson would say that answering a question with a question was some sort of giveaway.

"Almost everyone," she said. "He's OK. The Roosevelt I really like is Eleanor. She's a saint."

"Catholic?"

"No, smart-ass. Democrat. Ernest thinks Franklin is prissy, like a fussy woman secretary of labor."

"That reminds me of a line I read about A. E. Housman—'He was descended from a long line of maiden aunts.'"

"Yes. That's it. Once again, I'm impressed by your literary references."

"There's a lot of time to read aboard ship. And thank you for your letter by the way. I liked it very much."

"I'm glad. I like writing letters. 'That's what I'll do . . . when you . . . are far away.'"

"Nicely done. It fits the melody just right."

"Thank you. Since you mentioned Housman—do you read much poetry?"

"Hardly any. I don't like to work too hard to figure out what someone is saying."

"And you like to give and receive very clear orders, too. I remember. Like your captain."

"Yes, ma'am. But finish telling me how you know the Roosevelts."

"Oh. Well, my mother was a friend of Eleanor's in college. So I've known her for quite a while. Then I worked for the New Deal. I think I told you. I was doing stories on why the lives of working people were so wretched, especially down south. It was all completely useless. At one time the WPA had over five thousand writers working for them. Can you imagine the amount of bullshit they produced? My stuff included? But you felt like you were doing something. And we were getting paid, which was a novel experience for most of us."

"The technical term for that is boondoggle."

"I'm afraid so. Then the Spanish Civil War came along, and a bunch of friends and writers wanted to get involved, so we went there and reported on it. Almost everyone felt that we were doing something important, but in the end what we wrote was useless. No one in our government or the Brits or the French gave a damn."

"Did you expect that what you wrote would change things?"

"At first, we did. I did. Later, we all knew better. We also raised a little money and made a film about the fighting to raise more money for the Republican cause. It was called *The Spanish Earth*. Ernest wrote the narration and recorded it. It was supposed to be Orson Welles, but Ernest didn't like the way Orson read the lines. They got into a fight over it. So Ernest ended up doing it himself. He did a good job, too. We showed it out in Hollywood. Just think, you and I might have met there."

"I guess I didn't get invited to those parties."

"I wonder—if we had met out there, do you think we would have felt the same attraction?"

"Are you looking for a compliment?"

"Yes. Of course."

"Well then, if I had seen you standing in a room full of people, my expression would have inspired Cole Porter to write 'Night and Day . . . *You are the one, only you beneath the moon and under the sun.*'"

"Mmm. Very good, darling. I wonder who really did inspire that song. It's so beautiful and evocative."

From what I heard out in Hollywood, the inspiration could have been some pansy Porter met at Yale, but I didn't want to mention that and spoil the mood with Marty.

"Anyway," she said after a moment, "after Hollywood, we showed the movie at the White House. Everybody liked it, and all told we did raise money for some ambulances."

"Useful things in war." And highly symbolic. The Republicans got ambulances from Hollywood, and Franco got tanks and bombers from Hitler. I think the word for that arrangement is symbiosis. "Did you meet him in Spain?"

"Ernest? No, we met before that. In Key West, as a matter of fact, when he was living there. But I went to Spain to cover the war, and we met again there."

"By accident?"

"Not really. He was still married at the time."

"So 'not really' means 'no'?"

"Doesn't it always? But you know, for a while at least, those were wonderful days, even though it all ended so badly. The war, I mean. You really felt like you were a part of something meaningful. Have you ever felt that way?"

"Shall I tell you the truth?"

"Yes."

"I feel that way now."

"This minute?"

"Well, this minute I feel happy and exhilarated, because I am driving through a tropical evening with a beautiful woman who's incapable of cloying the appetite she feeds."

"My God. If you keep that up, you're going to spoil me for reality."

"Good. But I was really talking about the larger picture, and the Navy and the war. I feel that way about what I'm doing. That's why I joined."

Her large brown eyes studied me for a moment or two.

"Darling Riley, I believe you are serious."

"Darling Marty—I am."

"How sweet."

"That's one word for it, I suppose."

And it was true, despite the fact that I had complicated feelings about what had happened this past week—not about the morality of war or what we had done; that was all necessary. No, it was more disgust at the stinking, revolting mess it made, of people and their works, of the sea and the land around the battle. Black oil like a sinister leather blanket coating the sea where the tanker sank, white phosphorous smoke choking the jungle and everyone in its path—two ends of the spectrum of ugliness and stench. And Jose in the shithouse? The symbolism was so obvious as to border on sophomoric. Or was the better word jejune? Maybe. I liked that word but wasn't really sure what it meant.

But again, there was no need to mention all that to Marty.

"Now it's your turn to tell me something," I said.

"I thought I had been."

"Well, something you wouldn't tell anyone but me."

"What?"

"Where do you put my Eagle Scout badge?"

"Oh, dear. Why, sir! You'll make me blush."

"I doubt that."

"I'm serious. I won't tell, but I will show you, when we get where we're going."

"And where is that?"

"Short term? A little rocky cove on a deserted Caribbean beach."

"How about long term?"

"God knows. Why are you stopping?"

I pulled to the side of the road, put the jeep in neutral, set the brake, and leaned over and kissed her, very tenderly at first and then more urgently. She had a lovely soft mouth, and she responded in a way that made me hope that where we were going in this short term was not too far away.

"What was that lovely impulse for?" she said, after a moment.

"Because that kiss at the Finca was not enough."

"My God," she whispered. "A romantic. I thought they were all dead."

"Not yet."

The road finally ended at the seashore. There was another road that ran along the beach, but there was nothing in view in either direction. No houses, no villages. Nothing.

"Turn right here," she said, "and go about another mile. You'll see some trees and big rocks. That's the cove. There's a good place to pull over and hide the jeep, though there's no one ever around."

"Still, it's good to be careful. Car batteries are like gold, so they tell me."

We pulled in to an opening of palm trees and parked in the shadows.

"I'll get the basket, you take the duffle, please."

We walked through the trees toward the water and then along a path between two rocky outcroppings that were like a small amphitheater around the beach, with the ends going to the edge of the water. The little beach inside the rocks was only twenty yards or so wide and about that amount long. It was high tide, so we knew the water wouldn't come any farther up the beach. The rocks on the amphitheater were smooth and rounded from being pummeled by storms over centuries.

"This is beautiful," I said. "How did you find it?"

"Oh, just by driving around and looking. I like exploring."

"I know."

There was about an hour before sunset, and we opened the duffle and spread out a sleeping bag and unzipped it to make a blanket. Then Marty opened the basket and brought out two bottles of Tavel that she'd packed in ice and then some covered bowls of cold chicken and salad and a loaf of bread.

"Well done," I said. "And that's the Navy's highest compliment."

"Do you want to swim first or have a glass of wine or what?"

"Or what."

"I thought you'd say that."

"She pulled her scarf off and then her shirt over her head and slid out of her shorts and stood there looking exactly as I remembered her, tanned everywhere, tawny and golden, slim and lithe, smooth and taut.

"Your turn."

I did the same, and she watched and waited and then said, "I knew you'd have tan lines."

"And I knew you wouldn't."

"What fun."

We lay down on the blanket and tried to make the beginnings last, but weren't able to, not for long, and at the end she arched her back again, like the last time, but this time she held it for seconds with her eyes shut tight and her muscles quivering while I was finishing, and then she let out a sigh and fell back and lay there for a moment and then slowly opened her eyes halfway and looked at me, long and searchingly.

"No need to wonder, this time," she said, finally, with a soft, sweet trace of a smile.

"No."

We lay there for a while, not saying much, but being happy in the moment.

"Let's jump in the water," she said, finally. "There's not much of a drop-off here. I like to come here and swim and sunbathe."

We waded out, holding hands. The water was cool and felt wonderful. We ducked our heads under the surface and then swam about twenty yards out and then caught a wave and were pushed back toward the beach. We stood about waist deep in the water and let the waves splash against us, and then we held each other and said nothing until it was obvious the need had returned, so we waded to the shore and the blanket and began again. This time the beginnings lasted longer.

"Do you like the taste of salt?" she said.

"This kind."

"I see you've found the place I keep the Eagle Scout badge."

"Here?"

"Yes."

And if the beginnings were longer and slower, the ending was like the first time, and so we were finding ourselves lucky in how we were able to please each other. Then we lay still and she closed her eyes and I caressed her, trying to give her the kind of tenderness she told me she had always wanted, afterward.

"Oh, that feels good," she said. "But you know, I am liking the first part of things now, too. Maybe you noticed."

"I did. I'm glad about that."

"So am I, believe me."

Then we watched the sun go down and we drank the Tavel out of the wine glasses that came with the picnic basket, and we ate cold chicken and salad and bread.

"Taste good?" she said.

I had to smile. I could recognize a cue.

"Everything."

We went for another swim and then came back to the sleeping bag and dried off before lying down and pulling the side of the bag over us.

"Whose sleeping bag is this?"

"Mine. I had it in Spain. And in case you are wondering, you're the first."

"I was wondering if there was any significance to it. A sleeping bag instead of, say, a plain blanket."

"No."

I didn't really believe her, but I wasn't sure that it mattered, or if it did, just how it did. And then we both fell asleep. She was wrapped in my arms, or more accurately, we were wrapped in each other. Normally I like to sleep alone, but I found it was different with her. That was a little disturbing when I thought about it later, but I didn't think about it then.

We woke at around midnight. The stars were out in all their profusion. They were the only light because the coast there was uninhabited for miles in both directions. And the Milky Way arched over us like the earth's vaporous handle. The air was cool and smelled as clean as if there was no one else on earth.

"Do you have to get back?" I said.

"No. Do you?"

"No. I'd rather be here than anywhere else in the world right now."

"Really?"

"Really. 'Here will I dwell for heaven is in these lips . . .'"

"Shakespeare again?"

"No. Marlowe. Doctor Faustus. He conjured up Helen."

"God, Riley, you have to stop saying things like that to me. I don't want to fall in love. I can't afford it."

"Whatever you want, darling Marty."

"Good. Because right now what I want is for you to make love to me again. 'Please, sir. May I have some more?'"

"Dickens?"

"No pun intended."

The next time we woke, it was dawn. We went for a swim and then came back to the sleeping bag, clean and fresh. She looked at me.

"Are you serious?"

"'She makes hungry . . .'"

"My God, darling. You *are* spoiling me."

In an hour or so we started back to Havana. She was quiet for the first few minutes. Pensive.

"We're not going to fall in love, are we?" she said, finally.

"You said something about that last night."

"I know. I don't want to. It will only make things harder."

"I can believe that."

"You see, the problem is I don't know how much longer this thing with Ernest can go on. Are you surprised?"

"How could I be?"

She nodded ruefully.

"Well, yes. You have a point. But it has nothing to do with what's happened between you and me. I mean, if things were wonderful with Ernest, I suppose you and I would never have . . ."

"You don't have to explain about that." From the beginning I said I didn't need to know about her marriage, and I still didn't. But it seemed that I was going to, whether I wanted to or not.

"But the truth is," she said, "I never wanted to get married in the first place. To anyone. Never. I'd much rather live in what the church people call sin. It's much cleaner and more honest. And it is so much easier to get away from and leave behind, when things are over. And things are always over, one way or another. But he kept after me, and he is nothing if not persistent. It's not his fault. He wants to *be* married. He likes it. Oddly enough, he's very conventional that way. But I'm just not cut out to be anyone's wife. I mean, just three years ago I was in Finland covering the war against the Soviets. Then I was in London while the Germans were bombing it and the whole city seemed to be either burning or tumbling down. Now I'm making sure the cats are fed. I hate being at home looking after the house and servants and all the rest. And I hate being stuck in this little paradise while so many big things are happening. I was on my own for years before I met him. I want to be on my own again and do the kind of work I was meant to do. Do you understand?"

"Of course."

"I don't want to be Martha Hemingway. I want to be myself, with my own name. I know I sound like a selfish bitch, but that's how it is."

"You don't sound that way to me."

"I'm glad. The thing is, there are important events and important stories out there waiting to be written, and I'm in a tropical paradise thinking about menus. Or supposed to be. It makes me feel so guilty and frustrated at the same time."

"I thought you were writing a novel," I said.

"I am, but that's not what I want to do. It's no damned good, anyway. I want to go back to Europe, to the war. You know how last night you said you felt as if you were doing something of value? Well, I want that feeling, too. I've had it before. I don't have it now. Do you understand? Silly question. Of course you do."

"Yes. Of course I do."

And I did. She wasn't some cliché of a bored housewife longing for romance and a career in the wider world. Just the opposite. She had had those things and been plucked from them and dropped into a miniature world she was never cut out for. She had known it from the beginning. I had the feeling that almost everyone hears the little voice of doubt before the wedding day, and I'd bet more than a few should have listened to it.

"So we can't fall in love," she said. "I wouldn't be able to think or concentrate the way I'd need to. I'd be . . . distracted. And you . . . you'd be on your ship and we'd be apart and you'd be lonely and I'd be wretched and . . . oh, you know what I mean. Don't you? Do you agree? Is it a deal?"

Her eyes were soft and sad. There were no tears, but there was something that looked very much like longing. It would be very hard for me not to love her, I thought. But I didn't say anything. I pulled over to the side of the road and stopped. I got out and walked around to her side of the jeep and put my arms around her and kissed her as tenderly as I could manage, and then said, "Yes, it's a deal."

And I suppose that was the precise moment we fell in love.

Chapter Twenty-Four

We didn't say anything about it, though. We'd stick to the agreement. It was the only way, because she was right about all of it.

We got back to the Finca at around six in the morning. No one was there yet.

She got out of the jeep and took her duffle and the picnic basket and then came around to my side and kissed me.

"That was heavenly," she said. "The whole night."

"'Here will I dwell . . .'"

"Please tell me we still have a deal."

"We still have a deal."

"I was afraid of that. Call me later, will you? Let me know when you're leaving."

"What about tonight?"

"Yes, of course, if you're still here. I'll think of something fun."

She turned and ran up the stairs to the top and then dropped her stuff and turned around and waved, and I drove back to Havana, wondering if I'd ever see her again.

On the way back I also wondered if I should have told her about the tanker and Hermosa and the fact that there really was a war going on here, too. But it wasn't the kind of war she needed. There was censorship, and the action was all at sea. It was a small war, so far, and it was a war she could never watch or report on, except at second hand. She needed front lines, and there were no front lines in our war here. She needed generals and combat soldiers to interview, and she needed to watch artillery being fired and to see towns and villages that had been wrecked by bombing and roads filled with sad refugees hauling all that was left of their homes. She needed to see the big land war. She *had* to see it. I understood.

Then I wondered if I should have mentioned running into her husband at sea. But what would be the point of that? She knew more or less where he was and what he was doing, and she didn't think much of it. Well, that was between the two of them. Then I remembered Fritz and that I forgot to tell her where I got him. Not only that, I forgot to retrieve him. I wouldn't worry about it. If I didn't get back there, he'd be well looked after, and if Marty's husband wondered where he came from, she'd have no trouble coming up with some story. In her present mood, she might even tell him the truth. Maybe I'd pick him up sometime in the future. Fritz, I mean. I should. I felt I owed him for not barking, and I'd made a deal with him, too. But a ship is no place for a dog—no fire hydrants and cranky deck hands who don't like seeing messes of any kind. Not only that, the *Nameless* was the kind of ship that would roll on a wet lawn, as someone once said. Not the place for a dog with short legs.

There was a message waiting for me at the embassy: "Return soonest." So that answered that. I checked on the PBY. It would be leaving for Key West at sixteen hundred. They had room for me. That was kind of a shame, I thought. But there was no way around it.

I went to the Bachelor Officers Quarters, where I had stored my gear, and shaved and got back into uniform. By then it was time for Bill Patterson to be in his office, so I turned in the jeep and went back to the embassy.

Bill greeted me with his usual enthusiasm.

"Well done in Hermosa, old man. I saw the reports. Quite a show."

"Yes, it was."

"You'll be mentioned in dispatches, as the Brits say. You and the captain and the ship. I foresee a unit citation in your future. ONI was very impressed."

"That's good. The men will like it."

"When do you head back to Key West?"

"This afternoon. Sixteen hundred."

"You seem a little glum about that. Any particular reason? Hmmm?"

"You know me. I'm just naturally glum."

"Is she a real blond?"

"Who?"

"You know what they say about someone who answers a question with a question?"

"No, what?"

"They have something to hide."

"Me? Really?"

"Oh, I see. I must have you confused with someone else."

"It happens. Which reminds me—what do you know about the bartender at the Floridita? Name's Constante."

"We have a file on him. But there's nothing very interesting that I can see."

"Then why have a file?"

"We have a file on everyone, pretty much."

"Sounds just a wee bit sinister."

"Ever hear of a sinister bureaucrat?"

"I have now."

"A contradiction in terms, more or less."

"I don't know about that."

"Mostly it's just shuffling paper. But the thing is, guys like Constante hear things and then repeat them, and so whether they like it or not they're part of the system of underground information. We listen to what they say, and we watch what they do. It's routine."

"How much of that do you pass on to Batista's boys?"

"Not much of it. But they are doing the same thing. They don't need our help. The only time we overlap and share is in cases like Hermosa, when we have mutual interests. But we don't care too much about Cuban internal politics. At least, I don't. Batista and his gang are not that easy to like. But I can't speak for the other sly boys in the embassy."

"Can't say or won't?"

"Is there a difference?"

"You know damned well there is."

"Well, what would you say to a little lunch?"

"I'd say—'Hello, Little Lunch.'"

"That's not the way I heard that joke."

"Best I can do. But, yeah, let's have lunch. How about if I meet you at that *boliche* place around twelve hundred, which is noon to you civilians?"

"Good. I will shuffle papers till then. What are you going to do?"

"I think I'll go to the Floridita and have a few rum drinks and chat with Constante, now that I know he's not an official spy."

"Not for us, officially. But discretion in this country is always advisable."

"Point taken. You'd be doing me a favor if you let me use your phone for a few minutes—assuming it's not bugged."

"Oh, it's not bugged. I'll be in the library down the hall. Just pop in and let me know when you're finished."

I closed the office door and dialed Marty's number. She picked up on the second ring.

"Hello, darling," she said, and it sounded as though she meant it. "Where are you?"

"At the embassy. There was a message here for me this morning, calling me back to Key West."

"Oh. I see. Well, that's just as well. Ernest called me. He and the boys have arrived in Cojimar and will be coming out here later this afternoon."

"Oh. Well, in that case I guess I'm not sorry about having to go back."

"No."

There was a pause on both ends.

"Riley, darling . . ."

"Yes?"

"Have you thought about our deal?"

"Yes, I have."

"It's the right thing, isn't it?"

"Yes."

"And you're going back today, so that's lucky, because I might not be able to go through with it, if we had another night like last night."

"Neither would I."

"I'm glad. I better go now. I don't want to say anything more and spoil things. But I'll write to you. Will you write to me?"

"Yes, of course."

"Good. There is just one more thing, though."

"What's that?"

There was another pause.

"I *am* in love with you, you know."

"And I am in love with you," I said.

"I'm so glad. Now that we've said it, well, we've said it. It's real. But it can go to our lovely parallel life. Can't it?"

"Yes. Right under the apple tree."

"Nothing will spoil it there."

"No."

"Tell me it can stay there. And we can keep our deal here."

"It can stay there. And we can keep our deal here."

"Goodbye, darling."

And she hung up.

And I thought, Dammit all. I had no idea what it all meant or what we had just agreed to. What the hell was I saying about that apple tree? It was a pretty line, but what did it mean? Our original deal was not to fall in love, and that had not lasted very long. Now was there a new deal? I suppose it just meant that we would keep things secret between us and not press each other in ways that distracted us from what needed to be done. And when it was possible, we would get together and pretend that those few hours were all that mattered, and we would "make one little room an everywhere," and . . . so on. In the annals of love affairs, those were hardly original ideas. They weren't even original for me. But that was OK. I could live with that. Besides, what choice was there? But I wondered if we were trying to do one of those mental contortions and believing two different things at the same time. As for being in love with her—was I really? Well, yes. And who could blame me? Could I live with that? Well, as I said before, what choice was there?

I walked over to the Floridita. I could hear laughter coming from inside.

I stood at the door and looked in. The seat at the end of the bar was oc-cupied by the famous man himself. Apparently, he had come straight here from Cojimar. Sitting next to him was a very tall, nice-looking American. I recognized him as one of the others in Hemingway's boat. I went in and sat somewhere in the middle of the bar. Constante came bustling over.

"Riley, my friend. Welcome."

Hemingway and his friend both looked at me and smiled and waved.

"I remember you," said Hemingway. He had a deep, pleasant voice. I think they call it a baritone, but I'm not much on musical terms. "You were the officer with Captain Ford on the 475."

"That's right. Name's Fitzhugh. I'm the exec."

"Glad to know you. This is Wolfie, my exec." I thought it was odd that a thirty-six-foot civilian fishing boat would have, or need, an executive officer, but maybe he was just joking. "His real name is Winston Guest, but I call him Wolfie because he reminds me of that guy who played the Wolfman in the movie."

"Lon Chaney?" I didn't see much resemblance. Personally, I would not have considered that a compliment, but he didn't seem to mind.

"Lon Chaney. Yes. That's him."

"I'm pleased to meet you," I said. Hemingway didn't bother introducing himself, since we had more or less met at sea. He was also figuring correctly that everyone in this town knew who he was. It wasn't conceit, so much, as not being falsely modest about his celebrity. False modesty was not one of his flaws. I do not say that sarcastically. He disliked phonies and people he called the "ballroom bananas" in the military—guys whose principal role was wearing a uniform. I didn't know all that just then, but I learned it later. "I read your most recent book," I said. "I liked it very much."

"Really? Thank you. It's nice to hear that from someone who knows something about war. You know what Mark Twain said—he was always more interested in listening to war talk from a soldier who'd been to war than he was in hearing moon talk from a poet who'd never been to the moon. Ha, ha!"

"You can't beat Mark Twain," I said.

"No. But I'm going to try. I beat Tolstoy and Stendhal this last time around. Maybe I can beat Twain next. Huck Finn will be a tough opponent, though. Might go all fifteen rounds. Have a drink?"

"Thanks. I will."

Constante gave me one of the special daiquiris.

"I see you've been initiated into the Papa Doble," Hemingway said. "I invented it. The record is eighteen. Or sixteen. I forget."

"Who set it?"

"I think I did, but I can't be sure. Say, I heard there was some action at Cayo Hermosa."

"Really?"

He looked at me and smiled, nodding as if to say he understood and would shut up about it. There were legitimate reasons for suppressing news of the action. The fact that there were Cuban rebels involved was not something Batista wanted advertised, at least not until his boys figured out how to play it in the papers. And even a couple of German sailors on Cuban soil would make people understandably nervous. Since it took place in a remote area, it was easier to contain the news. So, all in all, we agreed with the Cubans that it was best to keep the lid on.

"Are you in town for long?"

"No, I just came for a meeting. I'm going back this afternoon."

"You'll have to come out to my place the next time you're here. Have dinner. There's usually a good crowd out there."

"I'd like that," I said, untruthfully.

"Have you ever shot live pigeons?"

"No."

"You'll have to try it. It's a challenge. We have a very fine club at Cazadores. I'll teach you. I taught Wolfie, and now he's a champion. Right?"

"Is that how you remember it, Papa?"

"Yes. But I may be wrong. Maybe you already knew how to shoot."

Wolfie looked at me and grinned as if to say, He's a good guy, but half the time he's full of it.

"Come to think of it, you probably did. Maybe I'm thinking about Marty. I *know* I taught her how to shoot. How to shoot and how to write. Two things I know about. Not the only things, though. I can fish a little, too."

I could easily imagine Marty's reaction to that.

"I met your wife in here a couple of weeks ago," I said. I didn't glance at Constante.

"Marty? Madame Eyeroll? Good-looking gal, isn't she? Legs go all the way up to her shoulders. She thinks our U-boat chasing business is a silly game. You know better. The bastards are out there."

"I do know that, for sure. I'm guessing you didn't see anything around Confites. We'd have heard if you had."

"No, we didn't get a sniff. But you know, coming back we saw this Spanish passenger liner, the *Marques de Comillas*. She was stopped dead in the water, and I'm positive we saw a conning tower come up right behind her and wait for ten minutes or so, then break off and head north. I'm sure they either put someone on board the liner or took someone off."

"Most likely took someone off," said Wolfie.

"Yeah. Probably. We chased them after they headed north. We were ready to take them on, right, Wolfie?"

"Yes. Ready, but I'm not sure how willing. I felt a certain puckering."

"Ha! You would have done your duty. Don't worry about that. A couple of grenades in the conning tower would have messed them up good. But they submerged before we could get close. We reported it, and the army sent some plane to check, but they didn't see anything. Well, how could they? By the time they got there the sub was two hundred feet down. But I'll bet that damned U-boat was headed right for the Mississippi, maybe to drop off saboteurs."

"Could be," I said. That was not at all farfetched. Submarines were the preferred way of inserting spies and saboteurs into enemy countries—a moonless night, a sub surfacing just offshore, an inflatable boat with a sailor to row and two spies dressed in civvies with forged papers. Drop them off and hustle back to the sub. Nothing to it. The Brits were doing it in Europe. Surely the Germans were doing it, too. That was probably how they first established the camp on Hermosa. Bill had told me the FBI had a special task force dedicated to catching those infiltrators. They caught four German saboteurs who were just dropped off by a U-boat on Long Island and another four in Florida. "How far away was the U-boat when you first spotted it?"

"Couple of miles, right, Wolfie?"

"No more than that."

"You know those Series Seven U-boats have a really low profile," said Hemingway, "so it was hard to see. They dip below the horizon in only a mile or two."

I smiled and nodded. I was being told stuff I already knew—and could be expected to know. Next to unsolicited advice, it was just about my least favorite thing. But, in fairness, it was just conversation.

"It sure as hell looked like a conning tower," he said. "What else could it have been? And why was the ship stopped, if not for letting someone off or taking someone on? The fact that it was a Spanish ship is significant. Adolf and Franco are tight. Hell, Adolf practically financed Franco's whole war effort. Do you know how Franco got his troops to Spain from Spanish Morocco and start the whole damned mess?"

"No."

"The Luftwaffe and the German navy. The Krauts gave Franco and his bloody Moors a ride. Talk about miserable bastards. The Moors were the worst. So what better way to get some saboteurs over here than to send them here on a Spanish ship and then transfer them to a U-boat for a quick trip up into Huck Finn country?"

"I hope you're wrong." I wondered if a U-boat could really navigate its way through the Mississippi delta. It was a maze of channels and false channels leading nowhere. Following the markers in the real channel would be tricky through a periscope. But maybe they'd wait and follow a merchant ship in. It could work.

"Me, too. But I don't think I am. What do you say? How about joining us for lunch?"

"Thanks, but I'm meeting Bill Patterson and then flying back to Key West."

"Patterson? FBI. They don't like me much. The feeling's mutual. Our homegrown Gestapo. I have trouble getting .357 ammunition because all the draft-dodging G-men use them. Well, maybe we'll see you again. If you're in town, be sure to give me a call. Constante knows the number. What did you say your first name was?"

"Riley. Riley Fitzhugh."

"Well, it was nice meeting you. I wouldn't be surprised if we run into each other again out at sea."

"I wouldn't either."

I left with more things to think about. As I walked away, I asked myself if I felt a little guilty, and maybe more than that, now that I'd met Marty's husband. He seemed like a nice enough guy—a little talkative, maybe, and not at all shy about his sense of greatness. Some of that could have been the rum. Maybe he was trying to break his daiquiri record. Then I suddenly thought of something Hemingway himself had written. I didn't remember where I saw it, but I did remember the line, because it was pretty straightforward and ironically apropos. He'd said, "I only know that what is moral is what you feel good after, and what is immoral is what you feel bad after." Well, that certainly was a simple enough formula. So the question became—was I feeling bad about anything that had happened with Marty, especially now that I'd met her husband?

Honestly?

Not really.

Chapter Twenty-Five

When I reported back to the ship the captain had been ashore at a meeting of some kind, but when he returned I was able to brief him on what happened in Havana, though not all of it, of course.

When I told him that we were in essence the fair-haired boys, he smiled his sardonic grin.

"Glad to hear it. I may make admiral after all. And speaking of promotion, you're no longer an ensign. When you have a chance, go on over to Supply and get yourself some silver bars and some new gold braid."

"Just when the old braid was getting salty."

"Well, you still got your hat. It's coming along. Won't be long before someone starts thinking you're real."

So now I was a lieutenant, junior grade. The promotion wasn't any kind of honor, though. Enough time had passed, and that was all it took. Merit didn't enter into the Navy's promotions until you were much higher on the totem pole. Then it became a factor, if only just one of them. But merit mattered even for junior officers when it came to assignments. You got regular fitness reports, and they were extensive evaluations of your performance across a wide range of criteria. And your fitness reports affected future assignments. So it wasn't all just seniority.

"Well, let's get down to business," said Captain Ford. "I just got a briefing from the intelligence boys. Seems a U-boat was spotted by a Navy blimp in the Crooked Passage between Long Island and Crooked Island." The Crooked Passage was one of the few fairly deep-water routes through the

Bahamas, and this particular place was due north of the eastern end of Cuba. "The blimp went in for a bombing run."

"Gutsy."

"Yes. Can you picture one of those things diving on a U-boat? Must have seemed like forever to the pilot and crew."

"Was the boat on the surface or just under?"

"Sunbathing on the surface. Don't ask me why. It was broad daylight. Overconfidence, maybe. Anyway, the U-boat was manning its guns, of course, and they shot down the blimp, but not before the blimp dropped a couple of bombs. Didn't hit the boat, but they exploded close aboard and killed a couple of U-boat sailors. Or at least blew them overboard. The sub didn't wait to pick them up and submerged."

"What happened to the blimp's crew?"

"Nine out of the ten were picked up by fishermen who were watching the whole thing. The tenth was killed by sharks. Hell of a thing. If that fishing boat hadn't been close by, the sharks would probably have gotten the whole crew."

"How about the Germans who were blown into the water?"

"No word about them. Anyway, it seems that the U-boat was hurt a lot worse than anyone thought at first, because about twenty miles or so south of the fight with the blimp, some turtle hunters saw the U-boat surface. And they watched the crew scrambling to get out of the sub like she was about to blow. Maybe a half dozen or so got away before she rolled over and sank. The survivors were bobbing around in the water wishing they'd gone into some other line of work. But most of the crew went down with the U-boat, apparently. They went down in deep water, so that's the end of anyone who didn't get out right away. Then one of the turtle boats did a stupid thing—they came over to give the Krauts a hand and got shot for their troubles. Seems some of the Krauts had remembered their sidearms when they abandoned ship. Another fishing boat watched the whole thing, but then got out of there pronto. They reported it to the base here."

"So the survivors are now heading somewhere in a turtle boat."

"Yep. Headed south. Wouldn't surprise me if they were pointed toward Hermosa. They might not have heard the news yet, and you can be sure all the U-boats in the area and all of them coming this way know where Hermosa is. Or used to be."

"There might be another place like it, too."

"Yep. There might. But wherever they're headed, we're obliged to find 'em and bring 'em in, dead or alive, just like the good old days out west. And if there's another fuel base, we're to take it on as well. Trouble is, their sub went down only about sixty miles north of Cuba. Those turtle boats are rigged with sails, so the Krauts could already be on the beach somewhere, unless they're creeping along the coast and in and out of the bahias looking for their supply station—either the recent Cayo Hermosa or some other one we don't know about. Sure as Satan's whiskers, they ain't still at sea. 'Course they could be somewhere in one of the Bahama islands, too."

"When do we leave?"

"Right now. You'll have to wait to get your new silver bars. We don't have much of a prayer of spotting them in the dark, but at least we can be in the general vicinity when the sun comes up."

So the *Nameless* got underway at twilight, heading back toward Cuba and the maze of islands and cayos along the north shore. Once we cleared the channel, I told the captain about meeting Hemingway and about the theory of the U-boat rendezvous with the Spanish passenger liner.

"Well, it's possible. Yes, it's possible. I don't know why any U-boat commander would be such a dumbass as to surface during the day right in a busy shipping lane. But the guy who shot down the blimp was on the surface, too, so I guess Fritz is feeling his oats. And maybe the skipper had no choice. He was ordered to pick up a passenger from the liner, and so he did it. Speaking of Fritz, what ever happened to that dog?"

"I left him in Havana, with a friend. I figured he'd like being on land better than being on board ship."

"Probably so. Your friend fond of dogs?" Was there something in the tone of his voice? I couldn't be sure.

"I think so, sir." Despite my best efforts, I had to smile. "Speaking of prisoners, what about Jose? Is he still aboard?"

"No. I turned him over to our intelligence boys. Last I saw, they were asking him some friendly questions. But they said they'd send him back to Cuba when they were finished."

"To a blindfold and a wall?"

"I doubt they'll bother with a blindfold."

"Kind of a shame."

"Yes, it is. Our boys may keep him, once they figure out what's waiting for him in Havana. I don't know. I told them he seemed harmless enough, but I don't know what good that will do."

"I wonder if he had time to show Blake how to make decent black beans and rice."

"Don't get your hopes up. Last I saw, Blake was teaching Jose how to make cornbread."

We headed for the general vicinity of Hermosa. That was as good a place as any to start looking.

The evening was as balmy as the chamber of commerce could wish for, and the sea was calm. We were heading south at a slow speed. There was no reason to get to the north shore before dawn with her rosy fingers showed up. From the wing of the bridge, you could see the wake of the ship, white and straight through the darkness of the sea. A straight wake always seemed like a good sign, sort of a metaphor for history—it was turbulent and roiling, but it was beautiful to watch and study, and it showed you perfectly where you had been, whereas the water ahead was dark and unmarked and was often full of surprises that you'd just as soon avoid.

"Yep," said Captain Ford, from his usual seat. "People pay as much as twenty dollars a day to do this, and here we are getting paid for it. If I had a stronger conscience, I'd feel guilty. Lucky for me, mine's a ninety-pound weakling and talks in a kind of shy whisper. A lot of the time I can't make out what it's saying. After a while, I give up trying to."

"I'd say that makes for a comfortable arrangement, Captain."

"Yes, it does. Very comfortable."

"Who was it that said conscience was a little voice that tells you someone might be watching?"

"Somebody who knew what he was talking about. That narrows it down quite a bit. Eliminates a sizable chunk of humanity. But I forget the guy's name. Speaking of names—you're a reading man, so I suppose you're familiar with the fella called Homer."

"Homer?"

"The Greek writer. Lived quite awhile back. Wrote some stories about the Trojan War and the boys involved. I've been reading about it. Very interesting. He often mentions the wine dark sea, which is what reminded me of him, just now. Good description."

"Yes, sir. I know the basics. But that's about it." Actually I knew a bit more than that, but I could tell the captain was in a talkative mood, and I didn't want to get in his way. And unlike Hemingway, who had told me things I already knew, I was pretty sure the captain's version of events would be different from the way I heard it.

"Then you probably know the whole thing started over a woman named Helen and a guy named Paris."

"Yes, sir. I do know that much."

"You've got to figure that anyone with a name like Paris is never going to turn out like you hoped, so I figure his parents are as much to blame for what happened as anybody. Call a kid Paris, and he's bound to be a disappointment."

"Do you figure when he was a kid, he went by that name, or maybe had a nickname?"

"Something like Jughead or Scooter? No, not according to Homer. Well, that tells you something right there. Nobody liked him, as a kid. But he was the kind that didn't care. His old man was the king of Troy, so Paris was probably full of himself. He had a lot of brothers, but he grew up to be the best looking, which made him even harder to live with, most likely. Anyway, one day Paris went on vacation in Greece, and on his travels he stopped in the town of Sparta, where he was bowled over when he met the queen."

"Helen."

"Yep. People said she was the most beautiful woman in the world. And although the world was quite a bit smaller in those days, there were still plenty of women around, and she was said to be the pick of the litter. Quite a compliment. 'Course they didn't have beauty contests in those days, but if they had, she'd of won, going away."

"I wonder if she was a blond or a brunette."

"I don't think Homer said. Or maybe I missed it. Well, anyway, Paris was smitten right then and there, and he decided to make off with her and take her back to Troy, which was across the Aegean Sea a little ways. Helen's husband was a king too. Fella by the name of Menelaus. There was no shortage of kings back then, mostly, I suppose, because communications were so poor that no one knew what was going on in the next town, so they all had to have their own kings, just to keep things running. They were minor royalty, though, probably not much more important than a mayor or alderman. If the Greeks had had better communications, those towns could have gotten by with just one king for all of them and saved some money on salaries. But they didn't. Anyway, the next morning Menelaus got a surprise. Like the old song goes: "He woke up and found her gone." But he figured out what happened and called a meeting of all the other Greek kings and told them that Paris had kidnapped his beautiful wife. So they organized a posse and set out after the lovers. It took the Greeks ten years to get her back, but they finally did get it done."

"Took a while."

"Yes, it did. And I imagine by the end of it, Menelaus was starting to wonder whether the game was worth the candle, because ten years is a long time for a woman to stay the most beautiful in the world. I mean, Miss America never wins even two years in a row, let alone ten. But as it turned out, he did find her, and he took her back to Sparta. The Greeks killed just about all the Trojans and burned Troy to the ground and went home satisfied, pretty much, although one of them got lost and took *another* ten years to make it back, and what he found waiting for him surprised him some, too."

"Odysseus."

"That's him. Though his nickname was Ulysses."

"Yes, sir. I remember that his wife was being bothered by a gang of suitors."

"Seems like it. There she was, sitting around for twenty years, waiting for her old man to get back. Mighty impressive. Even a dog won't be faithful that long. 'Course I figure she changed some, too, but it wasn't anything like the way her husband changed, because when he fetched up on shore nobody could figure out who he was."

"Twenty years is a long time."

"True enough. Anyway, it's all a good story. But I imagine when the various Greek kings all got together to drink and tell lies at their old soldiers' reunions, they asked themselves whether the whole Trojan War was worth it, especially since Menelaus was the only one that got anything out of it. And all *he* got was a wife who didn't like him in the first place. All the other guys got was ten years of work and fighting and living under canvas on a beach, which ain't as cozy as it sounds, especially for that long a time. It's very windy around there, I hear, and blowing sand is as irritating as a noisy conscience."

I had to smile at that, remembering a girl I knew out in L.A. She never liked to make love on the beach because "sand gets in places." Then I thought about Marty and our night on the south coast. But we were in a sleeping bag; there weren't any problems with sand. Well, it wasn't windy that night.

"So what's the moral of the story, Captain?"

"Moral? None that I can see. But I don't buy the idea that Paris just picked Helen up and slung her over his shoulder and hauled her off to Troy. I figure she was in on it, because she was tired of her old man and was glad to go. Menelaus was rumored to be a pain in the ass, and she wanted a change of scenery. She figured Paris would give it to her, which he did. Plus, Paris was a handsome fella, and that counted for something. Menelaus was known to have red hair, and she probably didn't care for it. You don't see many red-haired Greeks, even today. 'Course, the only Greeks I know are running diners, but all of them have black hair, or none at all."

"I wonder why she married Menelaus in the first place."

"Hard to say. I suppose she felt it was time to settle down, and he was handy. That's the reason most folks get married, if they're honest. And he did have a good job. She probably told herself she could get used to the red hair, or maybe talk him into dying it. But after a while, she realized she just couldn't do it. Plus, his habits probably got on her nerves. Even a king has habits. Gets ready for bed, puts his crown on the nightstand or hangs it on the bedpost, tosses his purple robe and shorts on the chair, kicks off his golden sandals, and all of a sudden he's just a red-headed guy who farts in his sleep."

"When you put it that way, you can understand her point of view."

"Yes, you can. Especially since the Greeks have a fondness for garlic."

"I'm surprised he wanted to take her back."

"I am, too. The way I hear it, he didn't intend to at first, and in fact when he and the boys finally came busting into Troy, he went rampaging around the town looking for her, intending to kill her. Ten years is a long time to stay mad, but he did it. Some things just don't get forgot."

"Sounds like a country song."

"Might be. Anyway, he found out where she was hiding, and when he came running into the room waving his sword, she stood up, cool as dammit, dropped her dress to the floor, and he changed his mind."

"She still had it."

"Appears that way. 'Miss World,' ten years running."

"What happened to Paris?"

"Somebody shot him. I forget who. Some guy with a funny name, though that doesn't narrow it down much. And stories differ. Some say it was one guy, some say it was another."

"It wasn't Menelaus?"

"No. That would have saved ten years of trouble, if he'd of done it right at the beginning. But he didn't." He stretched and yawned and put out his cigar. "Well, it's late, and I think I'll hit the sack. Call me if anything unusual comes up."

"Aye, aye, sir."

And I stood the rest of the watch in darkness, wondering what the captain's history lecture meant, if anything. Or was he just joking? He was a fox, not a hedgehog, and a fox knows many things—probably because he spends a lot of time with his nose in the wind.

Chapter Twenty-Six

In the morning we were on the west side of the Hermosa channel.

The captain called me up to the bridge.

"Riley, get the Fubars together and situate yourselves along the portside. We'll also man the three-inch and the forties and then poke our nose in the channel and see if anything is going on over on Hermosa. If there's some Krauts in a turtle boat in there, we'll give 'em a chance to surrender, so we don't have to blow up that boat. I expect the Bahamians would like to have it back. Their relatives, anyway. The Krauts'll probably see reason, but you never know."

"Aye, aye, sir."

The Fubars were called away from their regular duties. There were only five of them, because Smithers was still in Key West nursing his broken arm. The five went to the armory and drew their weapons, and when we were ranged along the portside and the guns were manned, the captain conned the *Nameless* very slowly into the Hermosa channel. We stopped just at the entrance to the bahia and looked east toward the former camp.

The merchant ship hadn't slipped any farther into the bay and was lying on its side where it had rolled over. Its rusted sides and bottom lay exposed to the sun, obscene and ugly, like a fat guy sleeping with no covers. During the attack the surrounding land had been ravaged by fire and explosion and white phosphorous, but the fires had burned themselves out by now, leaving blackened stumps, trees stripped of their leaves and branches, and scattered trash of all kinds—splintered wooden pallets and plywood panels, twisted metal gas cans and fifty-gallon drums, paper of all kinds, some of it still caught and tangled in the trees, even some spare uniforms and rags and patches of canvas. The tide had swept away most of the floating debris.

"All quiet," said the captain from the wing of the bridge.

"Yes, sir."

We scanned the deserted shoreline and the jungle behind for several minutes, but there was nothing moving. The ibises and flamingos and herons and most of the other local birds had abandoned the place. Maybe they didn't care for the smell of smoke and death. But the buzzards were there. We could see them roosting in the trees behind the camp. Well, it was their kind of place. The remains of the Germans, the Cubans, and some of the freighter's crew were scattered around there somewhere. The crew members who hadn't gotten out before the freighter sank were still down there. They were safe from the buzzards, but not from the crabs.

"Seems all clear," the captain said. "If there was anyone left after the fight, they'd have been glad to see us and glad to surrender. Even the Krauts. They'd have had enough of the bugs and going hungry."

We backed out of the channel and secured the guns and the Fubars, and then went out about five hundred yards from shore and anchored. There was a good holding bottom there.

I went up to the bridge to confer with the captain.

"We sure made a hell of a mess of that place," he said. "The jungle'll grow back quick enough, but that wreck will be there till doomsday. Maybe the next hurricane will slide her into the deep. I hope so for the sake of the tourists. Pass the word for Sparks."

In a minute Sparks, the radioman, reported.

"You get your radio fixed, Sparks?"

"Yes, sir. She's working beautiful. Got all the parts I needed and spares for each when we were in Key West."

"Get a new jeep battery from the MPs?"

"I couldn't really say where it came from, sir. One of the men got it for me."

"You didn't ask him where he got it?"

"No, sir."

"You'll go far, Sparks."

"Thank you, sir. It's a brand-new one."

"Glad to hear it. Now, do you feel like having a little more shore duty? Same as last time?"

"Yes, sir."

"I think we'll send two men with you for company, plus enough water and chow for five or six days. Bosun Wheatley's got the gear and supplies you'll need. We talked Supply out of a two-man tent and some bedrolls when we were in port. Wouldn't be surprised if they lifted 'em from the army. Pitch the tent someplace out of sight, like before, and just keep watch round the clock. One man on, two men off. We're looking for some Kraut survivors from a sunken U-boat. They stole a boat in the Bahamas, and I figure they're heading here or they're already around here, somewhere. There might be a half dozen or thereabouts. They'll be armed, but not very heavily. Pistols only, most likely. Can you recognize one of those Bahama turtle boats?"

"Yes, sir."

"OK. There's also the fact that they'll be white men, so there's not much chance of mistakes. You're not to take them on, if they show up. Just stay out of sight and radio us. We won't be more than a couple of hours away. Six at the most. Is that clear?"

"Yes, sir."

"Show the other two men how to operate the radio, when you get ashore."

"Sir, we can send Otto again," I said. "He's familiar with the radio. And Reynolds. He's a quick learner."

"No, pick another couple—guys who know which end of an M1 is danger-ous. But I want to keep the Fubars together. We're already down one man with Smithers gone. You and the boys might have some action coming up, and at least they have some experience shooting at live targets."

"Yes, sir."

"Now, Sparks, once you get ashore and get squared away, teach the other two how to send the letter K. K for Krauts. That's all we'll need to hear, and we'll come running. Keep sending until we respond. If we have to contact you, we'll send a message at zero eight hundred, twelve hundred, or eighteen hundred. So be listening at those times. Otherwise, switch off and save your battery."

"Aye, aye, sir. Would it be all right if I chose the men, sir?"

"Sure. Take anyone you want. And don't forget the bug spray and a good pair of binoculars. The island just opposite of where we are now has a decent-sized hill. You might want to pitch your camp at the top. There'll be a better breeze up there, and you'll still be able to see the channel entrance and the sea around for a long way."

"Aye, aye, sir."

He took off to get his gear together.

"I figure even if the Krauts catch a glimpse of them, they won't know who or what they are. Once Sparks spots them and sends the message, they won't get away. Their goose is wurst. Or what's that stuff the French are so proud of?"

"Pâté de foie gras, Captain?"

"That's the stuff. Ever had it?"

"Once, Captain. I don't care much for liver."

"No red-blooded American boy does. My mother used to try to get me to eat the stuff. Once a year, regular as clockwork, she'd serve it up with onions, and once a year I'd give it to the dog when her back was turned. He liked the liver. Not the onions. Speaking of dogs, I'll bet that little wiener dog you captured would like a bite of liver, raised the way he was with Germans. They're generally fond of organ meats. You don't want to know what they put in their sausages."

"No, sir. I think it was Bismarck who said something about that."

"Wouldn't be surprised. Isn't he the one that said, if you use enough mustard, you can eat anything?"

"I think so, sir."

"He would know. But you said the dog's got a new home. I assume he likes it there."

"Yes, sir. Regular meals and lots of company."

"That's good. Well, once Sparks and his buddies get squared away ashore, we'll start east and take a look at what's going on in these godforsaken cayos and bahias. If the Krauts try to hide out behind an island, let's hope they'll be dumb enough not to lower their mast. We might just get lucky and spot it peeking above the mangroves. Once the whaleboat gets back from delivering Sparks to the beach, I think we might as well leave it in the water. I have a feeling we'll be sending you and your gang into these little coves and bahias, one after another. There's no sense taking the time to bring it in and then relaunch it every time we see a likely spot. In fact, it might make more sense for you and the boys to stay in the whaleboat. It's calm enough and seems likely to stay that way. Just follow along with us, like a duckling after momma."

"An ugly duckling, Captain?"

"I ain't the kind of skipper to cast asparagus on my own men. Or even aspersions. Besides, you probably know what the ugly duckling turned into."

"Yes, sir. A handsome swan."

"Is that the way you heard it? I always heard he got a lot bigger, but stayed just as ugly. Well, you and the boys might as well get ready. Call away the Fubars, and we'll go find us some murdering Krauts."

"Aye, aye, sir."

I mustered my five guys on the quarterdeck and told them what we were going to do. The odds were that if we ran into the Germans we'd be at fairly close quarters, so I assigned two of the men to carry Tommy guns, the others M1s. All of them would carry three hand grenades as well as forty-fives. Everyone would have bandoliers of spare ammunition.

"We're going to sail along with the *Nameless* and cruise the coast. We'll go in close to shore where the ship can't go. We're looking for some German U-boat sailors who escaped from their boat when it sank. They killed some Bahamian turtle hunters and stole their boat, so they'll either be under sail or holed up in one of these inlets and cayos. So look sharp for a mast sticking above the trees and mangroves. We'll need to stay quiet. You know how sound travels."

"What about the sound of the whaleboat motor, sir?"

"Nothing we can do about that. We'll just hope they think it's a normal fishing boat or something. Maybe they'll even figure they can jump us—until they actually see us."

"What do we do if we find them?"

"It depends on the situation. If the *Nameless* is close by, I figure they'll give up without a fight. We'll give them the chance to surrender. But if we're inside one of these damned island mazes and the *Nameless* is outside somewhere, we may have to fight it out. But we think they only have pistols, so we'll have the range on them. The only wild card might be another hidden fuel dump that they know about. If we happen to stumble on something like that, we'll hustle back to the ship and treat the place the way we treated Hermosa. OK?"

The men all nodded.

"All right. Draw your weapons and bring me a Tommy gun and some grenades, if you please. We leave as soon as the whaleboat gets back from dropping off Sparks and the boys."

That first day we didn't see a thing. We were motoring slowly along the beaches of the barrier islands with the *Nameless* out to our left where the deep water started. The whaleboat was steered by a wheel amidships. The coxswain stood at the wheel and the rest of us sat on the benches and surveyed the shoreline and the tree line with binoculars. There was nothing but one tiny sand spit after another, with shallow inlets and flats winding in and around and behind the cayos. Now and then we'd come to an inlet that led to a miniature bahia. It seemed like the perfect place for another Kraut fuel dump, but it was always deserted. The small islands were just above sea level, barely, but now and then there'd be one with a hill or two covered with trees, the way it was at Hermosa. There were flats surrounding these places and here and there stakes marking a shallow passage through, but the markers were primitive and placed there by fishermen who knew the stakes and the channel would most likely be gone as soon as the next storm came through. It wouldn't even have to be a hurricane.

When the breeze died down, the heat and humidity settled on us like leaden gloom and a migraine. The trees and palms seemed to droop in the heavy air. We sprayed each other with the flit gun, and the smell and stickiness of the repellent was only just preferable to the attacks of mosquitoes and sand flies. You had to wonder what was in the stuff that would ward off those critters, which were otherwise fiendish and unstoppable. But there was no choice.

"Who the hell would want to live around here?" said Otto, as we motored slowly in and among the sand spits and flats.

"Take a look around, dumbass," said Boyle. "No one."

There were birds perched in the trees and mangroves. Others were wading and fishing. They weren't bothered by our presence, and I wondered if that was significant somehow. But there were no signs of any life other than the birds and the fish in the flats. There were plenty of sharks cruising in the shallows. They ignored us, too. Most of them weren't that big. Maybe three or four feet. Big enough, though. Now and then a barracuda would startle a school of bait fish and chase them around. Some of the guys said we should have brought fishing rods since we were in such likely territory. I made a mental note to get some gear once we got back to Key West. We saw some redfish, and I remembered the captain saying they were good eating. We saw a giant ray smoothly flapping by in three feet of water. I once was taken to a performance of *Swan Lake* by a woman with a taste for culture as well as the *Kama Sutra*. The ray's graceful motions reminded me of the ballerina dancing the dying swan. Strange, the things you think about. I wondered what that woman was doing right now. Most likely, number thirty-four. It was her favorite, especially in the afternoon.

At night we went back to the ship. The men and I all got hosed down on the fantail. No one wanted to take a swim after seeing the critters in the flats, but we needed to get the bug spray off us and our clothes. Afterward we'd send the clothes to the laundry and take showers to get rid of the sticky salt water. We left the whaleboat tied alongside and anchored the *Nameless* for the night. We darkened the ship and set an anchor watch. We figured even if there were a U-boat cruising around, the *Nameless* would be just another dark shadow against the dark shadows of the shoreline, for there was no moon to speak of and the humid air seemed to settle into a thin layer of cloud cover that blocked most of the starlight. We were in the midst of a barely translucent cloud.

That night I had dinner in the wardroom with the captain. Bosun Wheatley was on watch on the bridge, because even though we were at anchor, we wanted an experienced watch keeper ready to take whatever action was required at a moment's notice. I would have the midwatch. And we had one of the signalmen standing by the radio at all times.

Blake gave us something called gilli-gilli, which was rice and some sort of meat mixed together with some spice or other. The captain had picked up the recipe during a stint in the Philippines, and he had shown Blake how to make it. It wasn't that hard, and it was better than Blake's usual ideas.

"I don't know for sure what the Filipinos used for meat," the captain said. "I didn't really want to know. But I'm pretty sure this is beef. Or pork. 'Course it could be Spam. You put enough spice on it, you can't always tell. That's the secret of most Oriental cooking."

"It's not too bad, Captain. I don't think it goes so well with cornbread, though. But you can't have everything."

"No. That's true."

"Even so, after today, I don't think anyone would pay twenty dollars a day to do this, Captain," I said.

"Probably not. But look at it this way—we're not paying anything. They're paying us."

"So the joke's on them."

"Yep. Makes a nice change. But you know, every time I have gilli-gilli I'm reminded of Olongapo. It's a town next door to Subic Bay. We have a base there, or did, until the Nips overran the Islands."

"I've heard of it. Kind of a rough town, wasn't it?"

"Kind of. Probably still is, although the Nips are probably less easygoing about some things than we were. From what I hear they don't pay what they call their comfort women. Just put 'em in a house and let 'em wish they hadn't left the convent."

"Funny name—comfort women."

"The Nips are like that. Say one thing, mean something else. Anyway, back in the early thirties, we stopped in Subic for a few days of showing the flag and a little R&R. The boys got some liberty. I pulled shore patrol duty, so I got to see all the sights, firsthand. The town looked like they had something against paint when they built it. Had a unique sort of odor about it. Nothing but dirt streets. The whole place consisted of two-story shacks with bars downstairs and whorehouses upstairs. There were lots of women in colorful dresses in those bars. At least, I think they were women. There was some talk that maybe not all of them were. A sailor who drinks more'n he should sometimes can't tell the difference, which is a good way to get beat up and robbed. 'Course a sailor getting drunk is a rarity, but even so we had to be on the lookout for those guys in dresses."

"It was a disguise so they could roll the sailors?"

"Yep. They were called Benny Boys."

"It's a wicked world, Captain."

"Yes, it is. The time I was there, the mayor and his wife were having a war about who'd control the town's two main industries—those bein' women and booze. They weren't living together at the time, and I don't know if they ever reconciled. They each had their own gang, and shots were sometimes fired. Didn't bother our men, luckily. It would have been bad for business, if they'd accidentally shot one of our boys."

"Gives new meaning to domestic dispute—the mayor and his wife, I mean."

"Yes, it does. It was quite a place. There was a canal running between the base and the town. Well, they called it a canal, but that gives it too much dignity. It was an open sewer, and a big one. That accounted for part of the odor I mentioned. The sailors had to walk over this little bridge to get to town where the bars and the whorehouses were, and when it was time to go back to the ship, they'd pass over this same bridge and toss coins to the kids and their sisters who were underneath in little canoes. The girls were all dressed in skimpy spangles and that sort of thing. Some of the sailors thought it was funny to toss the coins in the water so the kids would dive for them. Not our boys' finest hour, seemed to me."

"Takes two to tango, Captain."

"Yes, it does. Sometimes I wonder how it all fits in the grand scheme of a benevolent Providence. Maybe when I make admiral, I'll be better fixed to figure it all out."

"What happened between the mayor and his wife?"

"I never heard. But now that I think of it, it was the wife who was mayor, and her old man was just a bartender and pimp. He had aspirations to go higher, but she didn't go along with it. I imagine he felt she was holding him back, and she felt he was trying to horn in on her business. I doubt they stayed married. It's a Catholic country, but I'll bet they got divorced anyway. I figure even the Vatican would agree that shooting at each other would be grounds for divorce."

"Maybe annulment."

"That's probably more like it."

The next day we went back at it in the whaleboat. The day was sunny, sticky, and hot. There might be a change of weather coming. A rainstorm would be welcome. But the morning went along as quietly as the day before, and it wasn't until the afternoon that we came on anything. We were passing between two clumps of mangroves hardly worthy of calling them an island or cayo. When we went behind to the landward side, we saw a group of five or six buzzards on the beach, all fussing over something.

"Take us over there, Reynolds," I said to the coxswain.

We ran the boat up on the beach and all got out. The buzzards all took off, but they didn't fly far. Just over to the trees.

It was obvious what they were after, because there was a shallow grave in the sand. And the dead man's body was half exposed. He was a white man, pale with wispy blond hair. Something must have unearthed the body just recently. Probably the tide or the wind or a local squall, because he wasn't too badly used up by the buzzards.

"Looks like the Krauts forgot to finish the burying job," said Otto.

"They probably put him all the way in, but something washed away some of the sand. Most likely they didn't have the right tools. Or maybe when they dug down a few feet they hit water."

I reached down and removed the German's identity disk. He was a kid. No more than twenty from the looks of him. His disk said his name was Gunther Schmidt. I put the disk in my pocket. He wouldn't need it; no one would come looking for his grave out here. Or if they did, they wouldn't find it, which was worse. I assumed that his officer took the other disk, so that he could report the death. Somewhere, someone had some bad news coming and didn't know it, yet.

"Do we have a shovel in the boat?"

"No, sir."

"Otto, run on back to the *Nameless* and get a couple. We can't leave this kid like this. And tell the skipper what we've found."

"Aye, aye, sir."

"Well, we're on their trail. The question is, which way did they go from here? East or west?"

"What do you figure, sir?"

"I dunno. But if I were the Krauts after sailing around in these flats and mosquito farms for a couple of days, I'd sail due north and turn myself in at Key West."

Chapter Twenty-Seven

The next morning we were getting ready to get underway.

"The way I figure it," said the captain, "if they're heading east, there must be another fuel dump. Otherwise they'd have no reason to head that way. At least I can't think of one, offhand."

"Maybe there's a prearranged rendezvous spot with a friendly freighter. Somewhere at sea."

"Maybe. But that seems unlikely. They have no radio, I'm guessing. I suppose they could have sent some sort of SOS as the U-boat was going down, or when they realized they were in trouble. That's possible. If that's the case, they're aboard some bucket hiding out as regular sailors, safe as houses. Could be anywhere by now, including on their way back home. If so, we can't do anything about it. But—it seems more likely to me that they're heading west to Hermosa and somehow slipped by us in the night. Maybe they swung out wide and passed us over the horizon. Or maybe they picked up a local guide who took them through a back way, on the other side of these barrier islands and cayos. If so, we're in good shape, because Sparks is there on watch. I think our best course would be to keep searching east in case there's a second fuel dump, while we rely on Sparks to contact us if they show up at Hermosa. That means more whaleboat time for you and the boys."

"Aye, aye, sir."

"If they show up at Hermosa, I figure that means there's no second fuel dump—at least not on the north side of Cuba. So let's hope they *do* show up and Sparks's jeep battery is still working. Probably is, but you can't always trust army MPs."

"I remember we had a hell of a time finding Hermosa the first time, and we had its coordinates. The way it was tucked in there made it hard to see from the seaward side. How are these guys going to do it? They probably don't have any charts or navigation equipment."

"I thought about that, too. And the fact is, they may never find it, and if they're wandering around like the Flying Dutchman, we'll get them eventually. If not the *Nameless*, then someone else. But . . . suppose that was the U-boat that dropped their men off originally. They would have hung around for a while and gotten used to the landmarks."

"That's possible."

"I figure we'll find out one way or the other."

"Sir, I don't think we need all the Fubars in the boat. If it's OK with you I'll just take Otto and Reynolds. Otto speaks a little German, and that might come in handy. And if we bump into the enemy, we can call for help easily enough."

"That's fine. Suit yourself."

So the third day was more or less the same as the first two. The three of us in the whaleboat coasted the shoreline, looking for a mast or for likely inlets, and finding neither. The day was just as hot and humid and the insects were just as annoying, the insect repellent just as repulsive and sticky. There was very little breeze and what there was smelled of dampness and jungle rot. Even the fish in the flats seemed dispirited. Now and then we touched bottom, but we were going so slowly it didn't matter. The bottom was mud and marl, seaweed and half shells. The *Nameless* was following along only a few hundred yards away on the edges of the deep water.

"You know, guys," I said, "the captain's always telling me that people pay twenty dollars a day to do this. Just to float around in the Gulf of Mexico's turquoise waters."

"I agree with him," said Reynolds. "And all we need to make life complete is to have the Andrews Sisters singing 'Nice Work If You Can Get It.' Over and over and over."

"'Nice Work'?" said Otto. "I know that song. Who wrote it?"

"Morey Amsterdam. Either him or the Gershwins. Sometimes it's hard to tell the difference."

"Didn't he write *Porgy and Bess*?"

"Morey? No, he wrote *Archie and Veronica*, the tragic opera."

"Hey! Speaking of the Andrews Sisters," said Otto suddenly. "What's that over there?"

We had just come around a little bend and opened on a small cove. There was a woman wading knee-deep in the flats. Apparently she was harvesting something, shellfish or edible plants. She was dark brown, the color of bitter chocolate, and she had black, shining hair tied behind and hanging straight down to her waist. She was wearing a thin calico shift, and when she saw us coming her way, she stood and waited. I had the feeling that she and I were both looking at aliens from another world.

"Take us over to her, Reynolds," I said, "but go slowly. No sense scaring her. Maybe she can tell us something."

"Which one do you think she is?" said Otto.

"Which of the Andrews? I'd say it's Maxene," said Reynolds.

"No way. It's Laverne."

"Either of you boys speak Spanish?" I said.

"No, sir," said Otto.

"I know a little sign language, sir. I used to go out with a girl who was deaf."

"And blind?" said Otto.

"You should know. You were married to her."

"She wasn't blind. She just had a glass eye."

"Which one?"

"The blue one. There was nothing wrong with the other one."

"Yeah, I remember now. It gave me the creeps when she took it out at night and put it in a water glass. I felt like someone was watching me all night."

"I know what you mean. If we'd have stayed together, I definitely would have said something to her about that."

"You didn't want to wake up in the dark thirsty, that's for sure."

"Tell me about it."

As the officer in charge I suppose I should have told them to knock it off, but I didn't want to. What would be the point? Just to prove that officers could be jerks? They already knew that.

We pulled up to where the woman was wading, getting as close as we could, which was about ten yards.

"Buenos tardes," I said. I wondered if she even spoke Spanish. I figured she was a sea Indian. They lived in remote areas and a lot of them had very little contact with the outside. Most of them wanted even less than that. You couldn't blame them. They were descendants of the Indians who were here when Columbus and the boys arrived—before they were "Indians." They had all heard the stories and remembered.

She said nothing, and her blank expression didn't change.

"Give her a try in sign language, Reynolds. Maybe she's seen a boat with some white men."

Reynolds went through the motions, and she made some simple gestures in return.

"I couldn't make out much of what she was signing, sir," said Reynolds.

"Maybe because of her Cuban accent," said Otto.

"She did say she thinks Adolf's a pussy."

"Thank you, Reynolds," I said. "Your efforts will be noted."

The woman went back to harvesting whatever she was after and ignored us from then on.

Just then we heard the *Nameless's* loudspeaker: "Mr. Riley! Return to the ship!"

"Maybe they heard from Sparks," I said. "Let's go."

"I still say it was Maxene," said Reynolds, as he spun the wheel and gunned the engine.

"You had the chance. Why didn't you ask her?"

"You really are a dumbass, Otto. There's no way to say 'Maxene' in sign language."

We hurried back to the ship, and while Bosun Wheatley supervised bringing the whaleboat on board and securing it, I went to the bridge. The captain was reading a message and grinning.

"We got 'em," he said. "Sparks sent a string of K's, and we answered back, asking for details. The boys spotted the turtle boat approaching a good half mile outside the channel. They could make out they were white men, and so they started sending. The Germans are still maneuvering their way into the channel entrance. I'm guessing they don't teach them how to handle a sailboat in U-boat school. There might be an officer who has some clue about sailing. They got there, after all. But making an entrance into a narrow channel might pose a problem for them, especially with the breeze coming offshore. We sent a message to Sparks to stay under cover. The Krauts could say the hell with it and just beach the boat outside and work their way through the jungle on the barrier island, thinking they could get someone from the camp to come get it later."

"We can't be more than sixty miles away."

"Correct. Once we get the whaleboat on board, it'll be all ahead full. Three hours at most."

"Whaleboat's secured, sir!" said a bosun's mate from the main deck.

A signalman came into the pilot house.

"Another message from Sparks, Captain. There's a black man aboard the Kraut boat. And they're towing a skiff."

"Ah. That explains it. The Krauts picked up a fisherman and a guide. And maybe a sailing master. Well, that doesn't change things, much. Tell Sparks we're on the way and to keep his head down. Let's go. Left full rudder! All ahead full! Come to course two nine zero."

The helmsman repeated the order. The *Nameless* shivered a little as the screws took hold and we pivoted around. We were underway, and in a hurry.

"Riley, take the deck."

"Aye, aye, sir."

Three hours later we were off the channel entrance to Hermosa. We couldn't see the turtle boat, but the Germans were probably on the other side of the barrier island where the camp used to be.

"I imagine the sight of that camp and the freighter was a disappointment," said the captain. "Launch the whaleboat and go pick up Sparks and his buddies. We'll just sit here a spell. They're not going anywhere, unless there's a backdoor we didn't notice. I doubt it, but I suppose there could be."

In just a few minutes the whaleboat returned with the three radiomen.

"Good work, Sparks," said the captain when Sparks came up to the bridge.

"Thank you, sir. I'm ready for a shower. We all are."

"Any idea how many there are?"

"Yes, sir. We counted three on deck, plus the black guy."

"Not so many as we thought. I wonder if they have injured men in the cabin."

"We couldn't tell that, Captain."

"OK. Riley, we'll nose the *Nameless* into the channel, like before, and take a look around. If they have any sense they'll give up. But we'll leave the whaleboat in the water in case the Fubars have to go in and have a word with them."

"Aye, aye, sir."

Slowly we went forward, guns manned. The Fubars were lining the rails on the portside. I was on the bridge, but the other five were armed with M1s, in case they needed greater range than a Tommy gun gave them.

In a few minutes we were through the channel. We could see the entire bahia and the wrecked freighter and the former camp. But there was no sign of the turtle boat. Not at first. Then we noticed a small inlet on the far side of the bahia. We turned left cautiously and moved ahead slowly. The fathometer told us the bahia had deep enough water in the middle, but we couldn't tell where it began to get shallow on the sides. The water in there was black and gave no hint of the bottom. It was no place to run aground. When we got opposite the inlet we saw the turtle boat. It was aground and listing at about a twenty-degree angle.

"There's the trap," said the captain. "But where are the mice?"

212 ❈ Terry Mort

"If they were towing a skiff, Captain, they must have taken it. I don't see any trace of it now."

"You'd best take the whaleboat and the boys and go have a look. I don't want to take the ship any closer than this."

"Aye, aye, sir."

"You men ready for a boarding party?" I said, as I gathered the Fubars at the quarterdeck.

"Yes, sir," they said. They seemed pretty calm about the prospect.

"The Krauts are around here somewhere. We're going to give them a chance to surrender, but not a big chance." I remembered the captain's story of the duck hunter and the SHOO. "Get aboard. Make sure those rifles are unloaded before getting in. But once we're all aboard, load up and be ready."

I had my forty-five, but that was all. I figured we had enough firepower.

"Reynolds. Take us over to that turtle boat."

"Aye, sir."

We motored slowly toward the grounded boat. It was black with age. About thirty feet long, it had a high mast, but the sail had been lowered and lay unfurled and flapping idly on deck. The sail was patched and dirty. There was a small cabin on the main deck. We couldn't see anyone moving.

"*Achtung!*" I yelled, melodramatically. "Come out and surrender. Hands up! You will be treated as prisoners of war. If you do not come out immediately, we will destroy the boat with grenades."

"*Fich Dich*, Yank!"

"That means fuck you, sir," said Otto.

"I figured. Back off about twenty yards, Reynolds."

It occurred to me that if we tossed grenades into the cabin they might just come flying back to us. They usually took about ten seconds to explode, and in close quarters like these it was possible to start up an unwanted game of catch. There was a simpler solution.

"We're going to blast the hell out of that cabin, guys. Just like the radio shack before."

When we were in position, I gave the order to open fire on the cabin.

All five M1s unloaded eight shots apiece. The noise was deafening and continuous. The cabin blew apart in clouds of splinters. Then the men reloaded and fired again. If the Germans were hugging the deck to avoid bullets they were getting showered with dangerous splinters. We put eighty thirty-caliber bullets in that cabin, and there wasn't a lot left of it. One thing should have been clear to the Krauts—we were not bluffing.

"Cease firing! Reload," I said. We watched and listened, our ears ringing from the shots. There was no sound or movement on the boat. "Put us alongside, Reynolds."

When the whaleboat bumped against the tilted side of the turtle boat, I jumped aboard. I had my forty-five in my hand and I stood beside the shattered cabin door, just out of sight. I reached my hand around the door opening and fired seven quick shots into the cabin. Then I quickly shoved in another magazine and peered around the opening.

"*Hilf mir*," I heard someone say.

"Otto! What does *hilf mir* mean?"

"It means 'Help me,' sir."

I looked inside. There were three German sailors stretched out on the deck of the cabin. They were not moving and appeared to be dead. But one was moaning. "*Hilf mir*," he was saying, over and over. The other two were past help. Both were missing parts of their skulls. All three had some nasty-looking wounds on their legs and torsos, but they were old wounds, blackened with dried blood. But they had some fresh wounds, too, undoubtedly from our fusillade.

I went down the three steps into the cabin and checked the wounded man. He was hardly conscious. He wasn't much older than the kid we buried in the sand. They were all in their twenties, from the looks of them, even though they'd had some hard experience over the past few days. They all were burned by the sun, blistered and red. They were a mess. And the smell in the cabin was enough to make you retch.

Hell of a way to die and a hell of a place to do it, I thought.

I went back out on the tilted deck and jumped into the whaleboat.

"Let's call for Doc. Maybe he can do something for the one that's left. There are two others in there, dead."

"Think that's all of them, Mr. Fitzhugh?"

"Nope. Whoever's left made off with the skiff and the guide. Probably three of them, according to what Sparks saw. Once we get Doc over here with a couple of guys to stretcher the Kraut back to the *Nameless*, we'll go after the others. They know we're here now, so they'll either hide somewhere or try to run for it. Either way, they'll be somewhere along this inlet. This may open up into another bahia for all we know."

We shouted for Doc and two men to come with a stretcher in the inflatable, and when he got there he assessed the situation.

"Any chance for him, Doc?"

"I doubt it. Maybe in a hospital. Probably not in the ship's sickbay. I'll do what I can, though. I think these other guys have been dead a while. I'd say gangrene in their legs probably killed them before we got here. The head wounds didn't matter."

"Gangrene cause that smell?"

"Yes, sir. It's very distinctive."

"OK, Doc. Take him back and see what you can do."

Doc and the two men he brought with him lifted the German and carried him moaning out of the cabin, loaded him on a stretcher, and strapped him in. Then they put him in the inflatable and returned to the ship.

I started thinking about what I would do, if I was in the Germans' shoes. They'd tried to escape in the turtle boat but had run aground in the shallow inlet. One thing I wouldn't want to do is row a skiff from here to anywhere, but until we showed up they had no choice. But now, with a little luck, they could steal a US Navy motorized whaleboat and some uniforms and rifles and then worry about where to go next. It wouldn't matter if the uniforms had some holes in them. The *Nameless* sure as hell wouldn't be able to follow, and there was a guide to lead them—where? Somewhere. Anywhere was better than right here.

So the odds were, they weren't running. They were hiding and waiting. Maybe they figured if they could steal a better boat, they could go back and get their wounded shipmate. Maybe they figured he was too far gone. Either way, they needed what we had.

"I'll take the bow. Reynolds stay at the wheel. Otto and Griffiths on the starboard side, the other two on the port. Hunker down. If you see any movement in the bushes or whatever, shoot it. There aren't any civilians around here, except that fisherman they grabbed. We can't worry about him. I figure they'll only have handguns, but in these close quarters they'll still be dangerous. Take no chances and don't hesitate or wait for me to say something or give an order. They could have set up on both sides of this water, so keep your concentration on your side. They could easily start firing on one side to distract us and then open up on the other. They won't set up directly across from each other for fear of the crossfire. But they'll be close."

"Sounds like you know how to set up an ambush, sir."

"I knew some gangsters in a former life."

"Yeah," said Reynolds. "He used to go out with Lana Turner."

"Is that true, Mr. Fitzhugh?" This came from Griffiths, the youngest and probably the most gullible of the men. He looked younger than his eighteen years.

"Do you want it to be true, Griffiths?"

"Yes, sir."

"Well then, it is. I bought her a milkshake in Schwab's drugstore."

"Wow." To Griffiths, a milkshake at Schwab's was almost as glamorous and exotic as a martini at the Copacabana.

"All right, guys," I said. "Let's go find the rest of them. Reynolds, hand me your M1. It'll be more use than a forty-five. You just keep us in the center of this channel. And slow."

We motored very slowly down the narrow waterway that the Germans in the skiff must have taken. It was a straight passage, almost like a canal cut in the jungle. It looked to be about two hundred yards long, and beyond we could see an opening, so there was a bahia or some open water at the end of it. If so, that might give them a chance to get back to the sea or maybe even give them a safe passage within the barrier islands, either to the east or west. We went cautiously because the jungle and swampy land on both sides were thick. A perfect place to hide. Lots of them. In some spots, they could pull the skiff in among the reeds and we wouldn't see it, until the last second.

Standing in the bow with my rifle, I had the absurd sensation that my shirt was very thin. It was decent protection against mosquitoes, most of them, but that was all, and I felt it sticking against my skin from sweat. And it wasn't just the heat. I clicked the safety off the M1 and looked hard at the reeds and mangroves on both sides of the little channel.

We were about halfway down the channel, when on the right, about fifteen yards ahead, a huge black guy came flying out of the bushes and dived into the canal. I heard someone shout "*Scheisse!*" And a shirtless white man stood up and fired at the swimming fisherman. The German was only twenty yards away or so, and I aimed at him and fired twice. He went down hard. On the opposite bank another man stood up and aimed a pistol at us. At me, really. But I still had the rifle on my shoulder and I swung around and pulled the trigger three times, and the man on the left bank flew backward. By this time, only a matter of split seconds, the Fubars were unloading in both directions on both banks. A second man on the right bank waved his hands above the bushes and shouted, "*Kamerade!*" But Otto and Griffiths were firing, and they must have hit him with a half dozen shots because we could see the way the bullets tore through the underbrush after he fell. The whole thing lasted no more than a few seconds.

"Anybody hit?" I yelled.

"No, sir."

"Reload!"

We crept forward to about where the Germans had been hiding on both banks. Even though the bushes were thick, we could see the three bodies. They weren't moving.

The fisherman who'd given the alarm, either because he wanted to or because he was just trying to escape when the Germans weren't paying attention, lay in the water facedown. We motored up to him and Otto turned him over.

"I don't think so, boss," he said.

"Too bad. He sure as hell saved us."

We pulled over to the right bank, and I got out carefully and went over to the two Germans. I checked their pulses, but they were both dead. I took their identification disks. I don't know why. Certainly not as a souvenir. I had a vague notion that the International Red Cross did something or other about things like this.

"Can we keep their Lugers, Mr. Fitz?" said Otto, forgetting protocol in the excitement of the moment. "They both have two. Probably took the ones from the dead guys in the turtle boat."

"Yeah, sure."

"You want one?"

"Save one for me, Otto. Make sure they're unloaded. We don't want some dead guy's pistol going off accidentally."

Then we went over to the other bank. The one man there was still alive, but he had some pretty bad wounds in his legs that were bleeding freely and a nasty gash across his hairline and another one on his rib cage. He was groaning but I couldn't make out what he was saying.

"A couple of you guys give me a hand. We'll take this one back and give him to Doc. He may have a chance. Collect his pistols."

"Sir, I'm sorry I shot that one who was trying to surrender," said Griffiths.

"That's OK, Griffiths. In the heat of the moment, you didn't have a choice. I would've done the same thing. Fact is, I might have, now that I think of it."

The fisherman's skiff was pulled up in the weeds.

"Drag the skiff out. We'll put the bodies and the wounded man in it and tow it back to the *Nameless*. The captain can decide what to do about the dead. I imagine he'll want to bury them on Hermosa, but it's his call."

It occurred to me that there might be one or two Germans still alive and hiding in the jungle or the reeds. I figured I'd give them a chance to surrender.

"*Achtung!* If there are any of you left, this is your only chance to surrender. Otherwise we're taking your boat and leaving you here to starve. Come out with your hands up." More melodrama, but what else are you supposed to say in that situation? "Now or never!" I shouted.

There was no answer. Well then, the hell with them, if they were there. I doubted it, but it really didn't matter. If they were alive, they wouldn't be for long.

We got everything together and tied the skiff with the dead and wounded in it to the stern of the whaleboat and went back down the channel to the ship. On the way we stopped at the turtle boat and retrieved the other bodies and put them in the skiff, too.

"Man, these guys are ripe," said Otto. "I don't suppose we could leave them here, sir."

"We could, but we won't."

Nobody said much on the way back. Even Reynolds said nothing.

Finally, as we were approaching the side of the ship, I said, "Well done, men. And you know that's the Navy's highest praise."

"Thank you, sir," said Otto. "But I have to say I don't feel all that great."

"Nobody does, Otto. Nobody does."

"But I'm sure glad we got through it OK."

"Me, too."

I had the identification disks in my pocket. I could feel them against my leg. That feeling would be my souvenir, long after I turned the disks in, whether I wanted it to be or not.

Chapter Twenty-Eight

The wounded man in the skiff died on the way back to the ship. I think an artery in his leg had been cut by a bullet and he bled to death pretty quickly, even though we tried to wrap the wound with the sleeve of his shirt.

We left all the bodies in the skiff. There was no sense bringing them aboard, especially the ones who'd died from gangrene. The captain ordered us to take the bodies and bury them on the seaward side of the barrier island that protected Hermosa. He sent a working party along to help the Fubars, who, for reasons best known to themselves, wanted to be part of the burial detail. They wanted to put a period to the chapter, I suppose.

"Take them far enough up the beach so that the tide doesn't wash away the covering," the captain said. "Drag the skiff up on the beach and leave it. Somebody'll come along and notice it, sometime."

"Any markers for the grave, Captain?"

"Well, I imagine the next storm would just blow them away. But suit yourself about that. If you're feeling grateful to that fisherman, you might leave a note secured in the skiff somewhere, explaining what happened and where he's buried. Maybe his relatives will come along and be interested."

"Yes, sir. I'll take care of it. What's the condition of the German Doc brought back?"

"Still in sickbay. Last I heard, he was hanging in there. I hope he lasts, because he might be able to give us some information about hidden fuel dumps. I'd sure like to know whether Hermosa was the only one or not. Soon as the burial party gets finished we'll hightail it for Key West. Get that guy to a hospital and maybe save him."

"Ironic, isn't it, sir? Trying to save him, I mean."

"That's one word for it." He smiled at me in an almost fatherly kind of way. "You and the boys did well today. *Nameless* is proud of you. I am, too."

"Thank you, sir."

We reached Key West late that afternoon.

"I figure we're due for a little liberty," said the captain. "The Fubars especially. I don't suppose you'd mind a little time off, too."

"Yes, sir."

"Well, that's a shame, because I'm afraid I'm going to have to ask you to go to Havana and do a little politicking with the locals, meaning our boys as well as Batista's fellas."

There was the barest trace of a smile on his face when he said this.

"I don't mind."

"Well, that's good. But be sure to watch out for dangerous characters. It'd be a shame to get shot by some Cuban criminal after today's business."

"I didn't think Havana was that dangerous, Captain."

"Just some parts. Anyway, I'll put together the report for the ONI. It's good to keep them in the loop. You can take it with you tomorrow."

"Aye, aye, sir."

We both knew there was no real reason for me to fly to Havana. No official reason. But it was a short, easy flight in the PBY, and the ship was going to have liberty, anyway.

The yeoman went on shore to pick up the mail. There was one for me. It smelled good and had no return address.

Darling,

Hello from under the apple tree. The blossoms are blooming, but you know that these blossoms bloom all year round. Can trees blossom and still have fruit at the same time? I don't know about the others, but this one can. Do you know that in Celtic mythology the Isle of Apples was a place of eternal life? One story has it that they took King Arthur there, after the last battle. Apparently he's still there, waiting until the Brits really need him to return. I'd say it's about time he showed up, what with the Blitz. But it's a lovely old story about the apples, don't you think? Yeats makes a big deal out of the theme in some of his early poems, too. You'd like those, I think, because you can actually make out what he's saying. Not like the later stuff. And then, because I was thinking these things, I looked up the ode "To Autumn," because I remembered reading these lines: "To bend with apples the moss'd cottage trees/And fill all fruit with ripeness to the core." Goodness! Keats was feeling his oats when he wrote that, I think.

Are you planning to come to Havana soon? I hope so. I'm feeling rather Keats-ian, myself. And I have a bit of news.

Love,
Marty

I wasn't sure I liked the sound of that last line. There was an old Spanish saying, a wish or a prayer, really: *Que no haya novidad.* "May no new thing arise." You pictured it being said by a wrinkled grandmother in a black shawl, but there were times when I felt that way, too.

The next morning I took the short flight to Havana and checked into the base BOQ and changed out of my uniform into some presentable civvies. It was just about lunchtime, so when I went to the embassy, everyone was out. Bill Patterson was out of town doing something or other. His secretary wasn't sure about when he'd be back. I left Captain Ford's report with the ONI's secretary and then wandered over to the Floridita. It was just about noon, but there was no one sitting at the bar. Then I noticed there were two men sitting at one of the tables in the rear. Hemingway and Wolfie Guest. They were both dressed for the boat—khaki shorts and shirts. Hemingway wore a khaki hat with a long black bill. A fishing hat.

"Riley!" he boomed. "Come and join us. We're just about to have lunch."

Well, I thought, why not?

Constante gestured to me, asking if I wanted a daiquiri. I said I'd rather have a Hatuey and then went over to their table. We were the only ones in the place. It was still early.

They both stood up and shook hands, which I took to be very polite and friendly. They had drinks in front of them, but had not been there very long, by the looks of them.

"In town for long?" said Hemingway.

"No plans. I have a couple of day's liberty, so I'm not sure. I thought I'd look around the city a little. See the sights."

"Where are you staying?"

"The Bachelor Officers Quarters at the base."

"Oh. That makes sense. I was going to recommend the Ambos Mundos Hotel. It's only a few blocks from the harbor. It's a good place to write, if you feel like writing letters or something. I'd invite you to stay at the house, but we're leaving after lunch."

"Thanks. The BOQ's OK."

I looked through the menu.

"The club sandwiches are good," said Hemingway.

"All right."

Constante took our order, and we settled down to the drinks.

"What did you do before the Navy?"

Hemingway seemed to be genuinely interested and not just making conversation. My English friend once told me that appearing to show sincere interest in other people was the essence of charm. And when I asked him whether *appearing* to be sincere wasn't something of a contradiction, he said, "Why, of course." But it was an attractive quality that Hemingway apparently could turn on, when he wanted to. And for all I knew, maybe he actually was—interested, I mean.

"I was a private investigator in L.A."

"Really? How did you get into it?"

"The usual way. Drifted in from something else."

"Well, that's interesting. Sam Spade. Philip Marlowe. I like that stuff. Do you like that sort of writing?"

"Some of it."

"I remember reading a Chandler story where a guy says 'Lift the dogs,' meaning 'start walking.' Ha! He's great with smart-ass slang. Sometimes his plots are confusing, but that's not why you read him. You just read him for the style. Like PG Wodehouse, in a funny way. I like Simenon, too. Very different, of course. I often wonder why Hammett doesn't write more. I hear he joined the army. It's funny they let him in. He's a Red. Speaking of Reds, did you have much contact with the movie business?"

"Some. It's hard not to, when you're a PI."

"I'll bet. Lots of shenanigans. I'm surprised you didn't try your hand at acting. You've got the looks."

"Well, the fact is, I gave it a shot, briefly. That's where I drifted from. But it wasn't for me."

"How come?"

"Too many people telling you what to do. Too many hysterics. Too many insecure people worried they're going to get found out—worried that someone's going to notice they're not worth the money they're making. Makes them nervous and hard to be around."

That got a laugh from both of them.

"What's the *mot juste* for that, Wolfie?"

"Phonies."

"That's it," he said. "They're making a movie out of *For Whom the Bell Tolls*. Gary Cooper and Ingrid Bergman. It could be all right, but probably won't be. The other movie they made of my stuff was unwatchable."

"Coop was in that one, too," said Wolfie. "With Helen Hayes."

"I know. Don't remind me. Or Coop, for that matter." He looked at me for a moment. "So, what have you been up to? Any interesting action?"

I looked around. There was still no one else in the room. Constante was behind the bar, but he didn't seem to be paying attention, though he probably was. Then I figured there was nothing sensitive about the latest stuff. It would be in the papers soon enough. There was also something else—Hemingway and Wolfie Guest would be going back out in the *Pilar*, sometime soon, looking for U-boats. It may have been a self-appointed mission, maybe even ego driven, but it was sanctioned by the Navy and our ambassador. So it was legitimate, if unorthodox. I figured they ought to know they were getting into some increasingly serious business. It was one thing to imagine it, and something else again to know it. I wondered briefly if telling the story would seem like I was trying to build myself up in the eyes of the famous author and adventurer, but I dismissed that. I honestly didn't care about that. I still had the smell of the dead in my nostrils. Gangrene and bullet wounds leave a memory that lingers long after you've buried the bodies.

"As a matter of fact, we did run into some stuff," I said.

"Can you talk about it?"

"I guess so."

So I told them about the blimp being shot down and the loss of the one crewman to the sharks, and about the U-boat being damaged by the bombs and then surfacing twenty miles away and how some of the Germans got out and stole a turtle boat and killed the crew and then snatched another fisherman to guide them, how we found one body, and how we searched through the barrier islands and the cayos and found the turtle boat aground and then about the shootout in the mangrove swamp. They both listened intently, smiling slightly, but not with any humor or lack of seriousness.

"So you killed them all?" Hemingway said.

"Not all. We brought one back, badly wounded. He's in the naval hospital in Key West. I don't know whether he'll make it. We hope he does. We want to know if there are any hidden fuel dumps."

"You mean any *other* hidden fuel dumps. I heard about Hermosa."

"Well then, yes."

"You know, I'm surprised they didn't booby-trap the turtle boat once it was aground."

"Well, they left three of their men there. Two were dead, but one of them was still alive, barely. He died later, but I figured they were intending to come back for them, if they could steal our whaleboat."

"You're probably right. But you know what would have made a hell of a booby trap? One of those potato masher grenades under one of the dead bodies with the fuse cord tied to his belt or something. As soon as you moved him the cord would pull out, ignite the fuse, and the next voice you'd hear would be St. Peter asking how to spell your name."

"The Krauts are masters of the art," said Wolfie. "My brother's in the OSS, and he told me about a booby trap the Germans set in a French house. They tied a grenade to a cat's tail with a piece of string and locked him in a closet. One of our Resistance boys heard the cat meowing and opened the door. Cat ran out, the pin got pulled, and the grenade went off. Killed the guy."

"What happened to the cat?" said Hemingway.

"Got away."

"I'm glad I didn't know all this when we searched the turtle boat," I said.

"Well, you had a hell of a story, even without booby traps. What do you think, Wolfie? It's a hell of a story, isn't it?"

"Yes. A hell of a story," he said. "You should do something with it."

"You're welcome to it," I said, with a smile. I think it was a smile, anyway.

The lunch came and we ate the sandwiches and drank a couple of Hatuey beers and were all friends together, as the saying goes. There was no joking, particularly. Just ordinary conversation on the subjects Hemingway liked—hunting, fishing, and writing. It was interesting, and he didn't tell me things I already knew. He was damned likable when he wanted to be, and I had the feeling he felt the most relaxed and comfortable with guys who were serving in the military, especially if they'd seen some combat and knew what that was like. He felt he was one of them. One of us, I guess I should say.

As we were finishing up, he mentioned that a stray dachshund had shown up at the Finca Vigia, and he'd adopted him.

"I don't know where he came from," he said. "But he's a damned fine little dog. Never barks. Marty named him Fritz. Somebody's probably very unhappy about losing him."

He finished his beer and looked at his watch.

"Well, it's been nice seeing you again, Riley. We've got to take off. We're headed back to Confites this afternoon. Another couple of weeks of watching. Maybe we'll get lucky, too. Lunch is on me. And congratulations. As my old Wyoming hunting guide says, 'Ya done good.'"

"Thanks. My skipper says that, too. And good luck to you. But you know . . . it's getting to be very serious out there."

"Are you telling us to be careful?" He was smiling in a friendly way as he shook my hand.

"I guess so."

"Well, I appreciate that. But don't worry about us. The Krauts tried to kill me once. They blew it, and that's the only chance they're going to get."

They left, and I wondered if I was starting to feel bad about anything.

Chapter Twenty-Nine

I walked back to the BOQ. I didn't want to call Marty from the Floridita.

She answered on the first ring.

"Riley? Oh, this is so nice. Hello, darling. Where are you?"

"I'm in town. Just got here this morning. I got your letter. I'm sorry I couldn't answer it. We've been at sea the last week or so."

"I understand."

"I wondered about it, though. You said you had some news."

"Yes. It's very exciting. Can you get a car and come to the house? Ernest and his gang are off again looking for floating windmills."

"I know. I just had lunch with him and Guest. At the Floridita."

"Oh, so then you know. Did he happen to mention anything about me?"

"No. We talked shop, more or less. What's the news?"

"Oh, it's really great! I got a call from *Collier's Magazine*. I'm pretty sure they're going to send me on assignment. I'm leaving tomorrow afternoon for New York to work out the details. If all goes according to plan, I'm off from there to London. I'm really excited. What do you think?"

I figured it was something like this.

"I think it's exactly what you wanted."

"Yes. It is. But you know, darling, I have been wondering . . ."

"What about us?"

"Well, yes."

"It doesn't change anything."

"Still in that parallel place?"

"Sure."

"I'm glad. I don't know how long I'll be gone, but it'll still be there when I get back."

"Of course."

"You really believe that, don't you?"

"Yes."

"Good. I'm so glad. I guess I already said that, didn't I? Well, I am, and that's that. Can you come out to the house and pick me up? Maybe we can go to that place on the cove and have a lovely night with Tavel and the sleeping bag and the stars and everything. I'm feeling very . . . something."

Well, that was the reason I came here. And I knew by the sound of her voice what she meant by "something."

Then I heard myself say, "I'm afraid I can't."

"Oh." There was a long pause. "Do you have to go back?"

"Yes. I have a meeting at the embassy, and then I have to fly back this afternoon. The ship is getting underway again, tomorrow."

"Oh . . . Well, I understand, of course. But it's a damned shame."

"I know."

"So I won't be able to see you before I go. Hell. Oh, well. But I'll be back, and you'll be busy, and the time will pass quickly, and I'll write to you. Will you write to me? I'll send you my address, when I get to London."

"I promise."

"Oh, dear. 'What'll I do when you are far away . . .'"

"You'll do what you do best. Or should I say, second best."

"Mmm. Thank you for that. I always thought I wasn't very good at the other thing."

"Now you know better."

"Yes. And I'm glad about that, too. I have to go now. There's a delivery man at the door. And I have so much to do. I'm . . . I'm sorry you can't come out here. I would love to see you. I would love for us to . . . well, you know."

"Yes, I know. I am, too. Sorry, I mean."

"What I said to you the last time still goes. You know what I mean."

"I know. Me, too."

"I'm so glad. Oh, God, I've said it again. But it's true. You will remember that, won't you?"

"Yes."

"Goodbye, darling."

"Goodbye."

I left the BOQ and walked back into town, back to the Floridita. What the hell, I thought. I might as well go for the record.

THE END